DAWN WIND

Rosemary Sutcliff

DAWN WIND

Illustrated by

Charles Keeping

New York

HENRY Z. WALCK, INC.

1962

First published by Oxford University Press
in 1961

First American Edition 1962

Printed in Great Britain by Richard Clay and Company, Ltd.,
Bungay, Suffolk

Contents

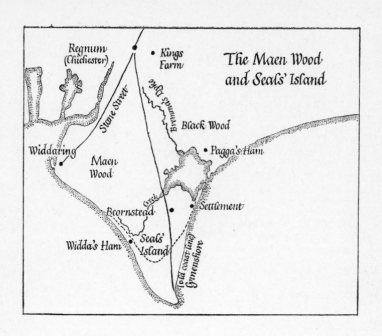

The Maen Wood and Seals' Island

Regnum (Chichester) · Kings Farm · Brunn's Dyke · Black Wood · Pagga's Ham · Stane Street · Widdaring · Maen Wood · Creek · Beornstead · Settlement · Widda's Ham · Seals' Island · Old coast line (Cymenshore)

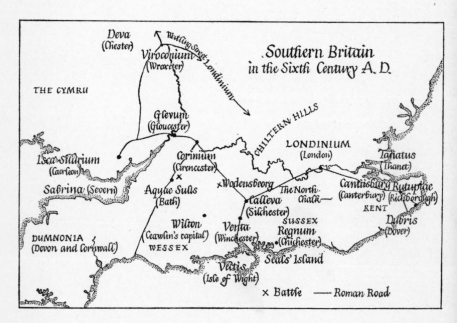

Southern Britain in the Sixth Century A.D.

Deva (Chester) · Viroconium (Wroxeter) · Watling Street Londinium · THE CYMRU · Glevum (Gloucester) · Chiltern Hills · LONDINIUM (London) · Tanatus (Thanet) · Isca Silurium (Caerleon) · Corinium (Cirencester) · Wodensborg · Cantiisburg (Canterbury) · Rutupiae (Richborough) · Sabrina (Severn) · Aquae Sulis (Bath) · Calleva (Silchester) · The North Chalk · KENT · Dubris (Dover) · DUMNONIA (Devon and Cornwall) · Wilton (Ceawlin's capital) · Venta (Winchester) · SUSSEX · Regnum (Chichester) · WESSEX · Vectis (Isle of Wight) · Seals' Island · × Battle — Roman Road

The Breaking of Britain

THE moon drifted clear of a long bank of cloud, and the cool slippery light hung for a moment on the crest of the high ground, and then spilled down the gentle bush-grown slope to the river. Between the darkness under the banks the water which had been leaden grey woke into moving ripple-patterns, and a crinkled skin of silver light marked where the paved ford carried across the road from Corinium to Aquae Sulis. Somewhere among the matted islands of rushes and water-crowfoot, a moorhen cucked and was still. On the high ground in the loop of the river nothing moved at all, save the little wind that ran shivering through the hawthorn bushes.

For a long while that was all, and then in the dark heart of the hawthorn tangle something rustled that was not the wind. It stirred, and was still, and then stirred again with a kind of whimpering gasp, dragging itself forward little by little out of the black

shadows among the thorn roots, like a wounded animal. But it
was no animal that crawled painfully into the moonlight at last, it
was a boy. A boy of fourteen or so, with a smear of blood showing dark on his forehead, and the same darkness clotted round the
edges of the jagged rent in his leather sleeve.

He propped himself on his left arm, his head hanging low between his shoulders; and then, as though with an intolerable
effort, forced it upward and looked about him. Westward along
the high ground the ring of ancient earthworks where the British
had made their last night's camp stood mute and deserted now,
empty of meaning as an unstrung harp, against the ragged sky. Far
down the shallow valley, the camp-fires of the Saxons flowered
red in the darkness, and between the dead camp and the living one,
all along the river bank and over the high ground and along the
line of the road to Aquae Sulis, stretched an appalling stillness scattered with the grotesque, twisted bodies of men and horses.

Only a few hours ago, all that stretch of stillness had been a
thundering battle-ground, and on that battle-ground, the boy's
world had died.

One of the tumbled bodies lay quite close to him, with arms
flung wide and bearded face turned up to the moon. The boy
knew who it had belonged to—rather a comic old man he had
been when he was alive, always indignant about something, and
his grey beard had wagged up and down when he talked. But
now his beard did not wag any more, only it stirred a little in the
night wind. Beyond him another man lay on his face with his
head on his arm as though he slept; and beyond him again lay a
tangle of three or four. Last night they had told stories of Artos
and his heroes round the camp-fires. But Artos was dead, almost
a hundred years ago, and now they were dead too. They had died
at sunset, under a flaming sky, with all that was left of free Britain
behind them, and their faces to the Saxon hordes. It was all over;
nothing left now but the dark.

The boy's head sank lower, and he saw a hand spread-fingered
on the ground before him. The fingers contracted as he watched,
and he saw them dig deeper into the moss and last year's leaves, as
though they had nothing to do with him at all. But the chill of
the moss was driven under his own nails, and he realized that the

hand was his, and understood in the same moment that he was not dead.

For a little, that puzzled him. Then he began to remember, and having begun to remember he could not stop. He remembered the brave gleam of Kyndylan's great standard in the sunset light, and the last stand of the fighting men close-rallied beneath it. His father and Ossian and the rest, the desperate, dwindling band still holding out, long after those that gathered to Conmail of Glevum and Farinmail of Aquae Sulis had gone down to the last man. He remembered the inward thrust of the Saxons yelling all about them, and the sing-song snarling of Kyndylan's war-hounds as they sprang for Saxon throats. He remembered struggling to keep near his father in the reeling press, and the hollow ringing peal of the war-horns over all. He remembered the glaring face and boar-crested helmet of a Barbarian warrior blotting out the sky, and the spear-blade that whistled in over his shield rim even as he sprang sideways with his own dirk flashing up, and the shock of the blow landing just below his sword-arm's shoulder. Everything had gone unreal and strange, as though the whole world was draining away from him, and suddenly he had been down among the trampling feet of the war-hosts. A heel, Saxon or British, it made no odds, had struck him on the head, and everything had begun to darken. He remembered dimly a gap opening as the battle reeled and roared above him, and crawling forward with a blind instinct to get clear of the trampling feet, and then nothing more. How he came to be where he was, he did not know. Maybe the slope of the hillside had taken him. And in the turmoil and the fading light among the hawthorn scrub, the battle must have passed him by.

But what of his father and Ossian?

All at once he was struggling to his knees, then to his feet, clinging to a branch while the moon-washed hillside dipped and swam around him. He did not feel how the spines tore at his clenched hand, nor the stab of the wound in his sword-arm which had ceased to bleed and clotted hard on to the leather of his tunic; all he knew was that he must find his father and Ossian. He was staggering uphill towards the place where Kyndylan had made his last stand, lurching, falling, and gathering himself up again, his breath coming in hoarse, whistling gasps. Once a body groaned as he stumbled over it, but when he checked and crouched down to look, the man was not his father, so he left him and staggered on, weaving his drunken way through the piled and scattered bodies.

Just below the crest of the ridge, where he had made his last stand, Kyndylan the Fair lay dead with his household warriors about him, and a goodly toll of Saxons to keep them company. His long pale hair flowing into the trampled bracken was stained and dabbled with blood, and the moon struck little jinks of light from the bronze hoops of the battered Roman breastplate he wore. But the boy paid no heed to him; he was looking for his father and his brother, not for any prince. And in a little he found them, lying close together among the thickest of the dead. His father was covered in wounds, like a boar that turns at bay and is savaged by a score of hounds before they pull him down; but Ossian was almost unmarked save for a little hole in his neck, and looked surprised, as though he was not sure how he came to be there at all. Ossian was not the warrior kind; the only thing he had ever really wanted to do was to make a garden of herbs and learn how to use them for healing people who were sick or hurt. But there was no time for growing herbs when Ceawlin, Lord of the West Saxons, was on the march, driving his grey-iron wedge towards the Sabrina Estuary, to split the last British position in two, and so make an end of the ancient struggle.

It had been almost two moons ago, early spring, when Kyndylan had sent out the call through all his territory; and the wind had been stripping the blossom from the pear tree against the south wall, when the messenger rode into the farm a day's march from Viroconium that was home to Ossian and Owain. And Ossian and their father had gone to the chest in the smoke-darkened atrium and brought out their swords. There was no sword for Owain—good blades were hard come by in these days, and reserved for the grown men who could make best use of them—but he had had his long dirk, when they had set out to join the rest of the war-host that was gathering to Viroconium of the White Walls.

The Saxons had taken their swords now. They had taken the

great war-standard of Kyndylan the Fair; maybe Ceawlin their
King slept warm in its gold-worked folds tonight, while Kyndylan and his warriors slept cold among the hawthorn bushes.
But it seemed that their looting had been hasty—maybe they did
not care much for a battlefield after dark and would come again
to finish the work by daylight—for as the boy Owain moved,
something on his father's hand gave off a spark of greenish light
under the moon. He bent forward with a gasp. The great ring
with its dolphin device cut in the flawed emerald of the bezel
was one of the first things that he could remember. It had been
his father's, and *his* father's before him, away back to the days
when the Legions first marched through Britain. It should have
been Ossian's after him, because he was the elder son, but now
Ossian was dead, too.

'I take the ring, my father,' Owain whispered. 'It is for me to
take it. I am your second son and it is mine, now.' It was not the
coldness of his father's hand he noticed, when he lifted it, so much
as the emptiness, like a lamp that has gone out. He fumbled the
heavy ring off, one-handed, and managed to get it on to his own
signet finger. It hung there loose and heavy, and he bent his
finger to keep it from slipping off again. There was nothing to
hold him here, nothing that he could do. He touched his father's
hand once more, and then Ossian's shoulder in farewell, not
feeling anything very clearly as yet, save a great coldness. Then he
stumbled to his feet and turned away, with no idea of where he
was going, knowing only that it was no good staying where he
was.

As he did so, something else moved in the hawthorn scrub.

He checked, his breath caught in his throat. What was it?
One of his own folk left by the fighting as he had been left?
Saxon marauder? Angry ghost? He was just starting forward
when a long slinking shape oozed out of the shadows. He saw the
pricked ears and open panting jaws, the eyes like twin opals in
the moonlight, and all the blood in his body seemed to fly back
to his heart. Wolf! His left hand went fumbling to the place
where the hilt of his dirk should have been. But it was not there;
he had lost it when he was struck down.

And then the creature whimpered, and in the same instant he

saw the broad bronze-studded collar about its neck. It was no wolf, but a dog. One of Kyndylan's great war-hounds. Perhaps it had escaped death by some such chance as Owain himself, perhaps it had merely been frightened and run away; Owain did not care, it was something alive and maybe even friendly in the cold echoing emptiness of a dead world. It stood with one paw raised, ears pricked, looking at him; and Owain called, hoarsely, with stiff lips and aching throat: 'Dog! Hai! Dog!' The great brute lowered its head and whimpered again, then came, slowly and uncertainly, crouching like a hound that has been whipped. 'Dog!' Owain called again. Once it stopped altogether; then it finished at the run, and next instant was trembling against his legs.

He was a young dog; the beautiful creamy hair of his breast-patch was stained and draggled, and his muzzle bloody in the moonlight, and Owain could feel him shivering. 'Dog, aiee, dog, we are alone then. There's no one else. We will go together, you and I.'

Dog—the great hound was never to have any other name—looked up, whining and bewildered, and licked his thumb.

'Come then,' Owain croaked. 'There is nothing to stay here for—nothing here at all.'

He never remembered afterwards where they went or how far, he and the hound together, only that it was away from the road and the river and the red flowers of the Saxon camp; and that they came at last to a little busy stream brawling down from the hills, and collapsed side by side on the bank and lapped the cold quick-flowing water that was webbed with living silver in the moonlight. When they had drunk their fill they crawled together into the midst of the streamside tangle of alder and osier and last year's willow-herb. And the last thing Owain knew before the blackness flowed over him, was the delicate tracery of alder leaves and the dark alert shape of the hound's ears pricked against the stars and a vague feeling of surprise that the stars still looked as they had done last night.

Most likely the boy would have died before morning, partly from shock and loss of blood, but mostly for the very simple reason that his world had died and there was too little life left in him to go on living on his own. But the hound lay half on top of him and kept him warm with his own warmth, and licked and licked at the wound as far as he could come at it through the rent in Owain's leather sleeve. And because the hound was alive, the little flickering life in the boy did not go out.

It was full daylight when he drifted up through the blackness that had been half sleep and half something deeper. And the first thing he saw, as it had been the last, was Dog's rough grinning head just above him. But now the pricked ears were outlined against a sky of drifting grey, and the alders swayed in the wind and a little spitting rain blew in his face. Maybe it was the day after the battle, or maybe it was the day after that, he did not know. The fighting seemed a long time ago, even longer than the time when the war-host had gathered to Viroconium; but he knew, confusedly, that that could not be so, because his father and Ossian and the rest had been alive when they hosted, and when the fighting was over they were dead—all dead—all dead.

And then in swift denial, the thought came to him, stopping the breath in his throat, that he did not know they were all dead. There might be some left, as he and the hound had been left, the few tattered remains of a broken army. And if that were so, surely they would make for the place where they had hosted in the spring. Maybe if he could get back—if he could only get back to Viroconium, he would find them again.

He propped himself up painfully on his sound arm, his wound stabbing wildly as he moved, and remained a while with hanging head, while the hound sat back on his brindled haunches, his pink frilled tongue drooling from his open jaws, and watched him.

Presently, when the world had steadied a little, he dragged himself to his knees and then to his feet, and staggered down to the edge of the stream. And there, lying full length among the alder roots, he drank again, lapping like the hound, for his right arm was numb from the shoulder down and so he could not make a drinking cup from his joined hands. He splashed the water into his face, and the cold of it cleared his head a little; and afterwards, sitting back on his heels, he pulled some woollen threads from the skirt of his under-tunic, and contrived with hand and teeth to thread his father's ring on to them and knot them round his neck.

B

It would be safer so, thrust inside the breast of his tunic, than on his finger where it was so much too loose.

Then getting unsteadily to his feet once more, he stood looking about him and sniffing, to get some idea of his direction. Viroconium lay to the north, several days' march beyond Glevum; and the old road from Aquae Sulis to Glevum must run somewhere beyond those low wooded hills. But it would be best to keep clear of all roads this side of the Sabrina.

He tried to whistle to Dog, who was snuffing among the alder roots, and could not make the sound break through his lips; but the hound looked up as he moved, and came bounding to join him, and they scrambled up the bank and struck out northward together.

Afterwards, Owain was never very clear as to the details of that long northward trail. Sometimes his thinking was quite clear, and he knew what had happened and where he was going and why; but at others, more and more often as the days went by, his head seemed full of a fiery fog that came in some way from the throbbing of his wounded arm; and nothing seemed real, and he stumbled along in a dream without any clear idea in his head save that he was going north. He could smell the north as a hound scents game. They were making their way through a world that seemed empty of all human life, but that might be only because he was instinctively keeping clear of all the places where men might be. Once, Dog caught a badger cub, and he managed to get some of it away from him before it was all eaten. Once, in some open moorland, they came on a dead lamb part eaten by ravens, and the hound gorged his fill, but the raw stinking flesh made Owain's stomach rise, and he could eat little of it. They crossed the Glevum road in the dark of the fourth night, and struck down into the fringe of the western marshes, and after that it was a little easier to get food, for the later wild fowl were still nesting, and there were eggs to be found without much trouble. Dog foraged for himself.

After the emptiness of the woods and marshes it was strange to come at last to Glevum and find it alive and thrumming like an overturned bee-skep. It was one of those times when his head was full of the fiery fog, and everything was shifting and unreal;

but something in him remembered where to find the Sabrina crossing, and he turned aside from the Southern Gate and drifted down on to the strand between the city walls and the river. The Water Gate was open, and people were heading in a steady trickle along the causeway over the mudflats, and away by the bridge of boats that spanned the river. Owain wandered into their midst because he, too, wanted the bridge, holding with his sound hand to Dog's collar, because he knew that if he and the great hound were separated, there would be no more hope in this world or the next for either of them.

He found himself one of the pathetic trickle of fugitives that he dimly realized was the life-blood of Glevum draining away. Tradesmen with their tools on their backs, whole families pushing their most treasured possessions on hand-carts, or pressing forward simply with what they stood up in; a girl carrying two pigeons in a green willow basket; an old woman on a mule— maybe some rich merchant's wife—with a face that showed staring grey under the stale rouge and eye-paint that had streaked with tears; a beggar with white blind eyes and bare feet. He saw them like the people of a dream, all with the same stunned masks for faces; and all around him, he heard one word repeated again and again: 'It is the Saxons—the Saxons—God help us! The Saxons are coming. . . .'

Somehow he had not thought of that, of the Saxons on his heels.

People were looking at him now, staring, their mouths foolishly open, asking questions. He heard his own voice answering, but was not sure what he answered. Something about the fighting on the Aquae Sulis road, something about Kyndylan's death, and Conmail's. They fell back from him a little, as though he were a ghost; as though he were the Breaking of Britain made visible to their eyes.

The bridge timbers sounded hollow under his feet, and there was a little gap between him and the people ahead and the people who came after. Then he was on the further shore, and the paved road ran out before him, thrusting westward into the hills.

2

The Hill Farm

NOT much more than a mile beyond the river, the road forked, the left hand branch running south-westward to Isca Silurium, the City of Legions, and the right striking off through the hill country to join at last with the great military road that ran like a frontier north and south along the wild marches of the Cymru. Once on that road, Owain knew that he would only have to keep walking long enough, to come to Viroconium at last. So leaving the pathetic string of refugees to go straggling off down the southern branch, he turned right, and lurched off north-westward, alone save for the hound padding behind him.

After that he lost all count of time, so that he did not know whether it was one or two days later, or even three, when he awoke to the certainty that he had gone astray. It did not seem possible, not with the road leading on and on in front of him, but somehow it had happened.

He stumbled to a halt, and stood looking about him like some-one who has just walked out of a rolling smoke-cloud into clear air and found himself not where he expected to be. But he knew that the clear air would not last, that was the trouble. He felt a cold muzzle thrust into the palm of his sound hand; Dog pressed against him, looking up and whining, and he rubbed the hound's rough head without thought, as he stood staring rather desperately about him. If he held on across country he was bound, some-where, some time, to strike the frontier road that he was making for. But quite suddenly he knew that he was very nearly at the end of his strength.

It was growing late, too, the sun low and glaring under brows of angry fire-fringed cloud, and the wind that swept towards him from the high hills of Cymru had the smell of storm in it as well as the smell of the mountains.

He was on the point of turning down-valley to try to find some sheltered corner of the woods before the storm was upon him, when a very small thing happened. A grey wagtail flew across his path. Caught by the quick movement, his eyes followed it—and he found himself looking at a little irregular corn patch on the hillside above him. It was roughly walled with stones grubbed up from the red earth of the hillside when the land was cleared; the wagtail had alighted on the wall and was flirting its tail up and down.

Where there was tilled land, the farm steading could not be far away. If he could find it, they would tell him how far he was astray; maybe if the woman was kind she would give him a drink of buttermilk—he was beyond wanting food, sick with the pain of his wound, but the thought of cool buttermilk tugged at him—and let him sleep in the barn until the coming storm was over. Perhaps from the corn plot he might be able to see the steading. He gathered up his wounded arm again, and leaving the track, began to stumble up the hillside, Dog, puzzled but willing, at his side. It seemed a long way, but he reached the plot at last, and stood clinging to the piled grey stones, while the world swam and jiggled before his eyes. But in a few moments the wind from the hills seemed to clear his head a little, and then with a sob of relief he saw the steading, which had been hidden from the track by the rising ground.

It stood at the end of a shallow combe, a cluster of two or

three turf-thatched bothies and a cattle fold, all within its grey encircling wall, like any other of the small hill farms; but its house-place walls were limewashed in the Roman manner, and shone harshly white in the sunlight. Owain remained where he was for a few moments, clinging to the wall and shivering, but he knew that if he was to reach shelter he must reach it soon. He thrust off from the wall like a swimmer thrusting off from shore, and began to stumble through the fern towards the blurred gleam of the distant limewashed walls.

For a long time the steading seemed to get no nearer, and then suddenly it was there. The gap in the low stone wall was clear, and Owain lurched through. He saw the dark opening in the house-place wall, and the dim red glimmer of firelight inside, and stumbled towards it.

Something moved in the gloom, and a woman appeared in the doorway. A tall iron-grey woman in a skimpy dust-coloured tunic, with a copper cooking spoon in one hand, and her hair knotted up on top of her head as though she would stand no nonsense from it or from anything else. 'Well?' she began before she had time to see who or what it was on her threshold. 'What is it? What do you want? Be quick, I can't stand here all day.'

Owain leaned his sound shoulder against the rowan wood doorpost. 'Viroconium,' he mumbled thickly. 'I—missed the road —can you tell me—tell me——' He saw her face very clearly, a long bony face with iron grey hairs sprouting singly here and there on the chin. But something very strange was happening to it, it was swimming towards him, growing larger and larger as though to overwhelm him. His shoulder seemed to lose the door-post, and with no more fuss and turmoil than a small tired sigh, he crumpled across the threshold.

He could not have been unconscious for more than a heart-beat of time, for dimly through the roaring darkness he heard the woman cry out sharply for somebody called Priscus, and Dog's warning sing-song snarl, and even managed to mumble some-thing that quieted and reassured the hound before he flew at anybody. He heard also the quick pad of footsteps, and a man's voice asking a startled question.

Then from a very great distance, the woman's voice again.

'How in Our Lord's name should I know who he is? Ceawlin of the Saxons or the Bishop of Gwynedd maybe; I can't have him cluttering up my threshold. Take his heels, man, or do I have to carry him alone?'

'Do but give me a moment, my dove,' said the man's voice. 'It is not every hour of every day one finds a stranger lying across one's door-sill. Where do you want him?'

'By the fire. Where else should I want him?'

Owain felt himself lifted and carried a few scuffling steps, and laid down again on the softness of strewn bracken. He tried to open his eyes, then shut them again hurriedly because everything was spinning. He tried to tell the woman that he would do well enough if she would just let him lie still for a while, but no sound would come. Yet when the woman spoke again, her voice seemed to come from a little nearer. But maybe that was only because she was leaning over him. 'Look now, he is only a child, after all.'

'Old enough to be at a man's work of kill and be killed, seemingly.'

The woman snorted. 'He's scarce dry from the egg for all that . . . Go now and draw some water and put it on to heat, while I get this stinking tunic off him. Milk too, today's milk; and leave me your knife. I shall want it.'

The agony of having the short leather sleeve cut away from his wound acted on Owain like a douche of cold water on the face of a sleeper, making him gasp and shudder but bringing him back to the urgent business of living. He opened his eyes again. The world was still swimming, but not so wildly, and he could see the woman's face bent over him, her lips tightly folded as she worked. She clucked sharply at the sight of the wound. He had not had his tunic off since the battle, and he supposed vaguely that it must be ugly to look at. Then she saw that his eyes were open, and said scoldingly, 'Hold still. If you are man enough to get yourself a wound the like of this one, you are man enough to bide still while I tend it.'

And a little later, slowly and grumblingly, as though she tried not to ask the question but something dragged it out of her: 'Was it the Saxons?'

Owain tried again to speak, and this time the words came, though thick and stammering. 'Yes—the Saxons.'

'Where?' she said. 'What happened?' and then quickly, 'Na na, I am an impatient old woman; let it keep for a while.'

But he contrived to stammer out an answer, all the same. 'Hard by Aquae Sulis. We—met the Saxons there. Kyndylan is dead, and Conmail and Farinmail—all our fighting men.' It seemed to him odd that the world had come to an end and she did not know about it; and he added accusingly: 'They knew in Glevum.'

'We are not Glevum,' the woman said. 'No one has come up the drove road for days before you came. How then should we know?'

The man she had called Priscus was back, accompanied by the rattle of a pail as he set it down, and she said to him: 'The Princes are dead, he says, and the Saxons have overwhelmed our men by Aquae Sulis. Pour some water into the crock and set it to heat, then bring me some clean rags from the chest yonder; is it that I have to tell you everything?'

'No, Priscilla my dove, but let us agree that you generally do,' said the man, with what sounded even to Owain's confused ear like a tremor of amusement.

The rest of that evening, and the nights and days that followed, passed for Owain in a queer hot dream. The storm that he had smelled at sunset broke over the hills before full dark, and the hushing of rain across the thatch and the booming of the three-day summer gale seemed to be part of his own wild unrest, while the throbbing of his wound somehow broke loose from his body and filled all the night with jagged fork-tongued flames. Sometimes the confusion rolled back a little and he was cloudily aware of lying on piled yellow bracken against the wall, of the sharp increase of pain when the wound was tended, and sometimes the woman's long grey face and sometimes the man's which was round and pink, bending over him; and always the brindled prick-eared shape of Dog sitting watchful at his side; the taste of milk and medicine-herbs mingling with the sour taste of fever in his mouth, and somebody pulling up the rug and scolding him as often as he threw it off because he was so hot.

Once he woke out of blackness to see the woman's face bending over him very close and hear her saying fiercely, 'That's better. Now drink this, and don't you *dare* slip through my fingers after all the care I've spent on you! There is no need for you to die now, and if you do it will be nothing but ingratitude to the Lord who gave you life—and ingratitude is a thing I cannot and will not abide!'

He thought, looking back on it, that that was near the end of the fiery time, and it was not long after that he woke in an early morning and found his wound cool and his head clear, and saw Dog's anxious ears pricked against the silken paleness of the doorway and heard the dunghill cock crowing, a shining lily-shape of sound in the grey dawn outside.

After that it was only a matter of getting well again; but it took a good while. The wound itself would not have laid him by for long if it had been tended at the first, but with long neglect it had become very sick, and he had been in a raging fever when he fell across Priscus's door-sill. Now he lay flat and silent under the striped native rug against the wall, eating whatever he was given, and sleeping, and staring up at the smoke-hole above him that showed sometimes grey and sometimes blue and sometimes had a star in, seen and lost and seen again as the hearth smoke fronded upward; scratching at the healing scar on his arm when he could do it without Priscilla noticing, while the life of the little hill farm went on around him, and slowly, day by day, the strength began to trickle back into his body.

Dog stayed with him almost all the while, sometimes sleeping with his warm chin on his Lord's chest, sometimes sitting alert and upright beside him, his tail giving a short burst of thumps every time he moved; and every time the woman Priscilla came to tend the wound, making a small soft warning in his throat, not deep enough for a growl nor menacing enough for a snarl, as though he would say only, very gently, 'Remember, if you harm him—I am here.'

'So it has been since the beginning,' snapped Priscilla. 'I'd have driven him away long before this, or tied him up outside, but well I know that if I tried to do any such thing the brute would bite me.' But she gave Dog the bones from the evening stew with quite a lot of meat still on them, all the same.

It was long past midsummer before Owain could get on to his feet again, and clad in an old tunic of Priscus's, he crawled out, feeling as though his bones were made of wet leather, to sit in the house-place doorway and watch the lean pig rooting in the midden, and busy himself with the odd bits of making and mending that are always needed about a farm.

One still summer evening with the swallows flying high among the shining midge-cloud, he sat in his accustomed place, with his back propped against the doorpost, and Dog sleeping beside him flat out with his creamy underparts to the last warmth of the sun. He was making a new ox-collar of plaited straw, working a little awkwardly because his arm was still stiff, but making a strong well finished job of it, all the same, for he had always been good with his hands. Priscilla, who was preparing the evening meal, had come out to see how he was getting on, and both of them were watching Priscus, who had just brought the little black cow in for milking, and was having trouble getting her through the steading gate.

Priscilla made the snorting sound in her throat that with her passed for laughter. 'A dear good man he is, and he never complains that this isn't the life he was bred to. But it's easy to see he's no farmer.'

Owain tipped back his head and looked up at her, the half made ox-collar in his hands. 'Not a farmer?'

'Does he look like it? He was a master potter—the best potter in Glevum, though I, his wife, say it. But folk don't buy fine bowls and pitchers for their tables any more.' She sighed. 'I miss the smells and bustle of Glevum sometimes, even now.'

Priscus had succeeded in folding the cow by this time, and in a little, Priscilla would go down to milk her. Owain took some more of the yellow straw beside him, and laid it into his braid. 'They were pouring out of Glevum when I came through,' he said slowly. 'They had heard how the battle went. There was a family with all their goods and the grandmother on a hand-cart—and a girl with two doves in a willow cage. They all stared at me as though I were a ghost.'

'As well they might,' said Priscilla. 'For sure enough you looked like one when you fell across my door-sill.'

Owain was silent for a while, his fingers busy with the plaited straw, his thoughts still with that pathetic straggle of refugees. 'They were heading south-west,' he said, 'all of them heading south-west. Where would they go?'

'Anywhere into Southern Cymru, or across into Dumnonia; or maybe those that can afford it, overseas to Gaul to join the settlement that Maximus planted with his old soldiers in Armorica, like many that have gone before them.' She sniffed acidly. 'Like enough they'll be calling it Brittany, by and by.'

'You would not go that way?'

'Do I not tell you it is a way for those that can afford it? It costs a fistful of gold, nowadays, to buy a place in a fishing boat making the crossing. Besides, we have each uprooted once, my old Priscus and I, and we are too old to uproot a second time and start life again in a strange land . . . Na na, we shall just abide here with our own fields, and trust that the Barbarians do not come so far westward into the hills.'

3

A Son's place by the Hearth

EVERY Saturday night Priscus shaved; a long and painful opera-
tion entailing the use of vast quantities of goose-grease to soften
the bristles, and the heating of much water over the fire, and next
day when the milking and the necessary morning work of the
farm was done, he and Priscilla retired into the small inner room
where they slept, and came out again in their glory, Priscus in
good russet cloth, Priscilla with a crimson border to her sheeps-
grey gown and a string of melon-shaped blue glass beads round
her scrawny neck. 'We are Roman citizens, and we might as well
look like it, at least on God's day of the week,' Priscilla said with
valiant pride.

And together they went off up the herding path into the next
valley, on their way to worship God, leaving Branwen the short-
legged cattle-dog in charge of the farm until they came home
again towards evening. On the earlier Sundays, Owain had of
course been left behind, but on the second Saturday after Priscus's
trouble with the cow, Priscilla came out of the inner room while
the master of the house was at his shaving, carrying something
blue over her arm. 'There,' she said to Owain, who was holding
up the big copper cooking pot for Priscus to see his round

agonized face in. 'This is his second best tunic; it will do for you tomorrow.'

'I can't wear out *all* Priscus's tunics,' Owain said without looking up. 'I'm wearing out his old working one as it is.'

'And you cannot come to Service with us in that one smelling of the byres. If you think,' said Priscilla with feeling, 'I am going to have it said that I grudged any member of my household a clean tunic to worship God in, you are mistaken!'

'To say nothing,' Priscus murmured gravely, 'of myself, the tunic's actual owner.'

Owain looked up slowly. 'Am I to go to Service with you tomorrow?'

He was born and bred to the Christian faith, and his faith had been dear to him. It was part of his heritage, part of being Roman and British, and standing for civilization and the light, against the Barbarians and the in-flowing dark. But now the last light had gone out, and it was as though something of his faith had guttered out too. Part of him wanted to go with Priscus and Priscilla and share in the familiar worship, but part of him shrank from it as from going back to a place where one has been happy, when the hearth is cold and the people one was happy with are dead. 'I think I will not go; I will bide here as I have before, and then nobody will say anything.'

'No one in my house stays at home on the Lord's Day, when once his legs are strong enough to carry him to Service,' said Priscilla simply. 'If you come for no other reason, you can come to thank God for leading you to my threshold in your sorest need.'

Owain said with a flash of rather dreary laughter, 'In actual truth it was a grey wagtail!'

'The Lord who knows when a sparrow falls will not find a grey wagtail too small to use for His purpose, I dare say,' said Priscilla briefly, depositing the blue woollen tunic on his lap.

And Owain knew that he would go to Service tomorrow.

He washed, and allowed Priscilla to clip off the strong dark hair that had grown long about his neck. And next morning, wearing Priscus's second best tunic, which was about the right length for him but roughly three times too wide, he set off up the green drove track, walking at Priscilla's left hand while

Priscus trotted at her right, and Dog, as usual, came padding along behind.

It was a good distance, following the winding drove-way that linked outland farm with outland farm among the hills, and Owain, whose legs were still apt to tire quickly, was not sorry when they came down through a tangle of low-growing woods into a shallow upland valley, and saw the village half-way up the slope on the far side, and higher up, where the field plots ran out into rough pasture, a little barn-like building with the tall grey finger of a preaching cross raised in front of it.

They were late, for Priscus had broken his shoe-thong on the way, and they had had to stop and mend it, and when they came up through the apple trees and kale plots of the village to the preaching cross, the rest of the little congregation were already assembled; maybe thirty or forty men, women, and children from the village and the outlying farms, gathered close about the grey stone shaft of the cross and the little figure in the long tunic of undyed sheep's wool who stood at its foot.

They looked round as the three latecomers slipped in among them, and many eyes were fixed upon the thin dark boy who had come with Priscus and Priscilla, and who wore—though he did not know it—an odd stillness on his face as though it were a mask, or a shield; but they had the courtesy of people who live very far into the wilds, and after the one look they did not stare any more, but made room for him close to the preaching cross, as though he had been one of themselves.

The priest had already begun the service, and Owain fixed his eyes on him, trying to take in his words. The man was worth looking at, small, fierce and fiery, with the head of a warrior prince on the body of an under-fed clerk; worth listening to also, for the fire that flashed from his dark eyes was in his voice, kindling the words of his mouth to a new aliveness. And yet Owain, listening to the familiar prayers, murmuring the familiar responses with Priscus and Priscilla, could not make them mean anything at all. The ground all round the cross and the priest's cell was hummocky, for the dead lay buried there, but there were few stones, and the little grey hill sheep cropped the rough grass to the very walls of the cell; and Owain heard their cropping

and the deep contented drone of bees among the opening bell
heather more clearly than prayer or psalm or litany; and remembered it longer.

But when the man began to preach, then it was a different
matter. The preachers of the Cymru were mostly gifted with
silver tongues, but it seemed that this man's tongue was of flame.
But indeed, Owain found that it was not a sermon he was listening to at all, but an exhortation, a cry that seemed to be for him
personally, as for every soul gathered there. 'Brothers, the Light
goes out and the Dark flows in. It is for us to keep some Lamp
burning until the time that we can give it back to light the world
once more; the Lamp, not of our Faith alone, but of all those
beauties of the spirit that are kindled from our Faith, the Lamps of
the love of wisdom in men's hearts and the freedom of men's
minds, of all that we mean when we claim that we are civilized
men and women and not barbarians.'

That was the message as Owain received it; it might have come
differently to the hill shepherd, differently again to Priscilla.

And listening to him, to the blazing urgency that could only
have flamed up from the need of the immediate moment, and
never been planned beforehand, the boy thought, 'This man has
heard something—some news that has only just come.' And he
thought, too, that the other people round him knew what it was.
In a short while the service was over; the people turned to each
other, no longer a congregation, but a gathering of friends and
foes and neighbours, and suddenly the priest was close beside them
with his hand on Priscus's arm, saying, 'You came late today, my
dears; have you heard the news?'

Priscus shook his head, his round face anxious at once. 'What
news is that, then, Little Father?'

'None that we were not expecting,' said the priest, 'and quite
stale by now, I suppose, but none the less dark for that, if it be
true. They say that Glevum is in Ceawlin's hands, and Corinium
and Aquae Sulis have gone up in flames. The Barbarians are over
all the country round Sabrina Head.' His brilliant gaze sought out
Owain, standing a little behind the other two. 'That is maybe
news that strikes nearer to you than to the rest of us, my son;
for the word that runs through the hills at any stranger's coming

among us, tells that you were at the last great battle, by Aquae
Sulis.'

'I and the dog here,' Owain said. 'It was the first fight for both
of us.'

And Dog, hearing his name, flung up his head and nosed
happily at the boy's arm.

'So.' The priest's gaze dropped to the great hound, and lifted
again to Owain's face. 'Kneel down, my son.'

Owain knelt, and felt the light touch of the man's hand on his
bowed head; the other was on Dog's; and Dog, who never
showed affection to anyone save his Master, nosed up under it
and licked the man's wrist. 'O Lord,' said the rough beautiful
voice above him, 'here are a boy and a dog who have fought Thy
fight according to the best that was in them. Therefore let Thy
blessing be upon them, and Thy courage bear them up, and
spread over them the mercy of Thy wings.'

The three of them walked home in silence; not one word ex-
changed between them until they came up between the midden
and the cow byre to the house-place door. But on the threshold
Priscus checked, and stood a moment looking away down the
valley. 'It would be useless, of course—perfectly useless; I dare
say I'd be no better skilled with a weapon than with a plough. I'm
not very good at anything save making pots, but I could find it
in my heart, just now, to wish that I was young again and had a
sword.'

'You were the best potter in all Glevum territory,' said his wife
bracingly. 'I'll say it to your face as I've said it behind your back,
and one skill should be enough for any man. Stop blocking up the
doorway now, and let me get at the stew pot if you want any
supper tonight.'

The stew, when it was ready, was a good one, but none of them
seemed hungry, and silence had descended on them again. Owain,
chewing his way through his bowlful without tasting it, stared
into the fire. The weeks that he had spent here in the shelter of
Priscilla's kindness had had a kind of battered peace about them,
like the lull in a storm; and the outside world, even his father's
death, had seemed a long way off. But now it had all come rushing back to him again, and the lull was over. He knew that even

if he stayed here, the lull would still be over . . . He wiped the last drops of soup from the bottom of his bowl with a piece of barley crust, chewed and swallowed slowly and deliberately, and set the bowl aside. 'Tomorrow,' he said, 'I must be away. I have stayed too long.'

Priscilla was collecting the bowls, which presently she would take down to the spring for scouring, and she pushed them together with a clatter. 'That is foolishness; you can scarcely walk as far as the village yet.'

'I can, you know I can; I—must go.'

There was a little silence, Priscilla looking at him tight-lipped. Then Priscus gently cleared his throat. 'I think, my dove, that ill fitting though the moment seems, you had best speak now to the boy of—the matter that we discussed a few days since.'

Priscilla's mouth tightened still further. 'You speak to him; it is for the head of the house.'

'Doubtless, my dove; also it is a task for a woman. I shall go and scratch the pigs' backs,' said Priscus, and got quietly to his feet and ambled out, Branwen trotting on her short legs behind him.

For a few moments Priscilla glared after him with the look of a woman who would dearly like to shake someone until his teeth flew out of his head; then she gave a small exasperated sigh, and turned back to the hearth. Owain could scarcely see her face now, for on these summer evenings the house-place became unbearable if one kept the fire up once the cooking was over, and candles were for special occasions. He waited for what she wanted to say to him, not wondering very much what it was, because his thoughts were turned towards setting out again tomorrow.

She said: 'We have never questioned you about yourself in all this while. It seemed both to my old Priscus and to me that if we waited, maybe one day you would tell us of your own choosing. But now it seems that there is no time left.'

Owain looked up quickly. 'I am sorry. I will answer anything you like. What did you want to know, Priscilla?'

'That ring you wear round your neck—I hung it on a new thong for you while you were ill; did you notice? Was it perhaps your father's ring?'

Owain nodded.

c

'Were you with your father in that last battle?'

'With my father and my brother,' Owain said, scratching the scar on his arm as he had got into the habit of doing, and staring into the embers of the sinking fire.

'Don't do that, you'll make it sore,' said Priscilla. 'They were killed?'

'Yes.'

'You have——' Her voice, softer than he had ever heard it before, hesitated a moment in a way that was not like her. 'You have a mother to go back to? She will have been thinking you dead with the other two, all this while, poor woman.'

'My mother died when I was small,' Owain said, levelly. 'I should not even know what she looked like, but my father made an outline in charcoal once of her head shadow on the colonnade wall, and kept it safe with a bronze grill over it. She had a very little neck and a lot of hair piled up high.'

Priscilla had taken up her distaff loaded with lichen-dyed wool, and when she spoke again, her words sounded against the soft background thrumming of the spindle. 'There's good land down the valley foot, and Priscus would have enclosed some of it before this, if he had had a son to work it with him. We would have liked a son, he and I, but the Lord never sent us any child at all, and there's no profit in questioning His ways. But the good land at the valley foot is still there, and there's a son's place empty by the hearth. If you have no one to go back to, you might do worse than bide here.'

Owain jerked up his head and stared at her. If the suggestion had come in a year's time, he might even have considered it—at least to come back to, by and by—but his father's death was still too near, so that the bare idea seemed like disloyalty. He shook his head. 'I might do very much worse, I know that, Priscilla. You have been kind to me—so kind all this while—but I must go on to Viroconium. If any of our men came through the battle and gather again, they will gather there. There's our own farm, too. I must see if anything is left of it. But first I must go to Viroconium.'

'If any gathered to Viroconium, they will have gathered and gone again before this; you have lain sick a long time.'

'Maybe the people of the city will be able to tell me where they are gone, so that I can follow.'

Priscilla teased out a few more strands of wool. 'There will be—there will have been no gathering to Viroconium or anywhere else, you know that. Here in the Western Hills we may remain free, but for the rest of Britain, the thing is finished and the lights are out. What can you do against the Saxon hordes?'

'Even Priscus wished that he was young again and had a sword.'

'Priscus is a fool.'

'So am I. I have no sword, but at least I am young. I must go, Priscilla.'

Silence hung between them, filled only with the thrum of the spindle. Then Priscilla broke it with a snort. 'A child you are, and a fool you are, and so you must go,' and was silent again so long that he thought she was angry. At last, quite suddenly, she laid aside spindle and distaff, and let her big hands drop into her lap. 'There's no more to be said. Go then, in the morning. But remember always that so long as my old Priscus and I are here, there's a place here for you, if you need it.'

'I will remember,' Owain said. 'And maybe I will come back one day, and maybe not. But either way, I will always remember.'

4

Shadow on the Wall

NEXT morning, so early that the hillside was still in shadow, Owain set out again for Viroconium.

Priscilla had given him food and the household's spare strike-a-light, and a good thick cloak, and Priscus had added three horse-hair snares and a good long hunting knife with a well-worn alderwood handle; and he had tried to thank them and failed completely, and whistled Dog to heel and come away. Now, as the rough hill track turned him over to the road that he had

missed so long ago, he wished that he had kissed Priscilla at part-
ing, because he thought that she would have liked it.

But already the past weeks were growing thin and distant to
him. There were plenty of other things to fill his mind. In two
days he struck the great double-track frontier road, and followed
it northward, keeping it in sight, but not too closely, for there
was no knowing how far west the Saxons might have thrust.
Dog trotted at his heel or loped on wolf-like far ahead, looking
round from time to time to make sure that he was coming. It was
late summer now, turning to autumn, and there were no more
birds' eggs, but he had the barley-bannocks and strong ewe-milk
cheese that Priscilla had given him, and when that was gone, he
had his knife and his hound and his snares, and his strike-a-light
to make a fire; and they lived on the country, hunting and
foraging as they went.

For the same reason as he avoided the road, Owain kept clear
of any place where men might be—and indeed the countryside
seemed almost as empty of human life as the forests and marshes
south of Glevum had been; and so in all that long trail north, he
never heard of the Saxons, nor how things went with the rest of
Britain.

He travelled slowly, as a man must who hunts as he goes,
and it was many days later when the road that he had been following along the east side of a great moorland ridge brought him
out into rolling wooded lowlands, and he saw ahead of him, so
far off that it seemed to have been moulded from thickened blue
air, the familiar wave-lift of the Virocon, which he had seen as
long as he could remember from the open end of the courtyard
at home.

That night he came down closer to the road, and found the
place where Kyndylan's war-host had encamped on their first
night out. The blackened scars of their fires were still to be seen
under the encroaching brambles, and he slept there with their
ghosts for company, and at first light was on the road again.

The last day of his journey started bright, with puffs of white
cloud sailing across a harebell sky. But as the day went on the
cloud thickened, and when at last he came in sight of Viroconium,
it was raining and the Virocon rising beyond the white walls of

the town seemed to have turned inwards on itself and sit brooding darkly on ancient sorrows, in its fleece of wet woods; while the Sabrina curling southward into its gorge was grey as a sword-blade, sullen and without light.

Owain crossed the river by the paved ford, and squelched on up the last stretch of the road, his shoulders hunched and his chin driven down into the wet folds of his cloak.

The gravestones, which were always the first things one met outside a town, were each side of the road now. They were dark with rain, and the first fallen yellow leaves of the poplar trees lay wet against their feet. He passed the turf banks of the Amphi-theatre, and then the double arch of the South Gate was before him, with the road leading through. There were no guards at the Gate. The walls looked much as usual save for a reddish stain spreading up one bastion that might have been the scar of fire; but as Owain, his chin still tucked down and the weary hound at his heels, trudged in through the archway and his padding foot-steps turned hollow in the enclosed space, they sounded like foot-steps in a house that is empty and hearth-cold.

He had passed two farms burnt out and deserted, that day. That should have warned him. But he had refused to understand what their blackened ruins meant; he had said to himself, 'It was a chance raid, no more,' and pushed on, with the dread that he would not look at thrust into the back of his mind.

There were no bodies piled within the Gate, no signs of a struggle that he could see. The townsfolk must have known that the Saxons were coming, and lacking their fighting men, fled in time. And the Barbarians, flooding into an empty town, had looted and burned to their fierce hearts' delight. Owain wandered on down the straight street towards the Forum, aimlessly, because he had got to the place he was making for and found it dead, and there was nowhere else to go. And as he drifted along, he looked about him.

Viroconium had been half empty when he came that way before. It had been falling into decay for a hundred years, be-coming slowly sleepier and more unkempt, the grass and the little dusty shepherd's purse creeping further out from the sides of the streets. But there had still been life in Viroconium when

Kyndylan's war-host had gathered in the spring; voices and footsteps in the streets, and children playing on doorsteps, and smells of cooking towards evening. Now, the city was dead. The streets were silent, and the houses stood up gaunt and gutted, with blind eyes and blackened roof-beams fallen in.

Owain found himself at the Forum Gate, with its proud inscription to the Emperor Hadrian, and halted there, staring dazedly about him, while Dog stood watching him expectantly and wagging his tail. It was growing dusk, and he thought suddenly—it was a thought that made the sick laughter rise in his throat—that he could sleep in the Basilica tonight, he could sleep in the Palace of Kyndylan the Fair, if he chose; he was free of all Viroconium. But the little low-browed shops in the Forum colonnade seemed to offer a deeper and darker refuge to crawl into. One or two near the Gate still had their roofs on them, and he turned to the nearest of these. It looked to have been a basket-maker's shop; everything that could be of use to the marauders had been stripped from it, but a broken pigeon basket and a bundle of withies still lay in one corner. The light was going fast, and the back of the shop was already lost in the shadows of the rainy twilight.

Dog, who was tired of being wet, padded in and shook himself, scattering a shower of drops from his thick brindled hide. Owain followed, dragging himself like a sorely hurt animal into the darkest corner, and lay down with his sodden cloak still about him. He lay curled in on himself and pressed against the wall behind him, his knees drawn up and his head in his arms, as though he would have shrunk away into the shadows and ceased to exist altogether if he could. He had thought that he knew it was the end of all things, in the night after the battle, but he knew now he had never quite believed it; always, all the long road north and while he lay sick of his wound, he had clung to some desperate hope that he had not really looked at; the hope that if he could only get back to Viroconium where they had hosted in the spring, there would be something . . . somehow life would go on again. But there was nothing. Viroconium was dead. All the world he knew was dead and cold, and he understood for the first time—he had never quite believed that either, even though

he had found their bodies—that he would never see his father and
Ossian again.

Dog sat beside him, watching with ears pricked and head a
little on one side, as though he wondered why his Lord made these
distressful muffled noises, and why his shoulders jerked.

Later, when Owain had cried himself into stillness, Dog lay
down beside him and licked his face; and the boy put his arm
round the hound's neck, feeling some kind of dim comfort in
the warmth and living strength of it under the harsh hide. And
sleep came for them both together.

Once in the night Dog roused, and Owain, woken by his
movement, felt the hair lift on the hound's neck as he raised his
head growling softly, and looked towards the entrance of the
shop. For a moment his own hair prickled on his nape, and his
heart began to race. But nothing happened, and there was no
sound save the rain on the roof.

Next time he woke it was full daylight; the rain had stopped
and there were smeared gleams of light on the wet herring-bone
bricks of the pavement. Dog was afoot already, and sniffing about
the doorway and the Forum Gate, as though after whatever had
been there in the night. Owain sat up, and drew his legs under
him, and got slowly to his feet. He was so stiff and weary, that
he felt as though he had been beaten, and for the first few moments he could hardly stand. He lurched across to the shop
entrance, and stood propped weakly against the fire-scorched
doorpost, looking out across the Forum. He did not know what
he was going to do now, he had not thought beyond getting
back to Viroconium. But meanwhile, his body knew that it must
have food, and even before food, water. Dog was lapping the
puddles that last night's rain had left in the roadway, but it wasn't
easy for a human to do that, Owain knew, for he had tried.
There was a fountain in the centre of the Forum; it was dead like
everything else, but when he went to look, the drain was choked
with leaves, and there was a little rain water in the green-stained
bowl. He managed to scoop some up in his cupped hands and
drink before it all ran back between his fingers. 'Food now,' said
his body, and he felt inside the breast of his tunic for the snares of
springy plaited horsehair that Priscus had given him. Evening was

the time to set a snare, but if he waited until then he could get nothing until tomorrow; if he set the snares now, there was a chance, though only a slim one, that there might be something in one of them by night, and if not, he had lost nothing. Anyway, he had nothing else to do.

It seemed a long way back to the South Gate, and he had not realized until now how footsore he was. Once he thought he heard footsteps behind him, very light and pattering, but when he looked round, there was no one there. The burial ground outside the walls had fallen into decay like the rest of Viroconium, long ago; saplings had sprung up between the graves, and here and there arched sprays of bramble and grey-bearded traveller's-joy laced the tombstones together, and looking about him, Owain thought that it would be as good a place as any for his snares. It was not long before he found what he wanted, the hollow line of a hare's run among the grass and brambles. While Dog stood by watching, he set his first snare at the foot of a stone to one Marcus Petronius of Vicenza, Standard Bearer to the 14th Legion, aged 39 years; and wondered, as he drew the crimson-leaved bramble sprays down to conceal his handiwork, if Marcus Petronius would have been angry or pleased, or cared at all, to know that one day somebody was going to set a snare for Lord Longears on his grave.

He set the two remaining snares in different runs, ate a couple of handfuls of blackberries, not more, hungry though he was, because he had learned by now the unwisdom of too many blackberries on an empty belly, and then turned drearily back to the town.

All that day, with Dog padding at his heels or turning off to investigate odd corners, he wandered about Viroconium, up and down the silent streets and in and out of the shops and houses, like an unquiet ghost.

He had not seen or heard anything more since that odd fancy or steps pattering behind him on the road to the South Gate, and yet all the time he had the feeling that he was being watched. It was just the loneliness, of course—though once or twice Dog had looked round quickly, or raised his muzzle to sniff the wind. . . .

By and by they found a breach in a high wall and scrambled

over into some gardens, which he judged were those of Kyndylan's Palace. There were apple trees close to the wall; some of
their branches had been scorched, but not badly, and the apples
lay in the grass around their feet. Owain picked one up and bit
into it, but the sourness of it dried his mouth like a quince, and he
threw it away, saying to Dog who was nosing at another, 'No,
you fool, come away. It is better to have an empty belly than the
bellyache.'

He was not much in the habit of talking to Dog; for the most
part they lived together in companionable silence; and the sound
of his own voice, which he had not heard for days, made him
jump. It was like a pebble dropped into a pool, the ripples of it
spreading out and out through the silence, and without knowing
why, he glanced behind him.

As he did so, there was a small fluttering in the heart of some
overgrown bushes beside the gap in the wall. His heart lurched
unpleasantly, and then steadied as a chiff-chaff darted out, and the
fluttering was explained. He hunched his shoulders and turned
away. 'Stop jumping at shadows,' he told himself. 'It is because
you want food, that is all.' But before he was out of sight of the
bushes, he glanced back once more. Nothing stirred among them
now; the chiff-chaff was darting and hovering after flies under the
apple trees.

Owain prowled on, his feet carrying him now towards the
fire-stained walls and colonnades of Kyndylan's Palace. On the
way, he came on a little grotto down three steps, with a grey
stone roof under an overarching tangle of hazel bushes; and
below the eaves, water still trickling from the mouth of a bronze
lion's mask. He had found water in other places in Viroconium,
but it was mostly foul and stagnant; this was fresh and sweet, and
he and Dog drank their fill from the ferny basin, and remembered
it for the next time they were thirsty.

Kyndylan's Palace was a shell; the walls stood up, empty and
fire-stained, roofed with the drifting blue and grey of the autumn
sky, the great chambers choked up with charred beams and all the
debris of the fallen roof. But at the end of the slaves' wing he
came on a small store-room two steps below ground level, which
still had most of its roof, though the tiles were broken and he

could see the sky through a jagged gap in one corner. And the part of himself that was concerned with such things recognized it for a good place to camp. He could even have a fire here to cook his hare if he caught one. That was as well, for the shop where he had slept last night was darkened in his mind as though the misery that had overwhelmed him there had filled it with a black cloud, and he knew that whether or not he found other shelter, he could not go back to it.

There was plenty of wood lying about in the ruins, and not all of it wet. He collected a good supply, and made ready his fire in the middle of the beaten earth floor; he even brought in a few armfuls of long grass and weeds from the nearest part of the garden, and flung them down in the corner furthest from the hole in the roof, to make a bed. Then he sat on it, and scratched the scar on his arm, and waited for dusk to come. It seemed the longest day that he had ever known.

Evening came at last, and he set out on the long journey back to his snares. Two of them he found empty, but in the third, the one set on the standard bearer's grave, there was a fat buck hare. He took it out, with a salute to the shade of Marcus Petronius, paunched it and let Dog eat the offal; and resetting the snare, set out for Kyndylan's Palace, his kill swinging in his hand.

He felt a vague unwillingness, now that he was outside it, to go back into the empty town in the dark—though to be sure the moon was rising—and as he

trudged wearily in once more through the dark gate-arch into the brightening moonlight of the street beyond, the sense of being watched was stronger on him than ever. He stopped to listen, as he had stopped so often that day, and a small sound that he had been hearing stopped with him; *splat-splat-splat*—but it was only a little blood dripping from the hare where he had paunched it.

The half-fallen rafters made queer shadows on the pavement of Kyndylan's colonnades, and he found himself avoiding them with care, or else deliberately wading through them to show himself that there was nothing there; a trail of ivy swinging in the little wind made him whirl round in his tracks, and the *kee wick-wick-wick* of a hunting owl set his heart racing and damped the palms of his hands. But he reached his corner of the slaves' wing at last, and squatting down, set to work to get a spark from his strike-a-light. It took a long time, and he tore one finger with the flint, but it came at last, and he got the fire going. He felt better after that, and while the fire burned up he set to work to skin the hare. He gave the skin with the head and paws still inside it to Dog, who leapt on it, tearing and worrying as though it were a full-grown buck, and choking himself with the fur. Then he poked the skinned hare into the hot edge of the fire with his knife, and began the difficult business of getting it cooked a little without burning it.

Presently there was a strong smell of scorching flesh, and when he managed to rake the thing out and get it turned over, there was a blackened patch on its shoulder. He must be more careful. He scraped off the charred surface, and put more wood on the fire, trying to build it a little round the hare without getting it too close.

It burned with small bright flames over a glowing heart, for the firewood was seasoned timber; the smoke curled upward to find its way out through the hole in the roof, and warmth stole out into the little store-room with the tawny light that fluttered over the intent faces of the boy and the hound.

At last, probing with his knife, Owain decided that the meat was cooked as well as it was ever likely to be; at any rate he could wait no longer. He had been beyond feeling hungry when he brought back his kill, only a little sick, but now with the smell of the baking meat curling up into his nostrils, the warm water was running into his mouth so that he had to keep swallowing. He raked it out from the hot ash with his knife and a bit of wood, and rolled it over on to the floor to get cool enough to handle. And as he did so, Dog, who had long since finished his share and was lying nose on paws watching the cooking, raised his head and looked towards the doorway, his eyes like green lamps in the firelight, and growled softly in his throat, as he had done the night before.

Owain also looked towards the doorway.

The moonlight made a bar of silver on the edge of each of the steps, and shone full on the wall just inside the door. The last time he looked that way, the moonlight had been empty save for the cracks in the plaster; now, on the milky light, he saw a shadow, angular and delicate as that of a grasshopper, but seemingly human.

5

Regina

OWAIN grabbed Dog's collar as the great hound sprang up, and scrambled to his feet, shouting something, he did not know what. The shadow started back as though to run, hung for an instant on the edge of the dark, then slipped forward across the moon-whitened wall. A figure with the same sharp-edged delicacy as the shadow appeared in the doorway, and a husky voice edged with fear, begged, 'Don't let the dog hurt me.'

'I'll set the dog on you this instant, if you don't come into the firelight and show me what you are,' Owain panted, strangling at Dog's collar with both hands. 'Peace, Dog! Be quiet! Quiet, I say!'

The figure came slowly down the steps and into the firelight.

Owain found himself looking at a girl of maybe twelve years old, a dark creature with arms and legs as thin as bare bone sticking out of the tattered remains of a filthy tunic. She had come close in to the fire, and they surveyed each other, while Dog, ceasing to growl, stood watchful at his Lord's side. The girl stood poised, flinching and wary, as though ready to run at any moment, yet at the same time defiant, staring back at Owain with the most extraordinary eyes, grey as rain and fringed all round with black lashes. He did not notice that she smelt, for he had grown used to smells since Kyndylan's war-host marched from Viroconium, but he did notice that there were dark sores round her mouth, and something crawled out of her matted hair and disappeared into it again.

'Who are you, and what do you want?' he demanded furiously. 'Is it you who have been spying on me all day?'

She answered the second of his three questions, which was the one most to the point as far as she was concerned. 'I smelled the meat cooking.'

There was a faint whine in her voice that he did not like. He stooped and picked up the hare, which was cool enough to handle now, tore off one of its back legs, and tossed it to her as though she were a dog. 'There, take it.'

She snatched it up and crammed it against her mouth with both hands, tearing and worrying at it; but all the while her eyes never left his face. In an unbelievably short time the bones were bare. She pulled them apart, licking the last threads of meat from between them, then dropped them and held out her cupped hands in the gesture of the trained beggar. 'I am very hungry. Let my Lord give me the other leg.'

So that was what she was: a beggar. Savagely, Owain tore off the other leg and dropped it into her pleading hands; then he began hurriedly to eat as well, lest she should ask for more and more until there was none of his kill left for him at all.

So they ate standing, staring at each other beside the fire. The girl finished first and stood sucking the bones, her eyes fixed on the remains of the hare which he still held; but Owain refused her silent pleading—fair was fair, it was *his* kill and he had given her nearly half of it anyway—and ate on to the end, stripping the nutty white flesh along the backbone; then he gave the carcass with a few rags of meat still on it to Dog. He was angry at having been frightened, even more than at having lost so much of his supper, but against his will he was a little glad to find that he was not the only human being alive in the dead city; and after he had licked his fingers, he demanded, 'What is your name?'

'Regina,' she said, licking her fingers also, and the greasiness round her mouth.

Owain had enough Latin, though people did not use it much in everyday speech nowadays, to know what that meant. He laughed. 'Queen! That's a likely name for you, isn't it? Were your father and mother of royal blood, then?'

'I never had a father nor a mother,' Regina said, as one stating a simple fact. 'I lived with an old woman, but she died last winter. She made me beg for her, and when I did not bring home enough, she used to beat me. Once I tried to kill her, but she tasted the killing-herbs in the broth, and beat me until I could not stand.'

Hearing her husky level voice and seeing the look in her eyes as she spoke, Owain did not doubt that the story was perfectly true. But for the moment there were other things about her that interested him more. 'What are you doing here alone in Viroconium?' he demanded, frowning. 'If you are alone. I thought the town was empty.'

'No.' She was rubbing her bare feet one over the other where the warmth of the fire fell. 'It was not empty. I was here all the time.'

'Since the Saxons came?'

'Yes, since—then.'

Owain said hoarsely, 'Tell me what happened.'

'There was a great stir all through the city, and they cried that the Saxons were coming and all the farms *that* way'—she pointed south and east with a bony finger—'were burning. And all the people caught up food and the things they wanted most to save, that were light enough to carry, and ran away into the hills. I ran with them, but only a little way, and when the Saxons had gone again and the fire died down, I came back.'

'Why?'

She looked at him with those strange rain-grey eyes wide and grave. 'It is the only place I know.'

Owain was silent a moment; then he said, 'Weren't you afraid to be here all alone, with the town dead and empty?'

'No. I would have been more afraid where the others went, into the hills. There were no roofs to hide you from the sky.'

'There aren't many here.'

'There are little dark corners. Besides——' and her voice hardened with vicious satisfaction, 'Viroconium I like better without people in it.'

In the complete silence that followed, Owain heard the wind rising, rustling the scorched leaves to and fro. Despite himself he was aware of a sudden ache of pity. He did not want to feel it, because he knew that it was the beginning of things coming back to life in him and that coming back to life would hurt like the blood running back into a frozen limb.

Regina heard the wind too, and shivered, creeping a little closer to the fire, her thin wisp of a face sharpened with entreaty; and he saw that she was afraid she had made him angry—and he had a fire. The beggar's whine was back in her voice. 'You'll not turn me away? The wind blows so cold now that it is autumn. Let me sit near the fire. See—not very near, just where a *little* warmth reaches.'

Owain glared, guarded and resentful because she was making things come alive in him, and it hurt; oh, how it hurt! But he knew that he could no more turn her away from his fire than he could have turned Dog. 'There is fire to spare for both of us. Stay if you must,' he said grudgingly. And she sighed and folded up on to her heels as though she had been there all along.

Owain sat on his haunches with Dog sprawled against him, and went on staring at her, while she leaned forward holding her hands to the flame. They were so thin that the fire shone through them red, and he could see the delicate shadows of the bones. 'Why have you followed me and watched me in secret all day?' he asked at last.

D

'I wanted to see what you were doing, and I was afraid if you saw me you would throw stones at me.'

'Did people often throw stones at you?'

'Oh yes, quite often.' She turned the backs of her hands to the fire. 'What *were* you doing? Why have you come to Viroconium?'

Owain stared into the fire and scratched the scar on his arm. 'I was with Kyndylan's war-host—I and my father and my brother—when we gathered here in the spring. And after—after it was all over'—his voice began to shake and he steadied it carefully—'I thought that if there were any more of us left alive, they might gather here again; and if I came back, I—might find them.' It was odd: with their sitting down by the fire together, something had changed between him and the girl. A little while ago he would not have told her that; he would simply have bidden her go tend her own business.

She looked at him quickly; all her movements were as though quicksilver ran in her veins. 'There was a battle? And the Saxons won?'

'Yes.'

'No one came,' Regina said.

Owain shook his head, still staring into the red heart of the fire.

She reached out in a little while, and pointed at the purplish scar that showed below his sleeve. 'It was in the battle you got *that*?'

'Yes,' he said again.

Regina gazed at it in silence. Then she thrust out one small bare foot and turned the sole upward for him to see. 'Look, I have a scar here. I got it on a piece of broken glass.'

Owain looked. Her foot was dusty and scurfed, ingrained grey and brown with ancient dirt; but through the dirt he could see the thin white scar running jagged from the arch down towards the root of the big toe. For a moment, because he had grown up in the past months and forgotten some of the things he once knew, he was not sure why she was showing it to him. Was she proud of it? Had she perhaps used it in her begging, to get sympathy and so more charity? And then he understood, remembering himself and Ossian comparing their backs after a beating. Comparing

scars was a companionable thing to do. It was a gesture of friendship; probably the first she had ever made.

He reached out and touched her foot, feeling it icy under the
caked dryness of the dirt. 'That must have hurt,' he said gruffly.
'Your feet are still frozen. Put them nearer to the fire.'

She did as he told her, sighing in the warmth, and asked, 'What
is *your* name? I told you mine.'

'Owain,' he said. And then, 'I set the snare again before I came
away. Maybe there'll be another hare tomorrow.'

When the little fire burned out, they spread the bedding-grass
wider, and shared Owain's cloak. It was ragged at the hem by
now, but thick, and big enough for two if they lay close together.
Dog slept with his chin across Owain's knees, and growled very
softly in warning, every time the girl moved in the night.

In the morning they were hungry again. They went, all three
of them, to the lion-headed fountain, and then to get some
apples. 'The one you tried yesterday came from a tree they used
to make apple wine from,' Regina said. 'That is why it was so
sour. But I can show you the apple trees that are sweet.' And if
the water and apples did not really satisfy them, it killed some of
their hunger for the time being. And when Owain went back to
the deserted burial ground, he found another hare in one of the
snares. So they were sure of full stomachs again tonight.

It was a piece of unbelievably good fortune, but he realized
that he could not go on snaring the same runs over and over again;
he must widen his hunting grounds. He reset his snares on the
edge of the woods above the river gorge, about a bowshot beyond the last of the gravestones, the girl Regina tagging along
behind him like a shadow, though he felt her scared unwillingness, and knew that she did not like to come so far beyond the
city walls. 'I might get a hedgehog hereabouts,' he said. 'We will
not cook the hare until this evening. It is better to eat at the end of
the day, and sleep with something in one's belly.'

And together, Owain carrying the hare, they made their way
back into the city.

In the Wild, Regina was lost and unsure of herself, but once
back within the walls, it was another matter. She slipped into the

lead, catching his free hand and pulling him after her by back ways and short cuts, in at the gaping doorway of one house and out through the broken wall at the back of another; and about every corner of every ruin she seemed to have something, mostly disgraceful, to tell of the people who had once lived there.

Down an alley off the street to the West Gate, they came to the blind-eyed shell of a house, with a fire-blackened hawthorn twisted as wrought-iron-work leaning over the doorway in its courtyard wall. 'That is the house of Ulpius Pudentius,' said Regina. 'He was very old, and they said he had bags and boxes full of gold under his bed. They said—everybody said—that his forefathers made it by doctoring broken-winded mules and selling them to the soldiers while they seemed all right.' She was leaning on the remains of the door timbers as she spoke, her pointed chin in her hands as she stared through. 'He once gave me a copper coin. I was the only beggar he ever did *that* to.'

'How did that happen?' Owain said, staring into the little courtyard beside her.

'I ran behind him in the street on all fours, and brayed,' said Regina. 'He threw it at me to go away.'

They hid the paunched hare in a convenient hole in Kyndylan's private colonnade, and spent part of the rest of the day making their lair more comfortable, getting in more firewood and more grass for bedding. They found an old rust-eaten sword in the ruins of a house, and brought it in to spike the hare on when the time came to cook it. It seemed to have become an accepted thing that the lair was for both of them now. Owain never asked her where she had slept before; maybe she had had no particular hideout but had merely curled up in a different corner every night.

He went back to look at his snares much earlier that evening than he had done yesterday, because of Regina, but even so, she did not come with him that time, but slipped off by herself at the last moment on some business of her own. The snares were all empty, and one of them had been interfered with by a fox. He reset it, and came back through the wild burial ground and the dead streets of Viroconium to the store-room at the far end of Kyndylan's Palace.

Regina was not there, and suddenly the little dark lair looked empty without her. But he had scarcely had time to notice that when he heard the patter of bare feet and saw her coming towards him along the broken colonnade, with her tattered skirt gathered up in front of her, very carefully, as though she had something precious hidden in its folds. Dog, who had by now accepted her into their company, swung his tail in greeting, and thrust a hopeful muzzle at whatever it was she carried; and Owain cuffed him away, but looked curiously in the same direction himself. 'What have you got there?'

For answer, she opened the gathered-up folds of her skirt, and he saw that the treasure was a few handfuls of yellow grain.

'Where did you find that?'

'It is in the baskets under the big baker's shop in the Forum. The rats eat it too. There are still a few cats—you can hear them singing sometimes at night when there's a moon. But there aren't enough to keep the rats down, and so they eat the corn. But there's still quite a lot left.'

So that was how she had kept alive all this while. He had not thought to wonder until now. When she first appeared, her coming had been so startling, and afterwards it seemed so much a matter of course, that either way he had not thought to wonder how she had lived before.

As she spoke, she had gathered the folds of her skirt into one hand, and with the other she was picking out a few golden grains. With a curious deliberate delicacy, as though she was doing something familiar that delighted her, and making it last as long as possible, she scattered them almost singly, a few on the broken pavement, a few more on the half wall of the colonnade.

There had not seemed to be any birds about when she started, but on the instant, with a purr of wings from all directions, they were there; dust-coloured sparrows cuddling to the ground, a robin perched on long legs, a rose-breasted chaffinch, a shy thrush hovering on the outskirts of the throng; and the grey flagstones were alive with them among the gold-spangling of the scattered barley.

And then, with a flash of jewel-blue through the air, a tit darted to her feet, where she had dropped the last grain of all.

Dog stiffened, thrusting forward his broad muzzle towards the impertinent feathered atom on the pavement; and the tit, waking to the presence of unknown monsters, started, spread its wings and made a sound like an infinitely small cat spitting; and losing its head, darted off in the wrong direction, through the dark store-room doorway, with Dog bounding in pursuit.

Regina dropped her skirt, scattering the precious barley far and wide, and let out a shriek. 'Oh! he'll catch it! He'll catch it!'

'No he won't.' Owain flung himself after the great hound. He had forgotten the two steps down, his feet flew from under him, and he plunged forward with a yell, landing with most of the breath knocked out of him, but his arms fast about the hound's neck. Dog threshed around with his tail lashing wildly behind him; the carefully built up firewood scattered right and left and above them the panic-stricken tit dashed itself from wall to wall.

He heard Regina cry out as though the hurt was in herself: 'Don't! Oh *don't*! You'll hurt your wings!' She slipped without speed across to the far wall, where the tit, ceasing for a moment its frantic darting to and fro, clung with wings spread to the broken plaster, and reached up her hands to it quite slowly. Owain sat among the wreckage of the fire, his arms still round the excited hound, and watched her as if he were seeing her for the first time.

'Come then, stupid,' she said, and gathered the tiny creature as though it had been a flower, closing her hollowed hands over it, and turned towards the door. Then she hesitated, and in the sudden quiet after the turmoil, came across to Owain, and stooped over him. 'Look!' she said on a clear note of delight, and parted her fingers a little. The last gold of the sunset streaming in through the low doorway, showed him the tit, captive but quite contented inside the globe of her thin brown hands; the bright eyes in the tiny painted clown's face, the jewel-blue cap of feathers. 'Isn't it *blue*!' said Regina. Then she went to the doorway and up the steps, and standing on the top one among the spilled barley, opened her hands. The tit sprang upward, hung for a moment on vibrating wings that were like tiny fans of blue-green mist against the low sunlight, and darted off. She stood for a moment gazing after it. Then she turned back to the darkening room.

She saw Owain still sitting among the wreckage, with Dog

clasped to his bosom; and flung herself down on the top step with her knees drawn up to her chin, and burst into shrill, hoarse, hooting laughter.

He began to laugh, too, though it was laughter that tore painfully at the misery within him, and for a little while they rocked together. Owain was the first to recover, and scrambling to his feet, took command of the situation. 'This will not get us any supper. Scrape up as much of the barley as you can, and I'll go and fetch the hare.'

It was dusk before the supper was cooking, for they had to remake the fire, and even when Owain had got a spark from his strike-a-light and managed to kindle it, they still had to skin the hare. But it was done at last, and the hare propped on its old sword-blade over the flames, while Dog worried the skin just as he had done last night. And Owain and Regina squatted beside the warmth, dipping turn and turn about in the yellow pool of very dusty grain in her lap and eating while they waited. Among the wood they had collected for the fire were some bits of a small olivewood chest that must have been brought from overseas long ago. The Saxons had burst it open in search of loot, and the little splintered planks were a good size for burning. (He must find something that he could break up bigger wood with, by and by.) It caught quickly when he fed the first bits to the fire, and burned with little oily flames that were blue as the top of the tit's head. No, that was the wrong blue, Owain thought, more like the colour of wild hyacinths.

Regina, glancing up from the grains of barley in her palm, seemed to notice something on the front of his tunic that she had not seen before. Then she pointed: 'What is that?'

And peering downward, Owain saw that his father's ring was hanging in full view. It must have tumbled through the neck of his tunic when he fell down the steps after Dog. His first instinct was to thrust it back out of sight, muttering that it was not anything in particular. But Regina had shown him the scar on her foot in exchange for his; she had not minded him seeing when she fed the birds—and remembering the wolfish way she had eaten last night, he had the sense to know how much feeding the birds must mean to her—and she had shared the blueness of the tit with

him before she let it go. He slipped the thong over his head, and
held it out to her. 'It was my father's ring. It is mine now.'

The light of the flames caught the flawed emerald and it blazed
into a flake of green fire between his fingers; and she leaned towards it with a little gasp, her dirty hand darting out to take it.
'You must have been very rich!' she said, and her fingers suddenly
looked like little brown claws. He had not thought of his father's
ring as being valuable, only as being precious.

'No,' he said. 'That's the only jewel we ever had; and look, it is
flawed. . . . There was just the farm, and it was all we could do to
keep the roof on the byres.'

'Farm? You had a farm all of your own? Where was that?'

'Over that way, maybe a day's march.' He jerked his head
towards the south-eastern corner of the little room.

Regina glanced in the same direction, as though she expected to
see the farm in the shadows beyond the firelight. 'The Saxons
came that way,' she said after a moment.

'I know,' Owain said, staring at the hare. He was thinking of
the burnt-out farms that he had passed two days ago. He had been
careful not to think of his own farm ever since. He knew now that
he would never go back to see what the Saxons had left.

Regina was turning the ring between her fingers, her head bent
over it. 'There's a queer fish-thing carved on it. Is it very old?'

'That's a dolphin,' Owain said. 'Yes, it is old. It came from
somewhere beyond the seas—Rome, I suppose—when we did.
And that was when the Eagles first came to Britain.'

But he saw that she did not know what he was talking about.
He knew, because his father had told him what *his* father had told
him; but there had been no one to tell Regina. Anyhow, it didn't
matter. It was all dead now.

'You should take better care of it,' said Regina, with a hint of
scolding in her tone. 'I could have cut the thong and stolen it
quite easily in the night, if I had known that it was there.'

'Thanks for the warning. I'll sleep with my hand over it
tonight.'

She looked up at him with those strange rain-grey eyes, and
said simply, 'No, you need not. It is no good stealing now. There
is nothing in Viroconium to buy with gold.'

'You could take it out of Viroconium and maybe buy a place in a boat crossing to Gaul. That's what the people who have any gold to spend, buy with it nowadays.'

It was said half in jest, half in unexpected earnest, but either way, Regina slipped away from it as though it were some kind of menace. She pushed the ring back into his hand, and turned away to the fire. 'Oh look!—the hare is scorching.'

6

The Cattle Raiders

OWAIN came to the edge of the trees that made a dark fleece about the flanks of the Virocon, a pair of wood pigeons swinging in one hand and Dog loping at his heels; and turned his steps, weary from his day's hunting, back towards the pale gleam that was the walls of Viroconium. He shivered in the thin east wind that parted Dog's hair in zigzags down his back, and thought of the cooking fire that Regina would have made ready.

He was hungry as well as tired, and the store-hole in the wall had been empty, so there would be nothing to eat until the pigeons were cooked. Once, he and Dog had killed a yearling roebuck—the sling he was carrying now, tucked into his belt, was made of its skin—and the three of them had gorged themselves for days. But there had been other times, especially when the snow came, when he and Dog had snared and hunted for days, desperately, without a kill and there had been nothing to live on at all save a little corn from the store under the baker's shop. The corn, stale and fouled by rats as it was, had kept them alive; but it was getting low now, and Owain knew that it was time to be going.

He had known all along that they could not go on living in their dead city for ever. The Saxons might come back any day, the woods were full of broken men, and the hunting was not good. But every time he tried to speak to Regina of what they should do, she slipped away from the subject with a kind of silvery whisk like a minnow. Viroconium was the only place she knew, and she was frightened of what lay beyond. And then it had been winter, and one could not travel in the winter.

But now the blackthorn was in flower. . . .

It had been a strange winter; hard and grim and hungry, but with a kind of light shining through it. They had simply lived from day to day, with not much thought to spare from warmth and food, just the business of keeping alive as the vixen who laired by the West Gate understood the business of keeping alive. But now it was over, he found himself remembering the rosemary seedling that Regina had dug up from the Palace gardens and planted in a broken crock by their doorway, and the blue flames of the burning olivewood. They had not burned it all. 'We will keep some of it for another time. It is too beautiful to burn all at once,' Regina had said. Owain scratched his head—there were things that walked about in his head now—and realized suddenly that he was thinking of their time at Viroconium as something that belonged to the past already; and of course it did no such thing; he still had to talk Regina into coming away. Well then, if she would not come, he'd go without her! But he knew he would not. He was not always sure that he liked her very much, especially when the beggar's whine crept into her voice, though that did not often happen now; but he knew that they belonged together, as he and Ossian had belonged together even when they fought.

The sun had gone and the light was thickening under a stormy sky as he came up to the North Gate, and the wind ran shivering through the long grass. And in the gateway he checked, sniffing. But it was nothing so tangible as a smell that had pulled him up;

it was the odd instinctive feeling one may have on entering a house that is supposed to be empty, that it is not empty at all.

Then Dog growled, soft and menacing, deep in his throat, and looking down, Owain saw the hackles rise on the hound's neck and down his spine. And suddenly his own heart was racing, and he did not know why.

He stooped, and slipped the bit of old rope that he used as a hunting leash through Dog's collar, and then went on. He was about a spear-throw from the Gate when he heard it; a distant splurge of voices somewhere ahead of him in the ruins that had been silent so long. He checked a second time, listening. Everything was quiet now, only a thrush singing in the gardens. And then as he stood straining his ears for any sound above the racing drub of his own heart, it came again, and mingled with it the distressful lowing of cattle.

The sounds seemed to come from the direction of the Forum. 'Quiet now,' Owain muttered to Dog, thankful that being a warhound he was trained to keep silent at command; and together they turned aside from the straight main street into the gardens behind the city's principal inn. No sense in going blundering down the open street into whatever was happening. Silent as a pair of shadows for all the speed that they were making, the boy and the hound crossed the garden and took to the maze of narrow alleys beyond, heading by back-ways and through the ruins of shops and houses in a bee-line for the Forum.

Round most of the Forum the streets ran broad and open, making of it an island, but on the north side the ruins of a tall house had fallen across the way and gave some sort of cover almost up to the side entrance against the wall of the Basilica. And in a short while the boy, with the hound still in leash, was stealing forward through the fallen timbers, into the gateway. On his left rose the wall of the Basilica like a cliff, on his right the blackened ruins of a garland-maker's shop, and at the end of the narrow cleft between, were sounds of men and beasts and the red flicker of firelight.

Owain slipped aside, crouching, into the ruins of the shop; and next instant, as he peered out through the charred tangle of the colonnade, the whole scene in the Forum was plain before him.

The light was fading fast, though overhead the storm-clouds had caught fire from the sun that was already way down behind the Western Mountains; and the great blaze that was leaping and crackling in the centre of the open space seemed to echo the gold and copper and ice-green of the sky. Upward of a score of men were gathered about the fire, a lean, ragged, wolfish crew, spears in their hands or lying beside them; and dim in the gusty twilight and the fringes of the fire, he saw the shapes of shaggy knee-haltered mountain ponies; further out still, fenced into the lower end of the Forum with a barricade of half-charred timbers, a huddle of cattle, brown flanks and wild eyes and uptossed wide-horned heads. Calves among them too, from the sound of it, and cows in milk.

'I still think we'd have done better to push straight on and get them across the river tonight,' one of the men was saying discontentedly, and Owain realized with a sense of shock that the words were not spoken in the guttural Saxon, but in his own tongue. Not a Saxon raiding band, but a British one; broken men out of the woods, maybe.

'So near to dark, and with the rain that there's been in the hills to bring it down in spate?' growled another, a small lean man with thatch of badger-striped hair, who seemed to be a leader among them. 'Milch cows with calves among them too? Don't be a bigger fool than you were born to be, Cunor Bigmouth.'

'Anyway, who is to follow us?' said a third, in the soft leaping voice of one bred in the mountains. 'I did not see many Saxons left when we had finished with the farm.' And there was a general laugh, snarling and ugly with the wolf pack note in it.

They had killed a half-grown steer out of the herd, and several of them were flaying it beside the fire, the flamelight striking on their fierce intent faces and the blades of the long knives. Owain felt the whimper rise in Dog's throat, despite his training, at the smell of the warm ox-blood, and strangled it quiet with desperate hands. He had seen all he needed to see; now the thing was to go and find Regina. But even as he drew his knee under him to slip away, he froze once more, as, with scarcely any sound of footsteps in their soft raw-hide shoes, three more men, returning probably from a foraging expedition, loomed in through the Forum arch.

What happened then was so quick that it was over almost
before he realized that anything was happening at all. As the latecomers entered, there was a startled movement among the ruins
of the colonnade, right in their path. One of the men pounced
on it like a dog on a rat; there was an instant's scuffle, and a burst
of fierce laughing voices, and then a scream. And the man came
striding on towards his fellows round the fire, with a small figure
fighting like a mountain cat across his shoulder.

Owain felt sick as from a blow in the stomach; too late to go
and find Regina.

The man swung her down into the midst of the group, holding
her fast with her thin arms twisted behind her back. 'See, lads,
here's something else beside cattle to carry back with us into the
mountains.'

They crowded close around her while in their midst Regina
twisted and wrenched at her pinioned arms. Owain caught one
glimpse of her, her matted hair falling over her face, as she
writhed round and doubled up to sink her teeth into a man's
wrist and hung on, worrying at it. 'Ah, would you, you wild
cat!' someone snarled; and he heard the sound of a blow followed
by a shriek and a stream of filthy gutter words in the girl's hoarse
high voice; and for the moment all sight of Regina was lost to
him.

His first instinct had been to loose Dog on them and come
flying out with his knife, but his brain was working cold and
quick, and he knew that would be a fatal thing to do. Even with
Dog's terrible jaws to help him, what could he do against a score
of armed men? And after he and Dog were dead, there would be
no one left to help Regina. If he could make a diversion of some
kind, that would be the thing——

The plan seemed to come to him ready-made, and next instant
he was melting back into the shadows, still clutching Dog's leash,
leaving the pigeons abandoned where he had laid them down. He
was slipping from one patch of dense shadows to the next, along
the ruined colonnade towards the far corner where the cattle were
penned; and as he went he plunged his hand into the little raw-
hide pouch at his belt, feeling desperately for the few sling pebbles
he had left from his day's hunting. Five or six by the feel of it;

that should be enough. In his ears were the voices and the ugly laughter about the fire, but he did not waste time in looking that way again. His business was with the cattle. . . . And a few moments later he was crouching close behind the place where they were penned. Dog was pressed against him, obedient to his orders, but he could feel the eagerness for battle, the rage and the bewilderment quivering through the great hound, as he drew out the first of his sling stones and lobbed it on to the broad back of the nearest cow.

She flung up her head and shifted uneasily, but no more; he chose a calf for his next target, throwing with all the strength and skill he possessed, and heard the young one bawl in pain and fright, as he ducked back behind the screening wreckage. Then he threw at the cow again before her unease had time to die away, and she snorted and flung up her head trying to turn full circle in the crowded pen. The fourth pebble caught a steer on its soft moist nose, and set it bellowing. The pen was a sea of tossing heads now, and he heard a warning shout from the direction of the fire as he lobbed the fifth pebble into their midst to keep the panic spreading. He had no need of the sixth pebble; a cow had gored one of the steers, the calves were bawling in terror, and the whole pen was in a milling turmoil. Suddenly the rough barricades burst and swirled aside, and the whole mass poured out into the open, bellowing and kicking and trying to horn each other as Owain, still clinging to Dog's leash, rose with a yell behind them.

'The cattle are stampeding!' 'Someone's driving the cattle!' 'Attack—it's an attack!' he heard men shouting.

'It's the Saxons after all——!' They were snatching up their spears as the lowing milch cows bore down upon them. The panic had spread to the ponies now, so that the poor little brutes threshed about neighing, terrified by the hobbles that dragged them to their knees. In a moment the entire Forum was a swirling and plunging chaos, shouts and cries, the lowing of cattle and the shrieks of ponies tore the air, and a bullock dashed right through the fire, bellowing as the flames scorched its hide and scattering burning fragments far and wide. And at that instant Regina twisted out of the slackened grasp of the man who held her, ducked under an outstretched arm, and came flying towards the Forum Gate.

Owain raced in the same direction, and reaching it first, turned for an instant to wait for her. She was running like a wild thing, her black hair flying behind her, and even in the dusk he saw the white terror in her face. 'It's all right—it's me!' he panted, and caught her as she reached him and stumbled, and swung her past him, just as a handful of the raiders, waking to what was really happening, came yelling out of the chaos after them.

Snatching one backward glance, he turned behind her, Dog racing leashed at his side, and together they hurled themselves across the street into the shadows opposite. A narrow alley-way opened to them, and they tore down it, then swerved right into another. They were in the street of metal-workers now, and squat forge chimneys rose along the way, dark and fireless against the sky; and they swung left again into a tangle of mean streets, just as the first of the hunters burst howling into the far end of the street behind them.

After that they lost all count of time or distance. It was like being hunted through the twisting ways of a nightmare; streets that seemed to stretch out to infinity with no cover in them, and the shells of the ruined houses crowding close to stare down at them with blind eyes as they ran; and always the yammer of the hunt behind. But Owain, who was choosing the way, knew every gap and short cut and dark corner of Viroconium now, as well as the girl did, and soon the dusk would be thick enough to cover them; and darting and turning and twisting in their tracks like hares, the time came when the cry of the hunt grew fainter and seemed to lose purpose behind them. And they knew that for the moment, at all events, they had shaken off their pursuers.

They were in the garden of a big house when they stopped to listen and draw breath. It was full dusk by now; the clouds were racing bat-winged overhead, and the rising wind was hushing among the dark masses of holly and juniper, driving the first chill drops of rain before it. And from the town, seemingly from two or three quarters at once, came the distant sounds of the hunt questing to and fro, faintly querulous like hounds that had lost the scent, while from the direction of the Forum they could make

out other shouts and the lowing of cattle where men were still
rounding up the scattered herd. Owain was catching great gasps
of air, and as the drubbing of his heart quietened, he heard
Regina's quick panting breaths like those of a little hunted animal.
But even as he listened, it seemed to him that the sounds of the
hunt were drawing nearer, and in the same instant Regina gave a
terrified gasp. 'They're coming this way!'

He reached out his free hand and caught hers. He knew that
she could not run much more, and they were a long way now
from any of the gates. 'Come!' he whispered. 'Up to the house.
Better cover among the ruins.'

She gave a little sob of exhaustion, but turned instantly to
follow his pull.

It was hard to run with both arms cumbered, but he knew that
if he let go of Regina she probably wouldn't make the house at all,
and he could not risk Dog turning back to give battle on his own
account. So he struggled on, desperately, his heart bursting against
his ribs. It seemed a mile, though in truth it was not much more
than a spear-throw, before they were panting against the half
wall of a colonnade from which most of the little painted columns
had fallen; and as they checked there, the sounds of the hunt swept
nearer behind them. 'Over the wall and get round to the back!'
Owain gasped. He thrust Regina over the fallen debris, scrambling
after her. The house doorway gaped before them and they
stumbled in over the jagged remains of the door timbers, groped
their way through the tangle of the fallen upper storey, found
another door and came out into the ruins of the slaves' quarters
and outbuildings behind. The first rain was spattering on the dry
pavement as they checked again to listen and look about them.

They were in a narrow courtyard, at the far end of which a
hawthorn tree leaned drunkenly across the broken wall that shut
out the street. Owain saw it jaggedly outlined against the last
stormy brightness of the west, and knew that they were in the
house of Ulpius Pudentius who had once thrown a copper coin at
Regina to buy her off from braying after him in the street.

Close beside them some steps led down into the ruined stoke-
house, where in the old days a slave had tended the hypocaust fire.
It was all overgrown now with brambles and the wreck of last

E

autumn's wild convolvulus. 'Wait,' Owain ordered, and letting
go Regina's hand, stumbled down the steps and ducked under the
fallen beam that leaned slantwise at the bottom. Other debris
had fallen across it, but the beam had held it up, and there was a
small triangular gap left, filled with the blackness under the house
floor. Bad air came from it, cold and dank, and he had no means of
knowing how secure the beam was. Maybe they were going to be
buried alive, but it was no time to be thinking of 'maybe'. Next
instant he was out again and reaching up for Regina's hand. 'We
can get under the house floor—the hypocaust—Come!'

He thrust her past him through the dark hole under the beam,
and pushed Dog after her, then turned to draw the brambles and
dead convolvulus stalks across the betraying entrance, and paused
an instant, listening. He thought the voices of the hunt sounded
fainter again, but that might be only the spattering of the rain
and the walls of the house, blanketing sound. Then he worked
his own way in, backwards on his stomach, pulling the last
bramble spray across as he did so.

A little grey light filtered through the tangle, but when he
pushed himself further back and turned about, the blackness was
like a tangible substance pressed against his eyes. Dog was licking
his face as though he had not seen him for a month, and he
reached out, groping into the dark beyond him, and found Regina
crouching where the narrow passage-way opened out under the
floor. 'Go forward,' he whispered, 'right forward as far as we can
away from the opening.' And they felt their way on, between the
squat pillars of the hypocaust, until at last they came to the blank
wall of the house's foundation, and there was no further to go.

Nothing to do now but crouch in the wolf-dark, stretching
one's ears for any sound of the hunt from the world above. Better
to lie down really, because if you sat up you found the floor
above pressing on the back of your neck, and that somehow made
it seem more like being in a trap. Beside him, Regina was pouring
out her story in a sobbing whisper. 'They must have been cattle-
raiding into the Saxon lands, and they—I suppose they came
because the Forum was somewhere to pen the cattle for the night,
and I crept up close to see if there were any milch cows because—I
thought we might have some milk—and then someone came up

behind me and caught hold of me before I could run, and he laughed and——'

'I know; I was there,' Owain whispered back.

'I guessed it was you that stampeded the cattle.'

'Regina——' he was not really listening to her, 'Regina, they were British, weren't they? Not Saxon?'

'They shouted to each other in our tongue. I know because I understood them.'

'Yes, that's what I thought. British gone wild, like dogs that run away to hunt in the woods.' Owain felt clammily sick. To be here in the dark hiding from Saxon raiders was no more than physical danger; to be here hiding from one's own kind, broken men turned wolf pack, was a hideous thing, an uncleanness like leprosy. 'Don't talk any more,' he whispered. 'We don't know how sound carries under here, and anyhow I want to listen.'

But listening did not tell them much, here under the ground, and when once or twice they did catch a sound from the outside world it always came from the direction of the entrance hole, because that was the easiest point at which sound could enter. Once Dog whimpered, and Owain, his hand on the hound's neck, felt the tremors running through his body, and wondered if danger was nearer than it seemed. But it did not feel quite like the quivering tension of the war-dog who smells the enemy; something else—another kind of uneasiness that he did not understand. . . . At last, bidding Regina to stay where she was, he crept back towards the stoke-hole, Dog belly-slithering beside him. It was not easy to find the opening now, for dusk had deepened into night, and there was no gleam of paleness filtering through the debris until he was close upon it. But he found it again in a little, and crouched there, his hand on Dog's collar, listening.

Far off, through the rain, he heard the intermittent lowing of a cow from the Forum, and that was all. The raiders must have given up the chase and returned to their fire and the cattle and whatever shelter there was to be found among the ruined Forum shops. Probably they would be gone at first light, for even though they had killed all the folk on the one farm it would not pay to linger on the way with raided cattle, and meanwhile, to hunt a girl through the streets was a thing that belonged to the hot blood of the moment; now that they had abandoned the hunt they would not return to it again. He drew a long breath of relief, but settled down to keep watch for a while, all the same.

It was some while later that he heard Regina calling him: 'Owain!—Owain!' in a whisper that seemed straining to burst free of her throat into the most dreadful scream.

7

The Olivewood Fire

'WHAT is it? I'm coming,' he whispered back. 'I'm coming, Regina,' and ducking round, he began to feel his way back with frantic haste, through the blackness towards where he had left her.

And all the while she kept up that little frozen call: 'Owain! *Owain!*' as though in that way she were clinging to him by a kind of life-line to save herself from some horror.

'It is all right! Hold on, whatever it is. I'm *coming*—I'm almost there.' He blundered into one of the hypocaust pillars, hurting his shoulder, scrabbled his way past it, and reaching out into the blackness that pressed against his eyeballs, found Regina's skinny arm with the lank masses of her hair tumbling over it. 'I'm here. Nobody's hurting you. What is it?'

'Make a light,' she whispered. 'A light—a light——!' It was almost a wail.

Owain hesitated, but the flash of the strike-a-light could scarcely betray them down here, even if there was someone quite close by, and the horror in Regina's voice could not be denied. He felt for the little leather bag at his belt, and fumbled out the flint and iron pyrites, a dry twig and the whisp of scorched grass he used for tinder. He got his first sparks quickly, and in the in-stant's tiny glow before they went out, saw Regina crouched against the wall staring straight before her with wide terrified eyes, and almost touching her knee, the bones of a human foot— just the bones, with nothing over them. Then the sparks went out.

Regina made a dry sound in her throat. And Owain, with a sudden feeling of suffocation, heard his own voice, shaking. 'Don't be afraid, he can't hurt you. I'm getting the light again.' His fingers were working frantically at the strike-a-light, made clumsy by his desperate urgency; spark followed useless spark, but he got the tinder to catch at last, and dipped the dry twig into it. A little clear tongue of flame sprang up and in the uncertain gleam of light he saw the skeleton of a man huddled, half lying, into the angle of the wall. It was still partly covered by the rags of a fine woollen tunic, and clutched against it by the delicate fan of bones that was one hand, was a leather bag. It was a little open, and something had spilled out from it. Something that gleamed faintly on the floor; and holding the light lower, Owain saw a scatter of coins, thick-furred with dust, but still showing at their edges a thin rind of gold.

Ulpius Pudentius, the master of the house.

The twig was burning down to his fingers.

'I want to go away,' Regina was whispering. 'I put out my hand in the dark and there he was. I want to go out of here.'

'We can't go out, not until those men are away,' Owain told her. 'We'll get back towards the stoke-hole, but we can't go further. There—isn't any harm in him, not now.'

'I wish I hadn't brayed after him in the street,' Regina said.

The flame burned his fingers and he dropped the twig. The darkness rushed in again as the tiny flame twisted and turned blue on the beaten earth floor, and guttered out. He reached out to where he knew Regina was, found her hand and pulled her towards him.

It seemed a very long way back to the stoke-hole, but they reached it at last and felt the wind clearly cold on their faces. The rain had stopped and the clouds parted, and one small white star looked down at them through the charred beams and the bramble sprays, which was somehow comforting. Owain put his arms round Regina and pulled her hard against him to stop her shaking. He wished he had his cloak to wrap round both of them. Dog lay warm and heavy across their feet, starting and twitching from time to time. There was no sound from the Forum.

The night took a long time to pass. Sometimes they dozed a little, huddled together, but never for more than a few moments at a time, and never deeply enough to forget where they were, nor what was in the darkness behind them. The rain came back, and then cleared again, and at last the chinks of sky overhead began to pale a little and turn ash-coloured. A willow wren twittered in the wild thickets of the garden. From the direction of the Forum a steer lowed, and then another. Dog pricked his ears.

'They're moving,' Owain said. It was the first time either of them had spoken in all the long night that lay behind them. Regina raised her head to listen. At any rate she had stopped shaking.

Presently they heard the confused sounds of a cattle drove coming nearer, nearer yet. To the lowing of the cattle was added the pelter of hooves and the shouting of men. They were heading down the broad main street towards the West Gate. To Owain and Regina, crouching tense in their hiding place, the sounds seemed to leap upon them in a burst, as the raiders swept past the narrow entrance of the alley-way; and Dog growled deep in his throat. Then it was growing fainter again, fainter, dying away into the gusty morning. And at last it was gone altogether. The light was growing fast, and thrush and robin were answering the willow wren in the tangled gardens, as though all that had happened had been nothing but an evil dream.

Owain waited a while longer, to be quite sure; then he straight-ened his arms from round Regina. They were so stiff and numb that for a few moments they did not seem to belong to him at all, and nor did his legs when he drew them under him. 'We can go now,' he said. 'Oh, but I'm stiff!' It was queer how ordinary his voice sounded.

They crawled out from under the debris, and without anything said between them, Regina and Dog looking on, Owain set to pulling and heaving at the fallen tangle of charred wood, until with a slithering crash, it came down over the beam, closing the little dark entrance behind them. That would at least keep out wolf and wild dog from the poor bones inside. Then they went back through the morning emptiness of Viroconium, through the Forum, where horse droppings and cattle dung and the great black scar of a fire was left to tell of the night that had passed, to the little store-room at the back of Kyndylan's Palace.

As they came nearer along the broken colonnade, Owain felt Regina begin to hang back a little; he was walking slower himself, wondering what they would find when they got there. But when they reached the low doorway, and he ducked down the two steps after Regina, with Dog bounding ahead, they found everything just as it had been yesterday. Clearly the raiders had not chanced on their hideout at all. Owain stood looking round him, seeing his ragged cloak spread over the dry grass against the wall, and the storage place he had made for the corn with a few boards in one corner. The fire burned out to grey ash—they always kept the fire going when they could, smooring it with turves at night, just as any household did, because it took so long to get fresh fire with the strike-a-light—and the wood piled beside it for last evening's cooking; the rosemary seedling with three pale flowers on it in its broken crock beside the door; the pair of raw-hide moccasins he had made for Regina from the skin of the roebuck, and which she never wore, for the soles of her feet were as hard as horn. The place smelled like an animal's lair, but in an odd way it had been home.

'The fire has gone out,' Regina said.

'We should have had to put it out anyway. If the Saxons came after the cattle it might betray us.'

'There are no Saxons to come; they killed all the folk at the farm.'

'There might be neighbours to avenge them.'

'If they were coming, they would have been here before this,' Regina said. She looked up at him pleadingly. 'Let us make the fire, Owain. I'm so cold; I want the fire here—just once more.'

Owain glanced at her quickly, and away again. So she knew it, too, that this was the end, the time to go.

'Please, just one more fire,' said Regina.

He squatted down and reached for some dry sticks from the woodpile to make the framework of their last fire in Viroconium.

Presently he had it going, the warmth stealing out into the chill of the little dark chamber, and Regina, who had been moving about making what few preparations there were to make for a journey, brought the battered copper pot they cooked in, with water and a few handfuls of grain in it, and propped it over the flames. A hot mush was more sustaining, they had found, than the corn eaten dry, and unless they wished to go hunting for the lost pigeons, which probably the raiders had found anyway, they had nothing else to stay their stomachs with before they set out. The rest of the grain she had scooped into the deerskin bag that Owain had made at the same time as the moccasins. Then she huddled closer to the fire, her thin arms round her updrawn knees, creeping closer as though she would get right among the flames in her efforts to get warm. 'He must have crawled under there because he felt too old to run,' she said, 'and so he died there all alone in the dark.'

'Maybe the smoke smothered him,' Owain said. It was better to think of the old man coughing out his life quickly, than lingering perhaps for days, under the ruins of his world, with only his useless gold to comfort him.

There was a long silence, and then Regina leaned forward to stir the unsavoury mush with a bit of wood to keep it from sticking. 'Where shall we go?' she asked.

Owain did not answer at once. He was thinking. But the strange thing was that he never for one moment thought of going back to Priscus and Priscilla. If he had found the remnants of a British host and marched out with them again to face the Saxon hordes, he might have gone back one day, if he had lived; even, perhaps, if the men last night had been Saxon raiders. But

Britain was a lost land and a lost cause, the swords were rusted and the lights were out, and nothing seemed left to do but to get away and leave it to the dark.

'I don't know. Perhaps we could get across to Gaul—to Armorica.'

'You told me once that that way cost gold,' Regina said.

Owain nodded, and his hand went without his being aware of it to the little hard knot under the breast of his ragged tunic that was his father's ring hanging there. But he knew that that could not buy a passage for even one of them, let alone three. Then slowly he looked up. 'Regina—the old man's bag of gold—I expect I could shift the beams over the stoke-hole, and get in again.'

'No!' Regina cried.

Owain did not like the idea himself, but still. . . . 'Why not? He does not want it any more.'

'That is just it! If he was alive it would be different. I'd steal his last denarius, but——' her voice broke into a little desperate wail. 'It's wicked, that gold. I'm afraid of it. If we take it, dreadful things will happen to us!'

He looked at her white strained face. 'Very well,' he said after a moment. 'We'll find another way.'

Silence again, until the water in the pot began to bubble, and Regina stirred the mush once more. Stirring still, she asked, 'What will you do about Dog?'

He was startled. 'About Dog?'

'Even if you had the gold, no one would sell you a place for a dog in a fishing boat.'

He had not thought of that, and he was blankly silent.

'Would you leave him behind?' she pressed. It was as though she wanted to make sure that he would not hold their need of the gold against her, later on.

He looked down at Dog, who had crawled closer and lay with his head on his knee. He put his hand under the great hound's neck, and felt the warm vulnerable place where the life beat below the chin. 'No,' he said slowly, 'I would not leave him behind.' Not for Dog, to be forsaken, to run to and fro searching for his Lord in a strange place until his heart broke and he knew that his Lord had betrayed him. 'If—if it had to be like that, I'd kill him, myself.' Dog gazed up at him with amber eyes, and thumped his tail, pleased because his Lord was taking notice of him; and Owain felt his throat swell, so that the words came gruffly. 'But I don't want to do that—I don't want to do that, Regina.'

They stared at each other, both taken up with the problem. Then Regina said, 'Maybe we could steal a boat? Just a little boat?'

'If we did, how would we know how to manage it—or which way to go?' But Owain answered his own questions almost in the same breath, his eyes brightening. 'I *have* handled a coracle on the river at home—I wonder if a boat is very different. And they do say that round the south-easternmost part of Britain the sea is so narrow that you can see the coast of Gaul. If we could get across in the narrow part, we could maybe work our way back along the Gaulish coast. There must be woods to hunt there too— until we came to Armorica at last.'

It was a crazy plan, but they had no means of knowing how hopelessly crazy it was. Owain knew that to head south-eastward would be to head straight into Saxon country, but so long as they kept to the wilds, and had nothing to do with roads and settlements, they might get through all right.

'That is what we must do then,' Regina said, as though the thing were as simple as walking across Viroconium.

Owain nodded. 'We'll try, anyway.'

Presently the mush was cooked, and they took it off the fire and tipped a good dollop out on the floor for Dog, and then with the pot between them, ate what was left, scooping it out in alternate handfuls.

Regina had brought out the last of the olivewood that they had saved for some nameless special occasion, and set it on the fire. The oily blue flames sprang up pointed and delicate as flower petals; and when they had finished eating she fetched the rose-mary seedling from its place beside the door, and tipping out the earth, smashed the crock to shards on one of the stones with which they had built their hearth, and dropped the seedling into the heart of the fire. Owain watched it twist and crisp and become for a moment a sprig of gold among the blue olivewood flames, and crumble into ash, while the aromatic scent of it stole out into the room like a farewell. He was not sure whether it was some kind of sacrifice, or just so that there should be nothing left. . . .

And he did not ask.

Anyway it was time to be going. He got up, making sure that his snares and his well-worn supple sling were in the breast of his tunic, and his knife and strike-a-light in his belt, and reached for the deerskin bag of grain. 'We must go now, while there is still half the day left to start us on our way.'

Regina looked up from the bundle she had made with the rest of their few possessions in his cloak. 'And before any more men come,' she said.

But Owain, taking a last look round while she scattered a few last grains of barley for the birds, knew that that was not all the reason for their going. Raiders might come again, yes, or Saxons come after the raiders or raiding in their turn, and that was the sensible daylight reason, the surface reason. But under the surface in the dark lay last night's discovery. And that was no good reason at all; yet they both knew that because of it, not because an old man had died in the ruins, but because of the manner of his dying, Viroconium was not a place to live in, any more.

The blue flames of the burning olivewood were sinking low, and soon the fire would be out.

'Come, then,' he said, whistled Dog to heel, and they walked out of the little room at the far end of Kyndylan's Palace, without looking back, on their way to Gaul.

8

The Forest of Thorns

THEY made slow travelling, for they had to stop to hunt as they
went. Several times they were halted by stream or river and had
to turn aside many miles out of their way before they could
find a place to cross, and from time to time, despite Owain's sense
of direction, they lost their way in the maze of marsh and forest
and open moor, for even when they found a road leading in the
right direction they dared not use it. Once Owain fell into an
ant's nest under a rotten tree-trunk and wrenched his ankle so
that they had to lie up for a few days, and once they passed too
close to a Saxon farm without realizing it, and set all the dogs

barking. But the wolves had drawn off into the deeper wilds, and for a long while they ran into no serious trouble.

It was almost summer already, though the distance they had covered would have been only six or seven days' march to a legion with a good metalled road underfoot and food at the transit camps at each day's end. But even so, Owain reckoned that they must be about half-way, when the bad thing happened.

It did not seem so very bad at the time. Just a sudden break in the weather, that was all; and in the high upland heather country that they were traversing, there was no shelter to be had from the wild summer storm; their rags were drenched through, and though they kept on walking because that seemed the best thing to do, they were chilled to the bone by the icy rain-swaithes, gale-driven across the heather. It would not have mattered much, for they were used to wild weather, but the rain went on and on, and that night, though they had left the uplands for the thin woods in the valley, they could find no sheltered place to sleep in, nor any dry wood to make a fire; and they had little in their stomachs to keep out the cold, for the barley was gone long since, and Owain had had bad hunting the day before.

They spent the night in the lea of a hazel thicket that gave them a little shelter though not much, huddled together with Regina in the middle and Owain's sodden cloak spread as far as might be over the three of them; and by morning the chill of the wet ground seemed to have soaked into their very bones. But by morning also, the storm had blown and rained itself out, and the world was quiet and spent, with even a pale gleam of sunshine to set the mist rising; and Owain, going down to the nearby stream to drink, met a hedgehog grunting back from a night's beetle-hunting, and hit it on the nose. At least they were sure of something to eat that night, though not overmuch between two of them—not three, for in the lean times the understanding was that Dog foraged for himself. Maybe by dark, if the rain held off, they would even be able to make a fire and cook it.

Regina came down after him to drink at the stream, looking white as bleached bone in the misty whiteness of the morning. He showed her the hedgehog, but she was shivering too much to be interested in anything else. 'Never mind; it's time we started out,' he told her. 'You'll feel warmer after we've been walking for a while, and the sun will come through again, too, when the mist has done rising.'

So once again they set out. And by and by the sun did come through, and their sodden rags dried on them as they walked, and the world seemed a kinder place than it had done last night. Owain found a hare's form with four leverets in it, and took two of them, quite ruthlessly; and that night they were lucky, for just at dusk they stumbled on the ruins of a shepherd's bothy in the fold of the hills, with part of its rough thatch of furze branches still on, so that there was shelter inside it, and they managed to make a fire with the branches of a dead thorn bush that had dried up in the day's sunshine, and scorch the hedgehog a bit. The leverets they cooked too, and pushed into the old grain bag and hung up out of Dog's reach, for next day. There was not much on them once they were skinned, but they would be better than nothing.

Next day there was no sun, and a little wet wind soughed through the moorland grass and heather. The whole lie of the land had been rising under them for days, and now it seemed that they were on the roof-ridge of the world; and as they came wearily plodding up and over the blunt skyline, far off southward, so far that save for the unnatural clearness of the air he would not have been able to pick it out from the sky, Owain saw for the first time in his life what he knew must be the sea.

His heart seemed to press upward in his chest. 'Look, Regina, there on the edge of the world—there's the sea!'

Dog swung his tail in response; on the slopes below them a green plover cried; otherwise there was no sound save the wet wind through the last year's heather. 'Look!' he said again, and pointed. 'Have you lost your eyes? It's the sea, Regina!'

'The sea,' said Regina, answering at last, but not as though the word meant anything. He reached out impatiently to give her a shake—and felt, despite the unexpected heat of her hand, that she was shivering.

He looked round quickly. 'What is the matter? Are you still cold?'

'No, I—I don't think I'm cold. My head feels hot.'

He saw for the first time that her face was queerly flushed, and the eyes she turned on him were very bright. She put up one thin hand and rubbed the back of it across her forehead in a confused way. 'It aches, too.'

A swift fear touched Owain like a chilly finger. He had dried off all right from that drenching, why should she take any harm from it? But supposing she had? Regina gave a little sigh, and sat down on her haunches. 'Tired,' she mumbled.

Owain stooped instantly and caught her hot hand and pulled her ruthlessly to her feet again. 'You can't stay here, Regina, there's no shelter, and the rain is coming back. Look, it's downhill now, and once we get into the woods we'll find a sheltered place and make a fire and you can rest until your head stops hurting— as long as ever you like. We'll take it easy for a day or two, and just hunt and live fat——' He heard his own voice, quick and urgent. He was not sure what he said, but he knew that he must get Regina down from this bleak upland into some kind of shelter before the next storm broke. He had forgotten about the sea; the dark shelter of the woods below them was all that mattered now.

Regina rubbed the back of her free hand across her forehead again. 'Everything was queer for a moment,' she said. 'It's better now,' and set off downhill beside him.

They reached the fringes of the forest ahead of the rain, and found a dry place, almost a cave, among the roots of a thicket of ancient yews, with plenty of dead wood lying about for their fire.

But Regina's head was still hot and the rest of her shivering, and she did not want her share of the leverets, so that it was hard to get her to eat, even when he picked the meat off the little bones and fed her as though she were a fledgling. She laughed about that, and then caught her breath and said that laughing hurt her. He ate the rest himself since there was nothing to be gained by wasting food, but he didn't taste much of it. Then he made her lie down on the floor of brown needles right at the back of their shelter as far under the branches as she could get, and spread the cloak over her. He sat up for a while with Dog propped against him, scratching the old scar on his arm and staring sometimes into the fire and sometimes at Regina. She had coughed a little when she first lay down, and now that she was asleep she still made little painful sounds in her breathing, and kept pushing the cloak down as though she was too hot, so that he had to be constantly on the watch to pull it up again. He wondered whether she was wrapped round in the same bright fog that blurred all his memories of the road north from Aquae Sulis when the wound in his arm was new. And he wondered very much, his head on his knees, what he should do if she was going to be really ill.

In the morning she seemed better, though she coughed again, and still said it hurt her to breathe; and they pushed on again, very slowly, getting what shelter they could from the rain squalls, and following the forest down-valley. It seemed a very old forest, this that they had come to; a spiny forest of ancient hawthorn trees for the most part, mingled with black thickets of yew and holly, such a forest as might have come into being if a mighty host of twisted dwarf magicians of some elder race had been overcome and turned by a greater magician into trees. And Owain tried to think that it was only the strange dark atmosphere of the place, and Regina's own fear of a world beyond city walls, when she said in a small fretful voice, 'I don't like the trees; they're pulling faces at me!' But he knew in his inmost heart, that it was not.

Soon after that she stumbled and would have fallen, and he put his arm round her to help her along, but she went on stumbling, more and more often, as though her feet did not belong to her at all. And when they came to a place where the bank of a forest stream had been torn away in the rains of some past winter, making a kind of dell among the thorn roots, he seized on it thankfully as a place to camp, though the day was not yet much past noon. He made Regina lie down as far under the cover as she could get, and wrapped the cloak round her. She heard the stream and said, 'Thirsty,' and he managed to get her some water in a big dock leaf, going back again and again. He gathered wood for the fire, but he did not go hunting. It was clear that whatever he killed, Regina could not eat it, and he had no heart to hunt for himself. Besides, he did not want to leave her. If only he could get some milk. . . . He almost laughed at the ludicrous idea of

F

milk in the forest, seeing himself trap-
ping a roe-doe and milking her while
her fawn stood bleating by.

If only he could get some milk—if
only he could do something to ease that
little dry cough. Honey was good for
a cough, but there didn't seem to be a
bees' nest handy at the moment, any
more than there was a roe-doe. Then
his head went up, his eyes brightening
with an idea, but it was not an idea so
much as a memory, something that belonged to his very young days, perhaps
even to the time before his mother died,
for it seemed to be connected with a
woman's voice, young and laughing,
saying, 'Suck! There, can you taste the
honey?' Just above their refuge, where
the forest opened out a little, he had
noticed a young hazel smothered in
trailing honeysuckle just breaking into
flower. He went and tore away great
ropes of it, and brought it back with
him; and squatting beside Regina while
she watched with eyes that were at once
bright and clouded, plucked off one of
the pink-tipped creamy horns and held
the narrow end of it to her dry mouth.
'Suck,' he ordered.

'Why?'

'Suck, and you will see why.'

Regina obeyed in a half-hearted way.
'It's sweet.'

'Why else do you suppose they call
it honeysuckle? Here's another. Suck
again.'

So squatting beside their little fire as
the day faded into twilight, and the

twilight deepened to dark, he fed Regina whenever she was awake, on the drops of sweetness at the base of the honeysuckle horns. But often he was not sure whether she was awake or not, for she moaned and muttered and tossed about with her eyes half open and half closed, and once when Dog nosed at her in bewilderment, she cried out in terror and beat at him with her hands, thinking that he was a wolf.

Once in the night, when the rain had stopped for a while, and there was a dark breathing quietness, Owain thought he heard a dog bark somewhere a long way off. Dog heard it too, and raised his head and listened. But there was nothing more to hear.

Morning came again, and he knew that Regina could go no further. She was not threshing about now, but it did not seem to him that that was a good sign, for it was as though the quiet came from weakness rather than any slackening of the fever. The wind had shifted its direction, too, and the rain which had not stopped all night (surely it must stop soon—they had had four days of it off and on) had begun to beat into their shelter. Owain sat for a long time shielding Regina as best he could. Then she began to cough again. It was a harsh tearing cough with not enough breath in it, and it hurt him to hear it; and though she was fully awake now, he did not think she knew him. He sat her up and held her tightly against him while she fought for breath, and when the fit passed, and he laid her down again, he knew, remembering the dog he had heard in the night, what he was going to do.

He pulled the old wet cloak round her, tucking it in as tightly as he could in the hope that she would not be able to push it down again, and whistling up Dog, who was rooting in the undergrowth, made him lie down close against her, between her and the stream. 'Stay,' he said. 'Keep. On guard, brother,' and got slowly to his feet, with the quietness of desperation on him.

Before he was more than a couple of spear-lengths down the streamside, he heard Dog whining piteously, and when he checked in his tracks and looked back, the hound was sitting up and staring after him as though making up his mind to disobey the order and follow. 'Stay!' Owain repeated fiercely; and Dog lay down again.

Owain scrambled on downstream in the direction in which he had heard the dog barking in the night. He was prepared for a long walk, for sound carries far at night when there is rain about, especially up or down a valley; but it seemed even longer than it was, for he was weak with emptiness himself, and stumbled and fell more than once in the rough ground. But at last his nose caught the whisper of wood smoke and stalled oxen, that does not belong to the forest unless man also is there. And as he halted, sniffing, he heard small but unmistakably the sound of a horse walking lame on a track, and again, quite near now, the baying of watch-dogs.

He pushed on with fresh heart, and in a little, the stream ran out into open air, not gradually as into a natural clearing, but with the abruptness that means felled timber.

Crouched among the tangle of the woodshore, Owain looked out over the clearing. He saw three fields, the sheen of young barley, the denser green of a bean patch, the brown of spring-ploughed fallow, and beyond a strip of scrubby pasture, the darkness of the forest closing in once more. And close beside a rough track, the bracken-thatched huddle of wattle-and-daub where the Barbarians had made their home. It all looked very settled. Here, deep in the Saxon lands, it had been like this for a hundred years.

His hatred of the Saxons rose in his throat like vomit, and for a moment it was in his mind that it might be better, after all, to let Regina die in the forest. At least she would die free, and with only himself and Dog, who were her friends—all the friends she had—beside her. But he knew even as the thought came to him, that he could not let Regina die, not while there was this one thing he could do that might save her.

There were signs of somebody having just arrived, a horse being led away. But Owain's attention was chiefly held by the figure of a woman in a russet-red gown, who came out of one of the huts bending her head against the rain. He wondered if she was the mistress of the house, and if so, whether she was kind—remembering the kindness of Priscilla, that had met him on another threshold. Then he slithered back into the darker shadows of the woodshore, and turned to make his way upstream again.

Dog, still lying as he had left him, greeted his return with

pricked ears and thumping tail, but Regina never moved; only
he heard her quick, painful breathing. It was very dark among the
trees, and he had to bend close before he could see her properly in
the gloom. Her eyes were half open, but she did not see him at all,
and her chest was quivering up and down in shallow gasps like a
small animal that has run to exhaustion. He felt the pain of them
tight under his own ribs. 'We're going now,' he said, in case she
could understand him. 'It is all right. We are going to a fine place
—where there will be milk.'

He gathered her up, awkwardly because he had never carried
anyone before, but as carefully as he knew how, and staggered to
his feet, wavering a little under her weight; not that there was
much weight to her now. He had not known how thin she was,
thinner even than when she had first come to his fire drawn by the
smell of the baking hare. The sharpness of her bones came not
only through her skin but through the folds of the ragged cloak
in which he had bundled her. But she was heavy enough, none the
less, for Owain who was only fifteen and far gone himself with
hunger and exhaustion.

The second journey down the streamside was a nightmare.
Again and again he had to stop to put the girl down and rest,
and each time it was harder to pick her up and struggle on again.
His heart felt bursting in his breast, and everything was darker
even than the rain should have made it, when he came at last to
the forest fringe, and stumbled to his knees. Regina slipped from
his arms to the ground, and he let her lie there, crouching beside
her and drawing his breath in great hoarse gasps that were painful
in their way as her little panting ones, until in a while he began to
feel less sick. Dog, poor Dog, stood beside them, looking from
one to the other, and trying, as he spent so much of his life in
trying, to understand.

A few yards back from the stream, among the hazel and crack
willow of the newly cleared land, one great thorn tree stood out
like a guardian over the trees behind; Owain had noticed it the
first time he came down to the woodshore, but without knowing
that he did so.

Now, as the world steadied and his breath came back to him, he
got up and stumbled towards it. It was so old that some of its

roots had pulled clear of the ground and spread about it in great arched and twisted limbs over the turf, and though it stood no more than four or five times the height of a man, its bole was thicker round than many a hundred foot forest giant, a Dwarf-King of the forest; maybe it was because of its royalty that the Saxons had let it be when they were at their wood-clearing. There, kneeling close against it, Owain pulled out his hunting knife and dug a little hole as far as he could get under one of the roots. Then he pulled the old battered signet ring from his breast, and cut the thong on which it hung. There was no light in the flawed emerald, only the surface reflection of the hawthorn branches and the pale glints of sky beyond. He wrapped it in a hanging end of cloth torn from the skirt of his ragged tunic, and thrust it down the hole, pushing it home with the point of the knife; and filled the hole in again. At least the Barbarians should not have his father's ring.

When he turned back to Regina, he found that her eyes were fully open and she was watching him as though she knew who he was and what he was doing.

For a moment, hope leapt up in him, and he scrambled across to her without getting off his knees. 'Are you better? Are you better, Regina?' But even as he reached her, her eyes half closed, and she had gone again, back to wherever it was that she had been these many hours past.

The brief flicker of hope made it all the harder to bear, and something very like a sob rose in his throat. Strength seemed running out of him like blood from a wound, and when he tried to pick her up again, he found that he could not do it. He gave up the attempt for the moment, and sat back on his heels, trying to fight down a rising sense of panic. Somehow he must get her up to the farm. It was not very far, not much more than a good bow-shot, maybe. He got his knee under her and his arms round her again. If he could have carried her over his shoulder it would have been easier, but he was afraid that that might harm her. He shifted his hold a little, set his teeth, and somehow, without much idea of how he did it, struggled to his feet. Regina's head hung back on her thin neck, but he could not help that. He set off, stumbling and lurching, Dog padding anxiously at his heels. Out from the

scrub of the woodshore and across the brown fallow towards the
track. Now that he was clear of the shelter of the trees, the wind
and rain swooped at him like live enemies, and the soft earth of
the ploughland clogged his bare feet and tried to hold him back.
He was blind and sick and dizzy, but somehow he clung to
Regina and struggled on, and suddenly the ground changed, and
the mire of the track was beneath his feet, and the gate-gap of
the stockade close before him. He turned in through it, and reeled
across the steading garth towards the gleam of a fire and the sound
of voices that came from the open house-place doorway. Two
guard-dogs—great red-eyed brutes—were baying the news of his
coming, but they were still chained up, for though the day was
drawing on, it was nowhere near yet to cow-stalling time, and
Owain paid no heed to them; nor did Dog, whose only concern
was to follow Owain.

A man had come striding into the doorway to see why the
dogs were barking. A second came up from the outbuildings, and
others, men and women and children, seemed to spring out of
nowhere like the people in a dream. He was in the foreporch
now, out of the wind and the rain. He let Regina slip from his
arms on to the guest-bench, and stood looking at the faces about
him as though they were indeed the faces of a dream, leaning
against the doorpost and bent a little over his own belly, like
someone who has been sick and wants to be sick again.

He heard voices coming out of the faces, speaking in a guttural
tongue, and the sound of the voices was questioning. 'She has—
the lung sickness,' he said in his own tongue, as soon as he could
straighten a little and speak; and remembered even as he did so
that they would not understand, and tried to gather himself together to show them. But in the same instant the woman in the
russet-red gown came from the fire, a woman with eyes of faded
blue in an old quiet face, and the rest made way for her so that he
knew she must be the mistress of the house. He had never seen a
Saxon woman before, and he noticed even in that unlikely
moment that her hair was covered with a kind of napkin, instead
of being bare, as the women he was used to. She looked at Regina
lying small and spent as a dead bird on the bench, with the cloak
fallen back from her and one arm trailing, and flung up her hands

with an exclamation that had the sound of kindness in it. Then it seemed that she asked questions, too, her gaze moving from Regina to himself and back again; and while he was still battling to clear the fog about him and make himself understood, a man who looked as though his brother might have been a fierce little mountain bull, grunted something in reply, and picked Regina up as casually as though she had no more weight than a dead bird and not much more importance, and turned into the house-place with her.

Owain, lurching after the man with no clear idea in his head save to keep close to Regina and see that they did not hurt her, had a confused impression of empty stalls as though the place were a cow byre and not a house, and then space opening out beyond them and the saffron warmth of the fire that he had glimpsed through the open doorway. Then the man had set Regina down on a pile of sheepskins in the corner, and instinctively he crouched down beside her, his arm across her body as though to shield her from harm. A boy with a handsome ruddy face like a bull calf pushed out from his elders to stare. He came too close, and Owain snarled at him much as Dog might have done; save for Regina it was a long time since he had had to do with human beings. Several of the folk laughed, and the boy scowled, then turned away shrugging, and went and sat down with his back against the upright loom and pretended to take no more interest in anything. The mistress of the house was already kneeling beside the unconscious girl, and very gently, smiling into his eyes out of her faded blue ones, she pressed his protecting arm away. He resisted a moment, and then let it drop to his side.

The man who had carried Regina in was talking with another beside the hearth, both of them staring at Owain and the girl while they spoke. Then the second man leaned forward from the stool on which he sat, and said in the British tongue, though with the broad guttural accent of the Saxon kind, 'Boy!'

Owain looked at him for the first time, and saw a fair, thick-set young man with a skin tanned and wind-burned to the colour of copper, and pale straight brows almost meeting across the bridge of his nose. He was sitting with legs stretched to the fire, steaming in their loose cross-gartered breeks, and a drenched cloak was flung down beside him as though he had not long arrived out of the storm. This, he realized vaguely, must be the rider of the horse gone lame.

'Boy,' said the young man again, 'what is it that you do, you and the woman-child, here in the Forest of Thorns? Is it that you run from someone?'

The sound of his own tongue, even spoken in that outlandish accent, pierced through the fog about Owain and seemed to clear his head a little. Relief swept over him at the discovery that there was someone here who could understand him. 'We were trying to get to the coast,' he said, and added on a note of defiance, 'We were running from no one save the Saxon kind; we hoped to get across to Gaul.'

The man nodded. 'That is boldly spoken, at all events.'

Owain said, speaking carefully to make sure that the foreigner understood, 'But now she has the lung sickness, and we can go no further.'

'So I judge,' said the foreigner.

'And so——' Owain's strained gaze went to the man like a bull, and then back to the other; he swallowed, and his mouth felt dry. 'Will you tell him, please, the master of the house, that if he will take her in and let his women care for her and—and give her milk—until she is strong again, I will stay and work for him and be his slave.' He knew that there were many British slaves on the Saxon farms, and always he had scorned them for having let such a thing come about when they could have died instead.

The man looked at Owain in silence for a moment, and then spoke to the bull-like one, and the bull-like one stared again at Owain, and said something, and shrugged.

But the mistress, who had pulled off most of Regina's drenched rags and was feeling her forehead and her heart, while the younger women went scurrying for milk and clean rags and medicine-herbs, glanced up and asked a swift question, and the man translated again. 'The mistress of the house says what is she to you? Is she your sister?'

Owain looked at Regina's still face and up again into the man's, and shook his head. 'She came because I had a hare cooking, and she was hungry. But that was a long time ago—last autumn.'

This also the man told to the rest; and he and the master of the house spoke together for a few moments, while Owain sat on his haunches and watched them, trying desperately to understand. Then the fair-haired man, who had been looking fixedly at Owain even while he argued—it seemed like arguing—with his host, leaned forward and reaching out, ran his thumb nail down the scar of the old spear-wound where it showed under the rags of his sleeve. 'That was gained in battle?' he said, speaking for himself now, not for the others.

Owain answered him in the same way, for himself, and not for the household watching and listening about the fire. 'By Aquae Sulis a year ago.'

'That was a great fight, as I heard.' The man was silent a long moment, studying Owain under his pale brows, somewhat as a man looks at a pony, for its spirit as well as its physical points. Then, as though suddenly he had made up his mind, he tossed three words, carelessly enough, over his shoulder to the bull-like master of the house. Then he spoke to Owain, returning to the British tongue. 'The master of the house says that he does not want another thrall. But the Gods have been good to me; there is a small son in my house, and because of that, I shall add to the Intake-land when I get home from this wayfaring, and because of *that* there is room in my house-place for another thrall. Therefore I have told him that I will take you off his hands—you and the dog together—for a gold piece. And he will keep his side of the bargain, and care for the woman-child.' His eyes narrowed a little, hard on Owain's face. 'But I say to you, and this is *my* bargain, that if she dies, that is the will of the Gods—and I have still paid my gold piece.'

Owain was silent a moment, looking at Regina. One of the women had brought something in a pottery bowl and the mistress had taken it and was trying to persuade her to rouse and drink. She seemed kind enough. His hand on the neck of the great hound who had crouched all this while watchful beside him, he stared into the fire again, seeing not the crackling red flare of burning furze but the little hyacinth-coloured flames that flowered from the burning olivewood, and Regina dropping the rosemary seedling into its heart, so that there should be nothing left—nothing left. . . .

'How shall I know whether she lives or dies?' he said.

'Unless she dies before we move on south tomorrow, you will not know,' said the man. 'My holding is many days from here.'

'They will be kind to her?' Owain said, putting the question simply as one man to another.

'I do not know them. My horse cast a shoe, and I am but a one-night's guest within the gates, but I think the mistress at least will be kind to her.'

Owain raised his eyes from the fire to the man's face, and said, 'I will come,' as though there was a choice to be made. But he knew that there was no choice in the matter. He was a Saxon's slave, bought with a gold piece. The choice had been in the woods, where he buried his father's ring.

The women got some milk into Regina, and Dog was fed with the watch-dogs before they were released, and Owain had a bannock and a bowl of kale broth at supper, and a place in the loft to sleep. They were a kindly enough household. Their animals would be well cared for and their bond-folk not beaten for the mere joy of beating; he was glad of that for Regina's sake, but he hated to admit it, even to himself, lying hot-eyed and wakeful while the wind and the rain hushed across the thatch and the long night wore away.

In the morning, when the early meal was eaten, and he had saddled his new master's horse—reshod by the man like a bull, for in the wilds every farmer must be his own smith—and brought it round to the foreporch door, they let him go for one last look at Regina. She was breathing more easily, and her eyes were properly shut as though she was asleep, the black lashes making feathery shadows on the white of her face. He knew that he must not wake her to say good-bye. But he pulled the little worn strike-a-light bag from his belt and laid it beside her. They had taken his knife and his sling, and it was all he had; it seemed fitting that he should give it to her, anyway; from now on he would come with the slaves and the dogs to warm himself at a master's fire; he would not have a fire of his own again. He looked at the mistress, anxiously, to make sure she understood that it was for Regina; and she nodded.

Then he heard his master calling from the doorway, 'Boy!'

And he went out with Dog at his heels, and an odd feeling that was not so much grief as a sense of physical loss—as though he had pulled off some part of himself, and if he looked down he would find the place was bleeding.

9

Uncle Widreth

A WARM west wind was buffeting across the tawny levels; there was a faint taste of salt in it, and the humming of the sea. But any wind, unless it came due from the north, had the taste and sounding of the sea in it, for anywhere in the flat lands thrusting southward from Regnum to the rocks of Cymenshore one was never more than a few miles from the sea on either side. Owain, with Dog loping at his heels, came up from the harbour—Windy Harbour, they called it—where he had been with a message to the boat-strand below the settlement; for Beornwulf his master, like most of the coastwise farmers, was part fisherman too, and had a third share in a boat. He sniffed the chill tang of salt mingled with the dry warm scents of the land that had grown familiar to him in the past year, and thought that maybe there would be rain before morning, with the sea sounding so loudly across the land from the westward.

His path dived from the open levels into the shadows of a broad belt of oak scrub that bordered the common grazing ground of the settlement. The leaves of the squat wind-twisted trees that had been salt-burned since high summer were blackened and shrivelled now, and the sea sounded louder among them than it had done in the open, as though the murmur of it was tangled in the branches. He came out on the landward side, turned up beside the narrow tidal channel that ran between banks of chalk and brushwood, and saw the steading in the distance.

One could see Beornstead from a long way off, because there was nothing save a thorn windbreak here and there to cut the view; a huddle of low roofs that seemed shaped, just as the oaks and thorn trees were shaped, by the prevailing wind; the house-reek driven sideways in a pale blur against the darkness of woods beyond. No one seemed to be about, as he came nearer on the levels, where Beornwulf's three brood-mares were grazing with their foals beside them, but as he drew towards the gateway of the thorn hedge, he saw Uncle Widreth sitting with his back against a pea stack out of the wind, with three children and a sheep-dog puppy squatting round him in attitudes of the deepest interest.

Uncle Widreth was something of an oddity, and to Owain, he was one of the things that made life bearable. He was almost as old as the farm, for his father had been a younger son who left the settlement and struck out for himself into the uncleared land, only one generation after Aelle had run his war-keels ashore and founded the South Saxon Kingdom. The household and the other thralls (there were two beside Owain) said that his mother was a British slave-woman who had left him on his father's door-sill as soon as he was born, and run away. But Uncle Widreth said that his mother had been a seal-woman and a princess among seal-women; one of those who laid aside their furred skins to dance and sing among the dunes of the Seals' Island on moonlight nights, and that his father had stolen her skin and so had her in his power and made her love him. But later, she had found her skin hidden in a hole in the wall, and escaped back to her own world. If he had been born after she escaped instead of before, Uncle Widreth said, he would have been a seal instead of a man. He was perhaps not quite right in the head, and certainly he was past doing a man's work on the family lands, but he was the best cattle doctor in eight farms, and could mend any broken tool; and he earned his keep, beside, by looking after the children whenever Athelis, Beornwulf's wife, could not do with them under her feet.

Just now, Athelis was laid by in the Bower, the women's quarters behind the house-place, with a squalling very new daughter; so Uncle Widreth sat in the shelter of the pea stack, telling stories to the children until the bondwoman fetched them for bed.

Owain had got into the way of going to the queer old man in his spare moments, especially when his shoulders ached more than usual under the drab weight of slavery; and though he did not particularly ache at the moment, he whistled Dog to heel and turning aside, went to join the little group in the warm lea of the pea stack.

Uncle Widreth looked up at him, his faded old eyes crinkling into a smile, then returned to the work of his hands. He did not look like a seal, Owain thought, more like a grasshopper. The children did not glance up at all; Helga and Lilla, the two little girls, were sitting on either side of him, watching what he did, with their chins almost on his updrawn knees, and Bryni, who was too young to be interested in watching somebody else do something for many moments at a time, was trying with enormous concentration to poke the puppy's eyes out. Presently, in all likelihood, the puppy would bite him; he had a good many tooth marks in the soft brown skin of his arms and legs already, but neither he nor the puppy ever bore malice. The enchanting thing in Uncle Widreth's hands was a bird that he was whittling from a scrap of driftwood.

'But the silver bird said to the chieftain's daughter, "I cannot spare you a feather from my wing, for I need them all to fly with, and I have a long way to go," ' Uncle Widreth was saying. 'And the chieftain's daughter burst out weeping with temper, and stamped and threw her bannock on the ground.' He always talked to the children in his mother's tongue (even if she was a seal, it would have been her human tongue) which was why Beornwulf had been able to translate between Owain and the people of the farm in the Thorn Forest.

'Was there honey on it?' demanded Helga.

'There was honey on it, and it fell honey-side down in the

very middle of her father the chieftain's best cloak, which was
spread out to dry in the sun because it was the time for the
summer washing,' murmured Uncle Widreth sadly.

There was a gasp of shocked delight from his hearers.

Owain, looking on and listening with half an ear while he
gentled Dog's head against his thigh, thought suddenly that it
would be good to be able to create something, even if it was only
a foolish tale for children or a rather crude little bird of silvery
driftwood that yet looked surprisingly as though it might be able
to fly. Dully he felt that the power to create would be a kind of
freedom. . . .

The story was drawing to a close. 'And so her father beat her
with his sword-belt, and her mother beat her with her spindle,
and she was very sore, my children, and so she deserved to be.'

'But the bird? What happened to the little bird, Uncle Widreth?'

'Ah now, the silver bird spread his wings, and flew home to his
own mistress across the sea, who had been waiting for him all that
time,' said Uncle Widreth, and dropped the scrap of carved
driftwood into the small eager hands stretched out for it. And
leaving the two little girls to huddle enchanted over their new
treasure, he looked up at Owain leaning against the pea stack
beside him. 'What are you thinking, way up there? Are you
thinking: What a very foolish old man; surely he has lived so
long that he has gone round in a circle and become a child
again?'

'I was thinking,' Owain said, 'that I wish I could make things.
Oh, I don't mean just things to use—I'm good with my hands;
I can make or mend any farm tool well enough—but things that
have life in them. I think I should not mind this thrall-ring round
my neck quite so much, if I could make things.'

Uncle Widreth's beaky old face was touched suddenly with a
gentleness greater than the gentleness he kept for the children. 'It
comes hard, when one is young. . . . I remember when I did not
like to be only poor silly Widreth, midway between the farm
folk and my brothers—knowing that I was my father's eldest
son.'

And looking down at him, Owain wondered for the first

time whether Uncle Widreth really believed in the seal-woman
mother, or whether she was just a young man's pitiful attempt to
save his pride. All at once he saw himself grown old too, and
clinging to some self-made heroic story of how he had been taken
in battle after killing thirty men with his own sword. And for a
moment he could have howled like a dog, both for Uncle
Widreth and for himself.

'When you are my age,' the old man was saying, 'when you
are my age, you will have learned how little all things matter.
Life is fierce with the young, and maybe more gentle with the
old. Only, while one is young, there is always the hope that one
day something will happen; that one day a little wind will
rise. . . .'

Even as the old quiet voice droned away into silence, Owain
felt Dog's ears prick under his caressing hand, and the great
hound raised his head to listen. For a few moments the sound was
too distant for human hearing, and then Owain caught it too, the
faint tripple of a horse's hooves on the old paved road from
Regnum.

He moved a long stride to the end of the pea stack, and looked
out in the direction from which it came. A man on a red colt had
appeared from the long shadows of the oakwoods and was heading towards the farm at a lazy hand-canter. It was not often that
one saw a horse on that stretch of the road, for not much more
than a mile northward the long curving sea-arm that made the
Seals' Island almost an island in truth as well as name, cut across
it, and travellers had to rouse up old Munna who had his bothy
and his boat there, to ferry them over. But at low tide the creek
ran almost dry, revealing here and there the sunken stones of an
old paved ford, and it was possible for a man who knew the land
and the tides and the drift of the sandbanks to get across on horseback.

Such a man was Haegel the King.

Three times before, since Owain had followed his new master
south, Haegel had come, unheralded and alone, as a man may drop
in to sit by a friend's hearth and drink his ale and re-fight old
battles or discuss the harvest prospects. Owain had thought it
strange, the first time, but that was before he knew that Haegel,

G

put out to foster after the way of the Saxon nobles, had been bred up here on the farm, so that he and Beornwulf were foster brothers. He knew that now, and that Beornwulf had been one of the young King's hearth-companions in his high Hall close to Regnum. (Regnum was like Viroconium now, and they called it Cissa's Caester, which sounded more like a sneeze than the name of a city; Cissa's Stronghold, after one of Aelle's fierce sons.) That had been before Beornwulf's father had died and the time had come for him to take over the farm and marry and settle down; but still the old friendship held, and Beornwulf continued to serve his foster brother not merely as a land holder with a spear serves his King, but in other, nearer and more private ways. Owain had a suspicion that it had been some mission for Haegel that had carried him up into the Thorn Forest, a year ago last spring. And still Haegel the King came to sit by Beornwulf's hearth with an ale horn on his knee and to laugh at ancient jests with him.

'It is the King,' he said over his shoulder to Uncle Widreth. 'I must go,' and strode off round the pea stack and in at the steading gate.

Beornwulf liked him to be there when a guest came, to take his horse if he had one, and when Athelis the mistress could not come, to pour the guest-cup for him. The bondwoman was a clumsy creature, and did little honour to a guest, but Owain had been well trained by his father, and carried himself even now like a ten point stag, which is to say like a king; and Beornwulf, had he known it, was proud of his Roman–British thrall. But Owain did not know it; he only knew that because the King had come he might not be free all evening.

A few moments later, Haegel swung in through the gate-gap, and he stepped forward to take the red colt from him as he drew rein. The King was darker than his foster brother, very dark for a Saxon, with level eyes set deep under his brows, and a thinker's mouth. The evening sunlight that turned the colt's hide to burnished copper glinted on the necklace of coral and gold beads under his beard, and the wind ruffled the colt's mane and the breast feathers of the hooded falcon on his fist.

Beornwulf's hounds, who knew him, ceased baying and came

with Dog sniffing round the colt's fetlocks, and Haegel swung his leg over and dropped into their midst, laughing as he turned to his foster brother who had come out to greet him. 'Ah, it is good to be home! Some part of my heart still cries out "Home again!" whenever I cross into the Seals' Island.'

'And all of mine cries out "My brother is home to his own place," for I knew it was you as soon as I heard the dogs bay,' Beornwulf said. 'How went the hawking?'

'Well enough. We have been flying at the wild fowl between the Haven Marshes and Bremma's Dyke. Now I have sent the others home with the hounds, and come to drink the bairn's health. Son or daughter? I have heard that there is a new bairn, but no more.'

'Another daughter,' said Beornwulf, and pulled a wry face.

'So? Ah well, we have each one son to carry our shields after us.'

Haegel turned towards the house-place, his arm flung across his foster brother's shoulders.

Owain took the horse round to the stable and handed him over to Caedman his fellow thrall, then went round to the store-room behind the house-place, to fetch Beornwulf's own drinking horn and a jar of their best ale.

When he returned to the two men they had not gone in, but were sitting on the bench by the foreporch door, their feet stretched before them, talking quietly in the way of men both tired at the day's end. Haegel the King was making much of his falcon, drawing his finger again and again down her back so that she bobbed her hooded head and hunched her wings in pleasure. They were not talking of family matters now, and nor were they laughing at ancient jests.

'I still think the day is not far off when we may have to defend our own,' Beornwulf was saying. 'It is as I told you; the West Saxon Kingdom grows over strong for safety—our safety—since Ceawlin broke the last of the British, two years and more ago.'

Owain checked an instant in his movements, then bent and set the great horn, with its copper and silver mounting, into the hand that Haegel held for it, and filled it to the brim.

'*Wass heil!*' Haegel said, and drank, and gave it back. 'Good fortune on the house and on the newest flower of the house!'

And then, returning to the thing that they were really talking of, 'I wonder—oh, I think with you that the day will come for calling out the warriors again; but I do not read the signs quite as you read them, for all that.'

Beornwulf took the ale horn in his turn. 'How do you read them, Haegel the King?' he said, and flung back his head and drank.

And Haegel put out his hand for the horn again, but when he had it, only sat with it on his knee, staring into the amber depths, while Owain, standing by with the ale jar, to pour for them again as soon as the horn was drained, felt his heart quicken with an odd expectancy, as though what passed between them had some personal meaning for himself.

'I read them—I think—in this way,' the King of the South Saxons said at last. 'Ceawlin is a great war-leader; one of those whose shadow stretches far like the shadow of a man at sunrise, but it is in my mind that he abides too much by his own strength, and does not understand the hearts of men, nor even see the need to understand them. . . . See now, his own sons and his brother's sons alike carried their shields for him in the Great Fight, when he broke the last power of the Princes; and to Coel and Coelwulf, his brother's sons, he has given maybe half of the new-won lands to rule between them; and to Cuthgils, the Chiltern uplands to hold. And for his own sons he has kept all else, from Londinium to the Sabrina's Sea, and from the Mid-lands to the coast.'

'They are his sons,' Beornwulf said.

'Yet his brother's sons will surely say, "We also fought for the Kingdom, and now Wessex is great. Why then is our share so small?" and so may come trouble on Ceawlin's threshold later. And that, I think, will be the chance of those who do not love Ceawlin—notably Aethelbert of Kent.'

'Aethelbert?' Beornwulf sounded surprised. 'Why the King of Kent, more than another one?'

'For the memory of Wibbendune.'

'That must be five and twenty years ago. Would he still carry hatred for a worsting in battle before his beard was grown, think you?'

'Quite easily. You know him only as a name, one of the mighty line of the Oiscings, great grandson of Hengest himself. But I am King of Sussex, and he is the High King and in some sort my Overlord, and I have sat at his table. He is not like the rest of his line, not a warrior at heart; he has the kind of cold merchant nature that hates well and hates long. . . .' He took up the ale horn and drained it, then handed it to Owain to be refilled, and fell to caressing his falcon again.

Owain wondered if they had forgotten that after a year and more among them he could speak their tongue; then he understood. It was because he was a thrall that they spoke so freely in front of him; a thrall who was of no account in the pattern of things, and whose word would carry less weight than a blade of grass.

'Also he is rich with the gold that his Frankish Princess brought him, rich enough maybe, to buy his revenge one day and set himself and his Kingdom above the West Saxons once and for all —and clever enough to know when and how to make the purchase. But if ever that day comes, the gold and the skill and the cunning will flow underground, like the seven secret rivers that flow through our South Saxon Land; and above ground there will be fighting, and it is we that shall be doing it, even as you say, my brother.'

He shook his head as Beornwulf offered him the horn again. 'Na na, I must be away before the tide drowns the ford. The red colt takes some handling, moreover; nor am I Vadir Cedricson to ride as well drunk as sober.'

Beornwulf laughed. 'Aye well, by your reading as well as by mine, it seems that the old fiery days are back. Now that there are no more British to fight, we fight each other.' He shook out the last few drops of ale in a dark spatter on the ground, which was instantly licked up by the dogs, and gave the horn to his British thrall, bidding him take it away.

And Owain, carrying horn and ale jar back to their places, heard the voices of the two men murmuring on, but could think of no excuse to come near enough to hear anything more that passed between them. He did not fully understand all that he had heard, for he had no knowledge of the way in which gold and the power of gold might be used in roundabout ways, to undermine loyalties or sow the seeds of distrust in men's minds, but he knew from bitter experience that one could not feed and arm a war-host without it. And echoing in the back of his mind, as he went to see that the red colt was ready when Haegel called for him, was something that Uncle Widreth had said a little earlier: 'Only while one is young, there is always the hope that one day something will happen; that one day a little wind will rise. . . .'

Yet it did not seem likely that a Saxon war would raise much wind in the fortunes of a British thrall.

10

The Silver Foal

B UT two years went by, and no more word of Ceawlin's nephews
came down through the Maen Wood, the Common Wood that
lay shaggy between Regnum and the Seals' Island. No wind
arose, only men and hounds grew older.

A spring evening came, when all across the marsh the hawthorn was in flower, the scent of it coming and going on the soft
damp air, breathing in at the open house-place doorway to mingle
with the tang of wood smoke and the all-pervading fish-reek of
the eels smoking over the hearth.

Owain, sitting at the lower end with Gyrth and Caedman, the
two half-bred farm thralls, looked up from the flail whose leather

hinge he was renewing, and glanced about him in the light of the seal-oil lamp on the roof-beam. The whole household were gathered about the hearth after the evening food, the master of the house and his thralls alike busy with the making and mending of harness and farm gear, Athelis the mistress sitting with her stool turned to catch the best light, finishing off the hanging ends of the piece of blue and brown striped cloth that she had cut from the loom that morning, while a little behind her the bondwoman, sleeves rolled to her shoulders, ground the next day's barley-meal in the stone quern. Uncle Widreth had been telling them a story, but it had got slower and drowsier as it went along, and now he slept, his back propped against the roof-tree, his thin grasshopper shanks drawn up almost to his chin, and his breath making little puffs in the grey hairs of his beard. The children too were asleep, like puppies tumbled with the dogs around the fire, Helga and Lilla and little Gerd, round and sweet as three brown barley-loaves warm from the bakestone, blue-eyed—when their eyes were open—and barley-haired. Bryni had abandoned his family to sleep by himself at the lower end of the fire, with his head on Dog's brindled flank—a freedom which Dog, lying sprawled in the best place beside the fire which he had won for himself by right of conquest from Beornwulf's hounds, would not have allowed to any other of the children. Bryni bore no re-semblance whatever to a barley-loaf. The hair tumbling across his forehead was gold with a rust of red in it. It was his mother's hair, but the devilish green glint in his eyes was all his own. Now, however, with his eyes shut and the flush of the fire on his cheek, it was hard to believe what Bryni was like when he was awake, hard to believe that only today, having been slapped for stealing honey cakes, he and Horn the Smith's youngest son had met half-way to the settlement and decided to run away together. Luckily for them, it had been Owain who found them.

The rhythmic grinding and grating of the quern was loud in the silence left by Uncle Widreth's half-finished story. No other sound save the small secret flutter of the flames and the cry of a marsh-bird far off, broke the quiet, until Athelis straightened from her work and shook out the cloth, folding it across and across with a snapping, capable gesture of finish. 'There! That is done,

and I might as well smoor the fire for the night. Half the household is asleep already, by the look of it, and the Old One will be
nodding himself into the flames if he sits there much longer.'

She rose, and laid the gay striped cloth away in the kist with the
carved worm-knots, against the gable wall; then caught up
Gerd, still half asleep, under one arm, and turned towards the
inner room, the Bower. The bondwoman was scooping the
coarse barley-meal into its bag, and at the lower end of the fire
the thralls, following Beornwulf, laid aside their work and
stretched. Gyrth and Caedman grunted their good-nights, and
stumbled away up the ladder to the half-loft in the crown of the
roof where they slept close under the thatch. But Beornwulf
himself took down one of the steading's two lanterns that hung
beside the foreporch door, and opening the horn pane, stooped to
light the candle at the fire. 'I think I will go and take a look at
Golden-eye before I sleep.'

'I'll go,' Owain said.

Beornwulf looked at him consideringly as he closed the
lantern. Then he nodded. 'Go then. But come and tell me at once
if she's uneasy.'

It was a measure of the place that Owain had won with him;
for Golden-eye was his favourite mare, and due to foal in a few
days, and most assuredly he would not have trusted Gyrth or
Caedman in the matter.

Owain took the lantern from him and went out with Dog at his
heels. Faint wraiths of mist lay across the levels, the thorn trees
rising knee-deep out of them, but overhead the sky was clear,
and the young moon floated like a curved feather above the
woods, as he made his way round to the back of the steading.
They had moved Golden-eye out of the usual grazing ground that
morning, for it was her first foal and the other mares were in-
clined to bother her, and put her by herself in the little close between the steading and the curve of the main windbreak.

Among the apple trees behind the steading buildings, the mist
rags drifted into his face like cool cobwebs, touched with gold by
the light of the swinging lantern. He came to the narrow gap
of the hind-gate, and pulled away the dead thorn branches that
closed it. He stood in the gate-gap, whistled, and waited. Usually

the little vixenish mare with the gleam of gold in her eyes would come to that call, but tonight there was no answering whinny, and no dark shape came trotting out of the mist. He whistled again, and then, as there was still no reply, strode out into the close, with the lantern held high.

It was only a slip of pasture between windbreak and steading, and even in the mist and darkness, a quick look round was enough to show him that Golden-eye was not there; and a torn-down place in the hedge told all too clearly the way she had gone. Owain stood for a moment, thinking. Curse the little beast; wilful and unsettled in the way of foaling mares, she had probably broken out to get back to the others. He ducked through the hole in the hedge, and headed for the grazing ground, whistling as he went. The other two mares were there safe enough, already lain down to sleep; but of Golden-eye, no sign.

Owain went back to the steading at a run, and burst in just as Athelis, having bedded the children down, was smooring the fire, while Beornwulf, who usually did most of his dressing and undressing in the house-place, sat on his stool beside her, un-binding the leather cross-garters below the knees of his breeks.

'Golden-eye——' He was panting with the speed he had made. 'She's broken out!'

Beornwulf looked up quickly, the garter strap in his hand. 'Has she gone back to the other mares?'

'No. I've been to look. There's not a sign of her.'

'Hammer of Thor!' the master of the house swore good-humouredly, and got up, one leg gartered and the other loose. 'Athelis, get me a cloak, there's a good girl; like enough we'll be out half the night. . . . Aye well, she'll likely come to no harm, unless she blunders into the dyke.'

'Or unless the foal starts early,' Owain said.

'Or unless the foal starts early.' Beornwulf was reaching for the second lantern. 'Gyrth! Caedman!' He lifted up his voice in a roar to the thralls in the loft. 'Down with you! Golden-eye's broken out, and the Thunderer knows where she is by now.'

In a few moments the thralls appeared, looking just as they had done when they climbed the ladder to bed, for they slept by night in the clothes and dirt that they worked in by day. 'Gyrth, go you towards the settlement,' Beornwulf said. 'Caedman, I shall want you with me. I'm afraid of the dyke.' Then to his British slave, stooping to coax a flame from the red embers of the fire: 'Owain, you had best take the woodshore and work along it westward. Get a spare candle, and keep that lantern. If she has got in among the trees you'll have more need of it than Gyrth will.'

And so a few moments later, the lantern swinging in his hand, Owain was heading for the woods above the winding creek. 'Find her,' he said to Dog, padding beside him. 'Find her, boy, find Golden-eye,' and the great hound looked up and whimpered in reply.

They came to the edge of the woods that skirted the Intake, and turned westward along them, Owain whistling from time to time, and stopping to listen, and pushing on again, alert for any sign of the mare having passed that way. After they crossed the Regnum road all sound of the other searchers died out behind them, and when he stopped to listen again, there was nothing to hear but the crying and calling of nesting shore-birds, and the rumour of the sea in the hollow quiet. In a little, a pale glimmer among the trees just back from the woodshore, told him that he had reached the place where a little ruined shrine stood forsaken, left unmolested from the past world that it belonged to, much as the great thorn tree in whose keeping he had left his father's ring, because the Saxons were afraid of it. It was a shrine to Silvanus the woodland god—one could still read the inscription from Virgil on a fallen column head—and the folk of the Seals' Island believed that it was haunted; even Owain had never cared to find himself near it save when the sun was high. But animals often seemed drawn to the place; and he turned aside to search the clearing, Dog sniffing among the ruins while the swinging lantern set the shadows flying. There was something there, something that seemed to cling about the ruined walls, tangible as the mist; another kind of shadow that lay cold on his heart. But still there was no sign of Golden-eye, and in a little, thankfully enough, he pushed on again.

Not far beyond the shrine, the long winding creek and the oakwoods which followed it swooped southward; a little further and the oakwoods thinned out and came to an end. They were far beyond the Beornstead Intake now, out into the Wild, the open levels of reeds and thorn scrub and undrained marsh that belonged to no man, heading over towards the settlement of Widda's Ham on the eastern coast of the Island. The moon was low by now, but the mist seemed clearer here, and out of it, a little way ahead, there loomed up suddenly a long curved line of wind-shaped hawthorns marking the boundaries of Vadir Cedricson, Vadir the Hault, of whom Haegel the King had once said that he could ride as well drunk as sober. Vadir, too, was an outdweller, but unlike Beornwulf's his family ran to many sons; his father had been the eldest of three brothers, and so by now the original farm steading had become something more like a village of kinsmen, with Vadir, young as he was, for its Lord. The royal blood of Aelle was in him too, from his mother's side, and altogether he was a powerful man in Seals' Island. Also he was one who thought much of his frontiers, an unchancy man to come up against, for the club foot that had gained him his second name had twisted his whole nature, and the red dogs he bred were the most savage in the countryside. It would be exactly like Golden-eye, Owain thought in exasperation, to drop her foal on Vadir's land, and at night when his dogs were loose.

The thought had barely crossed his mind, when Dog checked in his tracks, his muzzle lifted, sniffing the air. Seeing him, Owain checked also, sending out again that long-drawn shaken whistle, and again listened. Surely he heard something, a small stirring, out on the marsh; he strode forward in the direction from which it came, calling, 'Golden-eye! Hey, girl!' And from far out beyond the line of the hawthorn trees, he was answered by a shrill whinny.

Dog whimpered, and glanced up at him, then bounded forward. 'Easy then, easy, brother,' Owain said, and quickened his pace behind the great hound. He pitched into a soft patch and swore, gathered himself together and stumbled on.

He came upon the mare quite suddenly in the lea of an island of ragged furze. She was standing with legs planted wide apart, her flanks heaved distressfully, and he saw the dark sweat on her coat. She swung her head uneasily towards him, and her eyes shone puzzled and full of fear. Dog stood beside her with slowly swinging tail, and an air of triumph, his eyes like green lamps in the wolf-mask of his face.

Owain checked an instant and moved forward, speaking to her in quiet reassurance. 'So, so, here's a to-do all about nothing; easy now, easy my girl. . . .' He set his hand on her flank, feeling how she trembled and strained, and looked at her by the light of the lantern. Early or no, the foal was on its way, and the mare was having no easy time of it. There was no time to run back to the steading; he must simply do the best he could here and now, and hope that they would not need to get the ropes on. She was frightened more than anything else, he thought, for it was her first foal, and maybe she did not understand what was happening to her.

He hung the lantern on a furze branch and set himself to soothe and encourage her, caressing the sweating neck and talking to her as though she were a woman. It did not matter what he said, it was the sound of the familiar voice she needed. 'Easy then, take it easy my girl; nothing to be afraid of. . . . Ah, now try, and now again—soon it will be here, a fine son, a king among the horse-kind. . . . That was bravely done. Rest now, my girl. . . .' Presently, when the lantern had guttered low and then grown bright again with the spare candle, he was helping her with his own strength added to hers, Dog watching with prick-eared interest as they laboured together to bring the young one to birth. Owain had never actually delivered a foal before, but he had helped Beornwulf a couple of years back when one of the other mares ran into difficulties, and he knew what must be done. He had hold of the coming foal by its mushroom-pink fore-hooves, and taking the time from herself, he helped her every time she strained, letting her rest between efforts, and never ceasing all the while to comfort and encourage her.

It was hard work for both of them, and despite the chill of the misty night, Owain was sweating as much as Golden-eye, when at last it was all over and he found himself squatting beside the new-born foal that lay sprawled amid a tumble of disjointed-seeming legs on the turf. It was a son as he had said, a fine stallion foal whose coat, despite the birth-wet, had already a faint bloom as of dark silver in the lantern-light. He had never seen a foal quite that colour before. Having made sure that it had taken no harm from being born, he rose and turned his attention to Golden-eye who had begun nuzzling in bewilderment at the creature on the ground, and made sure that all was well with her.

He was still doing so when Dog sprang up, growling softly, the hackles rising on his neck, and stood staring into the darkness.

For a moment everything seemed unnaturally quiet, and then out of the quiet grew the flying beat of a horse's hooves over the turf. A faint lift in the land had somehow thrown off the sound until it was almost upon them, and Owain had barely time to stride forward and come between Golden-eye and the furious drumming when three red hounds leapt snarling into the lantern-light, and behind them a horse and rider loomed out of the mist.

There was a moment of yelling chaos as Dog sprang to meet the foremost hound. Golden-eye was trampling and snorting in terror, and Owain with his arm across her neck, trying to keep her clear of the little sprawled thing on the ground, was shouting, 'Hold off! For God's sake call your pack off—there's a mare here and a new-born foal!'

A sharp curse came from the rider, and the crack of a whip-lash; the man had swung his horse aside on the very edge of the pool of yellow lantern-light, reining it back on to its haunches with a savage hand, and leaning from its back, laid about him with the long whip he carried. The dark supple lash flickered out and curled with a vicious hiss into the midst of the dog-fight, and the fight fell apart, yelping, as the tip stung like a hornet across the neck of one dog and the haunches of another and the shoulders of a third. 'Sa! When I say kill, you shall kill, and not before!' said a cold voice; but the man kept the last and most savage cut of all for Dog, who, war-hound that he was, would have been at his throat next instant, if Owain had not called him off in a voice that reached him even through his red-eyed rage.

The red hounds slunk back to crouch, wolf-watchful, on the edge of the lantern-light; Dog stood against his Lord's knee, snarling still, deep and menacing in his throat, while the mare stood snorting and shivering over her foal. And in the uneasy pause that had followed the tumult, the two men surveyed each other. Vadir sat his fidgeting mount bareback, as though he and the horse were one—clearly he had not waited to saddle up; another man would have come on foot, but Vadir never walked a yard when he could ride—and looked down at Owain, his pale brows frowning.

'So it was not a marsh light,' he said coolly at last. 'You are one of the Beornstead thralls, aren't you? What do you think you are doing, playing corpse-candle on my land?'

'I came after the mare,' Owain said, his hand moving reassuringly on her neck as he spoke, 'and the mare has never learned to understand boundaries.'

'So it would seem,' said Vadir. He thrust his whip into his belt and dismounted, dropped the rein over the horse's ears, and tapped it on the breast to bid it stay where it was. Then he turned with his ugly, dragging limp to look at the mare. He did not speak to her as Owain had done, but it seemed that there was some power of quiet mastery in his hands, for though she started at his touch and was still trembling violently, she stood still for him to do what he would with her. Owain watched him a moment, very much on guard, but the man's touch was skilled and unexpectedly gentle; Owain left him to it and turned himself to the foal which was by now kicking all its legs in its first attempt to get up.

'Yes, she seems well enough,' he heard Vadir say after a few moments. 'Now to take a look at the young one,' and Vadir was beside him as he knelt supporting the creature on its long staggering legs, his hands moving with that same delicate sureness over the small body. 'Bring the lantern closer.'

It was not spoken as the Lord of Widda's Ham speaking to a thrall, but merely as one man to another. Owain knelt back on his heels and reaching the lantern from its furze branch, held it closer as the other bade him. The man's absorbed down-bent face caught the upwash of the light that fell soft and uncertain over the little creature under his hands; a thin face, older than it should have been, for he was only six or seven years older than Owain, with pale eyes, and faint lines that might have been either pain or a perpetual sneer running from the wings of the nostrils to the corners of the hard mobile mouth.

The foal was beginning to get some idea what its legs were for. It stood tottering, and blinking its long lashes over large bewildered eyes, while the mare licked and nuzzled at it between Vadir's hands.

'Who is the sire?' the Saxon demanded suddenly.

'A stallion out of the King's stables. Hugin the Raven.'

'So? It happens sometimes, with a black sire. Not often, but there are white horses in that strain.'

'He is going to be white?' Owain had had the same thought, seeing that strange silver shadow over the darkness of the foal's hide.

'By the time he is ready for breaking, he will be as white as storm water on the Seal Rocks.' As Vadir spoke, he was guiding the foal towards its mother's teats. Golden-eye, not yet fully understanding, began to sidle uneasily, and he spoke quickly over his shoulder to Owain. 'Take her head and keep her quiet until she gets the feel of the foal. It is better you should do that—she knows you.'

For a while they were completely absorbed in the shared task, Owain soothing the mare, while Vadir knelt with his head against her flank, steadying the foal and coaxing it to suck. For a few anxious moments it seemed that neither son nor dam knew what was expected of them, and then the foal got the taste of the warm milk. He sneezed, and started back a little, then butted into his mother's flank in search of more, his damp bedraggled feather of a tail beginning to flicker behind him; and the mare, her eyes soft and contented now, turned her lowered head to nuzzle him more securely into place.

Vadir gave a low, triumphant laugh. 'Aye, that is the way of it.' Then to Owain, as though he had only that moment answered his question, 'But he never will be truly broken, of course.'

'What do you mean?' Owain said quickly.

'Did I not say that he will be as white as foam on the Seal Rocks? Most of the white horses one sees have bleached with age —not that one ever sees many. It is seldom indeed that a foal is born like this one to be white in his young prime. Such horses are sacred to the God Frey who is the life in all living things, in corn and horses and men. No one save the God may ride the

God's Horse, and therefore he is never broken to the saddle and all that goes with the saddle.'

Owain had heard something of that before; he had heard vaguely that there was a white horse at the King's farm, kept apart. . . . He had not remembered much about it, but Vadir's words were enough to touch him with a faint chill as though a wraith of mist had drifted across his face. 'What does that mean? Will the King take him?'

'In his third year, yes, if he flowers into all that he promises to be, though the white horse that rules the King's mares is young as yet.'

'And what will—they do to him?'

Vadir glanced up, his hand still steadying the foal. 'Treat him as a God himself, and give him many mares, until the time comes that they have another need of him. There is always a price to be paid for Godhead.'

'And the price?' Owain was watching the foal butting at its mother's flank for the warm milk that meant life, and the words stuck a little in his throat.

'Once it was a man who died for the people,' Vadir said, 'then it was a horse who died, every three years; but now he dies only when there is some special peril or some special need, and for the rest we make do with a lock of his mane and a few hairs from his tail at the times of sacrifice—save that he must never be allowed to grow old and fail, lest the life of the people fail with him. So one day, there comes a new white horse to fight for the King-ship, and the old King dies. . . .'

Vadir withdrew his steadying hand, and got awkwardly to his feet. 'But we talk of things that lie beyond the years, and for the present it is enough that we get the mare into shelter. She is far spent, and scarcely stronger on her legs than the foal is; do you stay here with them and I will ride back to the steading and bring up some of my people and a mead-laced mash to put some heart into her. We'll get her into my stable for the night.'

Owain was feeling faintly sick at the things that the other had said, and the bond of the shared task that had held them together for a little while had snapped.

'To a man on horseback,' he said, 'the ride over to Beornstead is not so much longer than the ride to Widda's Ham. She is

H

nervous of new places, and I do not think that Beornwulf would wish her housed in a strange stable.'

They looked at each other a long moment in the lantern-light. Then Vadir said with faint amusement, 'You don't trust me, do you? You may be right.'

'There'll be no need to rouse them out,' Owain said, steadily. 'The household will be waking, and you'll maybe find Beornwulf along by the main dyke—he has a lantern.'

'So, I'll find him—and tell him what a splendidly dependable thrall he has,' Vadir said. 'Maybe he would sell you to me.' He whistled up his horse, who had been quietly cropping the grass at the edge of the lantern-light, and setting his hands on its shoulders, mounted with the steed-leap that men use who ride bareback, lightly enough despite his twisted foot; and in the same instant, with his hounds springing forward all about him, was drumming off into the misty darkness, in the direction of Beornstead.

Owain stood looking after him, though there was nothing to see once horse and rider were through the hawthorn bushes, hearing the hoof-beats die into the distance. Then he carefully unclenched his fists. He trimmed the lantern to make it last longer, and hung it again on its furze branch, and wishing that he had a cloak like Beornwulf, pulled off his own rough woollen tunic and spread it over the mare's back. Then he settled down, with Dog lying watchful against his thigh, to wait until someone came.

It was very quiet, now that the beat of hooves had died away; only curlew or sandpiper cried sometimes in the mist, and the air hushed in the faintest shimmer of sound through the dark masses of the furze behind him. From time to time the mare began to fidget and he spoke to her reassuringly. The foal, having drunk its fill, had lain down to sleep, its soft muzzle white-splashed with its mother's milk; and looking down at it, he was pierced with an aching tenderness. He had begun to love the little creature because it had, as it were, come to life under his hands; and the far-off gleam of the sacrificial knife added something, a kind of urgency, to his love for the silver foal, that it might not otherwise have had.

The candle in the lantern was guttering out in a pool of wax, when at last Dog raised his head to listen; and a few moments later, Owain, listening also, heard the distant long-drawn shout for which he had been waiting so long. He scrambled stiffly to his feet, and stood swinging the lantern above his head and shouting at full pitch of his lungs. 'Here! We're here! This way.' The lantern gave a last flare, and guttered out, just as the mist-blurred gleam of another lantern came bobbing between the hawthorn trees, and he heard Beornwulf hail in reply.

The sun was rising by the time Golden-eye and the foal were safely home. And a little later Owain stood beside the morning fire in the house-place, stretching the weariness out of his shoulders and smiling down at Uncle Widreth who sat with his back propped against the roof-tree exactly as though he had not moved since last night.

'You look different, this morning,' said Uncle Widreth, in his thin rustling voice. He was growing simple, in these days, so simple that he always said what he thought.

'How different?'

'As though,' said Uncle Widreth slowly, 'you had made something with life in it, after all.'

The Old King

In the ordinary way there was little coming and going among the settlements. Forest and marsh made for bad travelling, and each village lived for itself in its own clearing in the wild, wove its own cloth and forged its own ploughshares and grew its own food— or starved when the harvest failed. But between the coastwise settlements of the Maen Wood and the Seals' Island there was a certain amount of passing to and fro, for the business of dyking and draining, and clearing sand-choked channels; and keeping out the sea with turf and brushwood walls was a thing that concerned all the coastwise folk together. So the Beornstead folk had always seen more of their neighbours than was common among the Saxon kind. But after the birth of the silver foal they saw more of Vadir Cedricson than ever they had done before. He had always a good reason for coming, or had merely turned aside in passing, on his way to somewhere else; but Owain knew that he came to see the foal, to watch it growing to a long-legged colt, to a proud stallion, its coat paling from the dim grey of its birth until it was, as he had once said it would be, white as storm water on the Seal Rocks. He seemed drawn to the animal in some hidden way, so that looking back in after years Owain wondered whether he had already some instinct that his fate and the white stallion's were knotted together.

They called the foal Teitri, which was a name sometimes given to men but seldom to horses, for it simply meant a foal; because from the first it seemed that an ordinary name such as other horses bore would be too personal a thing for this horse who was never to know a human rider. And in his third winter—it was always in the winter that they broke the colts—Beornwulf and his British thrall, working together as they did in so many things nowadays, began the task of breaking him, so far as he was ever to be broken. He was used to being handled, for they had begun gentling him while he still sucked his mother; he was friendly and trusting, for no one had ever betrayed his trust, and would come to Owain's whistle, as his mother came. But when the breaking started, all that, it seemed, was lost. The touch of the headstall seemed to him betrayal; he was outraged and terrified and furious that the friends he had trusted should seek to impose their will on his in mastery, and he fought for his freedom like a wild thing roped and dragged in from the wilderness who had never felt a man's hand on him before. The greater part of the task fell to Owain, for there had always been a special bond between him and the grey foal he had brought into the world, and even now it was as though he could reach him better than Beornwulf could do. For most of that winter his life was centred round the struggle with the white stallion; a struggle that went on and on through days of triumph when it seemed that they were making some kind of progress, and days of despair when a small mistake or a moment's impatience undid all the work of the days that had gone before. It was a battle that was heartbreaking for both of them, and in the end it was not as though Owain mastered Teitri at all, but rather as though Teitri, coming to understand where before he had only raged and feared, at last gave freely what all the men with whips in the world could not have forced from him. After that the sessions with headstall and bit and guiding-rein were no longer battles but lessons, and he learned willingly and well; and so at last the

thing was done—as well as a thing could be done that might not
be carried through to completion.

That was a hard winter and a long one, and before it was over,
starvation, which was never very far off at winter's end, was
nearer than usual to the settlements along the coast. The young
and the strong went about with hollow faces and heads that
looked too big for their bodies, and more than usual of the old
and sickly died, and by the time Teitri had learned to move in a
circle on the guiding-rein, Uncle Widreth's place beside the
hearth was empty, and there was no one to tell stories to the
Beornstead household in the evenings, any more.

With spring, as so often happened after a lean winter, the grey
fever-hag came prowling across the levels from settlement to
settlement in the marsh mists, and as the winter had taken the
eldest of the household, so the spring took the youngest. Little
Gerd died on the night that the last of the grey geese flew north,
and all that night they heard the dark rush of wings overhead.
Her going made very little stir; death came so often to the settlements, and there was nothing to be gained by raising an outcry.
Her sisters howled for a while, but if Athelis wept at all no one
saw or heard her. They put the little one away as one might bury
a bird that falls dead out of a hedge, and the life of the farm went
on, through spring sowing and sheep-shearing—almost to hay
harvest.

On an evening of early summer, with the midge-clouds dancing
over the sunlit levels, Owain went down with the big wooden
pails slopping in either hand, to water Teitri for the night.

Between the oakwoods and the reed-beds and saltings that
fringed the harbour, a curved strip of rough pasture ran up towards the creek. Beornwulf had enclosed it in the year that Owain
first came to Beornstead. A bleak enough spot when the gales
blew in off the sea, but this evening the light lay long and golden
across it, and the long pale grass of the saltings scarcely stirred in
the salt-scented air.

Owain unhitched and lifted aside the hurdle that closed the gap
in the fence, and went through. Behind him he could hear Helga
and Lilla calling to each other as they went about the usual even-

ing hunt for eggs—the mallards in particular always laid abroad—
and the bleating of ewes and the lighter babble of half-grown
lambs, where Bryni, with Horn, the Smith's son, to help him, was
folding the sheep. They always folded them for the night, even
in summer, not for fear of wolves or wild men, down here in the
Seals' Island, but because of the dykes and channels that might
claim them in the dark.

Just inside the gate-gap stood a stone trough; Owain set the
buckets down beside it, and whistled, a long shaken shore-bird
whistle, and the white horse grazing at the far end of the horn of
pasture lifted his head and whinnied, then wheeled and came
trotting towards him. How often, Owain thought, Teitri had
come so, in answer to his whistle, breaking from a trot into a
canter; but this evening, watching him the length of the pasture,
he knew suddenly and with a painful awareness, that he had never
seen, and never would see in all his life, anything more beautiful
than a white stallion cantering between the oakwoods and the
sea. Teitri kicked up his heels like a colt, and broke into a lazy
gallop; he came up with mane and tail streaming, half circled
about Owain, and next moment was nuzzling against his breast.
'Greetings, brother,' Owain said, drawing his hand again and
again down the white nose from forelock to quivering nostril.
'It is thirsty work, this hot buzzing day. Drink then, it's cold from
the pond under the trees.' He took up the first pail and held it
for the horse to drink, before he tipped the rest into the sun-
warmed trough.

With his free hand he fondled the proud arched neck while
Teitri sucked up the water, noticing that the horse was getting
into better condition. He had been all bones at the winter's end.
Teitri was not a tall horse—there were dim half-legends of the
great horses that Artos the Bear had brought over from Gaul to
mount his cavalry, but the horses of today were seldom more
than thirteen or fourteen hands—but from the pride of his crest to
the sweep of his tail, he was magnificent. Nothing of his wiry,
vixenish mother in him save for a flash of gold in his eyes; a
creature who might have been one of the wild white horses of the
sea.

Owain gave the white neck a final pat, when Teitri had drunk

his fill, and stooped to pour the other pailful into the trough, while
the horse slobbered wetly at the back of his neck. Dog, who had
come down to the shore-pasture behind him, ducked his muzzle
into the trough and lapped thirstily. Suddenly the quick pad of
bare feet came over the turf, and looking round, Owain saw the
two boys heading in through the gate-gap. Bryni was first, Horn
just behind him—that was the usual way of it, though Horn was
the elder by two years and the taller by almost a head. Bryni had
been with the sheep all day, for as an outdweller Beornwulf had
no rights on the common grazing land nor the shepherd who
tended all the settlement's sheep, and now that he was ten years
old the task of watching them had fallen to the boy; and Horn, as
happened whenever his father could spare him, had come to
share it. Owain sometimes wondered if Brand the Smith ever
thought that there was a stranger at the hearth when his youngest
son chanced to be home for supper.

They came up, Bryni holding out his hand with a lick of greyish salt in it to the white questing muzzle that was advanced towards him, laughing at the feel of the delicately working lips in his
palm, while Horn, always a little slower, hung back behind him.

'You look as though you had been asleep in the sun all day,'
Owain said, looking down into the two flushed faces.

Bryni grinned up at him, shaking grass seed and bits of twig
out of his hair. 'No, only half the day. Anyway there are no
wolves to take the sheep, and Wauleye can keep them clear of the
dykes. There's a warbler's nest with five eggs in it still, among the
reeds just beyond the long turf stack, and look——' his hand went
to his belt, 'I've made an elder pipe and I can play three and a half
notes on it!'

'Can you so? Well even that's better than trying to steal wild
honey,' Owain said gravely. The summer before, Bryni had
tried to take a wild bees' nest unaided and very nearly been stung
to death.

Horn had come forward by that time, and was stroking Teitri's
neck, his square brown face serious and absorbed. 'He is beautiful,'
he said at last. 'He is the most beautiful horse that ever was foaled.
When the wind goes through the long grass and the old men say
"There runs the Wild Horse", he's just like the Wild Horse could

be if you could see him.' And then he turned fiery red at the
sound of his own words, and became very busy disentangling a
scrap of oak twig from the white mane.

'Teitri is the King of Horses, and he is my foster brother as
Haegel is my father's,' Bryni said, 'and Dog——' he ceased rubbing the stallion's muzzle, and swift and impetuous, as all his
movements were, flung himself down on the grass, nose to nose
with the great hound who promptly licked his face from ear to
ear—'and Dog is the King of all the dogs in Seals' Island, and he
is my foster brother, too.'

Horn looked down at them, and said in his serious pains-
taking way, 'Dog is growing old. He has got white hairs in his
muzzle.'

His arms round Dog's neck, Bryni jerked his head up, scowling. 'He hasn't, then! Can't you see he's been drinking and it's
only the wetness shining on his nose? And anyway he could still
beat every dog in Seals' Island in fair fight—even those red brutes
of Vadir's!'

Horn said something in reply, but Owain did not hear what it
was. He had been already turning to pick up the pails, but he
checked, and looked down at Dog also. The great hound must
be about ten years old now, the same age as Bryni, strong still,
milky-toothed and brave and cunning, and no hound as yet chal-
lenged his chosen place by the fire nor his king's share at feeding
time, but it had seemed to Owain lately that he was a little
slower than he used to be, a little fonder of sleeping in the sun.
No, it was not only the wetness shining on his muzzle. . . .

He picked up the pails. 'See that the gate-gap is closed after
you,' he said, and turned back towards the steading, leaving Dog
to follow with the two boys when they would. The sun was
below the oak trees now, and the gold was draining out of the
evening, and he had suddenly the odd feeling of a shadow lying
across his heart.

By the hind-gate of the steading, he met Beornwulf, frowning.
'Where's Bryni?' he demanded. 'I bade him always to come and
tell me at once when the sheep were folded, not simply leave them
and fly off about his own affairs.'

Owain jerked his head back the way he had come. 'Down in

the shore-pasture with Teitri, he and Horn; they took him a lick of salt.'

The master looked away in the same direction, his eyes narrowed under the golden brows, then he hunched his shoulders a little. 'Aye well, it is not so many more licks of salt they can be taking him,' he said in a different tone.

The thrall set the pails down carefully before he answered, and the shadow deepened across his heart. 'He—must go, then?'

'Aye, when the hay harvest is over.'

The last time Haegel the King had come that way, back in the windy spring weather, Owain was remembering how he had gone down with his foster brother to the shore-pasture and looked long at the white stallion. He had not asked any questions of Beornwulf afterwards; it had seemed better not to know. 'But why?' he burst out at last. 'The King does not need him. They say that the God's Horse is still in his prime and there is already a colt in Haegel's runs, ready for the day that he begins to fail.'

'I think that Teitri goes further afield than the royal farm at Cissa's Caester,' Beornwulf said slowly. 'It is in my heart that there is a higher place waiting for him—elsewhere. We should be proud.'

Owain looked round at him quickly; but Beornwulf's face was shut. No good to ask anything more. ' "Proud" has a cold sound,' he said heavily. 'Colder than the touch of a horse's muzzle on your shoulder when you saw him foaled.'

'All horses die one day,' Beornwulf said. 'Horses and hounds and men. Can I help it if you are a fool? . . . The evening meal was ready when I came out, and we might as well be getting back to it before the broth is burned and the women angry. The young ones will come when their bellies bid them.' And he turned in through the gate.

Owain picked up the pails yet again and followed him, walking heavily as though all at once he was desperately tired.

Hay harvest passed, and the day came for Teitri to go to the King's farm. They set out on a still grey morning, not long after sunrise so as to catch low tide in the creek, Owain riding first on Golden-eye with Dog loping ahead, Beornwulf following on another horse with Teitri on the leading-rein. It was an anxious out-setting, for the white stallion had never been off Beornstead land before, and they could not be sure how he would behave. But he followed Golden-eye easily enough, not because she was his mother, he had long ago forgotten that, and so had she, but because she was a mare. They got across the creek with little trouble, for he was used to being led in shallow water, and before noon they were at the King's farm.

And within an hour, Owain was riding south again down the old half-lost road from Regnum to the Seals' Island. He had not waited while Beornwulf finished his business with his foster brother; he had not felt that he could bear to wait, hanging about the high antler-crowned Hall, when Teitri had been handed over to the King's Horse Thegn, and Beornwulf had given him leave to start back at once. He rode slowly, knowing that the tide would not serve him yet a while for getting Golden-eye across the creek; but even so, the tide was not yet full out, when he came out from the Maen Wood and saw the levels lying pale under the grey sweep of the tall marsh sky.

He dismounted and sat himself down on the bank beside the roadway, his arm through Golden-eye's bridle, while Dog flung himself down contentedly at his feet. He was glad of the delay, for despite his eagerness to get away from the King's farm, he did not want to get back to Beornstead, not without Teitri. 'Can I help it if you are a fool?' Beornwulf had said. 'All horses die one day— horses and hounds and men.' But it was not the distant gleam of the priest's knife that hurt him so sharply; he had accepted that for the white stallion as a man might accept it for himself; it was that Teitri had come when he whistled, had been gentle and inquisitive and had known, save for that bitter time last winter, that men were his friends and to be trusted. And now they would treat him like a god, and he would become wild and fierce and men would be his friends no more.

But the sand-bars were laid bare now, and the stones of the old ford beginning to show. He stirred Dog gently into wakefulness with his foot, got up and remounted, and headed down over the wave-rippled sand into the shallows. Dog half paddled, half swam across, and splashed ashore ahead of him, shaking himself until it seemed that his four legs were about to fly off in different directions, then turned in behind Golden-eye, dodging from heel to heel as a dog does when following close behind a horse, as they set off down the last stretch of the road.

The steading was a place of women at that hour, for the thralls would be afield, but Bryni had brought in a couple of ewes for milking, and was hanging about the gateway with a scowling face. And when Owain rode into the garth, he found Vadir the Hault lounging on the bench beside the foreporch door, with two of his red hounds beside him, and an ale horn on his knee. Were they never to be free of the man, even now that Teitri was gone?

Vadir glanced up at him with those flickering curiously pale eyes, as he drew rein, and the dogs surveyed each other, snarling a little, their hackles raised. 'So, the God's Horse is gone already, they tell me,' he said.

'Aye. If you want to see him again you'll need to ride up to the King's farm,' Owain returned shortly. 'If it is Beornwulf you're wanting, he'll not be far behind me, or if he is, he'll miss the tide,' and dismounting he turned Golden-eye and led her away stable-ward to rub her down and give her a feed of beans before he turned her out to graze.

He did not notice for the moment that Dog had not followed him.

He had barely hitched the mare to the ring in the wall, as far as might be from Vadir's roan, when with appalling suddenness it seemed that all Hell broke loose in the steading garth behind him. The hideous snarling clamour of a dog-fight, the scream of a woman, and then Bryni's voice shrieking his name. 'Owain! Owain!'

But Owain had already snatched down the long-lashed whip that hung by the door, and was running—running as he had not done since an evening in the ruins of Viroconium, six springs ago. Just outside the stable door he all but crashed with Bryni, and the boy swerved, and whirled about beside him, sobbing out his story. 'It's Dog! They're killing Dog! It's Vadir's Fang—and the rest are with him—I tried to stop them—I——'

The sobbing voice dropped behind him as he raced, cold fury

and colder fear in his heart, for the end of the house-place, and the tumult beyond.

In the garth before the house-place door, Dog was fighting for his life, with not only Fang but three or four others upon him. The thing that always happened one day had happened now; the pack had turned under a young leader against the old one. He was fighting like a hero, flinging them this way and that, but the Red Killer was at his throat, and even as Owain burst into the garth, he went down and the battle closed over him.

Owain sprang in among the struggling, tearing, slavering bodies, yelling encouragement to Dog as he laid about him with a whip. What would happen if he missed his own footing, he knew well enough. Dog must have heard his Lord's voice, for somehow he got on to his legs once more, dragging Fang up with him; but the strength was pouring out of him through a score of wounds, and before Owain could reach him he was down again.

Owain brought the whiplash writhing and licking across this body and that; he kicked one hound—it was a Beornstead dog—in the belly and sent it yelping through the air. There seemed no weight in his body, as though he were borne up on the wings of the cold rage within him. He did not know that Bryni had joined him, wading valiantly into the fight with a piece of firewood, while the women huddled screeching in the house-place doorway; he scarcely knew that somebody had thrown a pail of water over them, deluging hounds and man and boy alike. He never knew what happened or how long the struggle lasted. He only knew that at last the hounds were falling sullenly back, and he heard the crack and crack and crack of another whip beside his own, and Beornwulf's voice, raised and cursing. He strangled Fang off Dog's throat with his naked hands, and flung the red brute aside.

After that was a sudden stillness. Beyond the stillness, making as it were a wall about it, he heard voices and the uneasy snorting and trampling of a horse, and beyond again, a sudden crying of gulls. One of Vadir's dogs lay still; Fang and the Beornstead hounds had slunk away to lick their wounds—they had plenty, for the old King had not gone down easily, though the odds had been five to one. Bryni was squatting beside him, whimpering a

little over an ugly bite in his arm, now that it was all over; and in
the midst of the stillness, Owain was kneeling beside Dog—Dog
bleeding from a full score of wounds, with his throat torn to rags.
The stubborn life and courage were in the old hound yet, and
even now he tried once more to get up; but his legs would not
answer to him, and he collapsed with a shudder, his head on
Owain's knee.

Owain was fondling the battered head, holding the beautiful
amber eyes with his own, while his free hand went feeling for the
knife in his belt. 'Good Dog! It was a mighty battle—a mighty
battle, brave heart——' Dog licked the caressing hand, and raised
his head a little to look at his Lord, the tip of his tail thumping
behind him. 'Good hunting, my brother,' Owain said, and drove
the knife cleanly home into the mangled throat.

Dog made a small surprised sound, and the life went out of him
with a great shudder, and the thing was finished.

Squatting beside him, Bryni rubbed the back of one brown
hand across his eyes. Owain remained quite still as though he
were stunned, looking down at the great brindled body with all
its wounds upon it.

At last he looked up, slowly. Beornwulf stood by with his
whip gathered into his hand, his horse fidgeting behind him.
The women and girls were still huddled in the house-place doorway, and on the bench, with Fang crouched against his knees,
Vadir Cedricson still sat, leaning back against the wall and looking
on as a man looks on at a show that interests and somewhat
pleases him.

Owain's mouth flinched and twisted sideways, and his throat
tightened a moment. He said, 'Could you not have stopped it?'

Vadir shrugged without troubling to lift his shoulders clear of
the wall. 'He was old and had his day; it is time there was a new
lord of the dog pack, and a worthier one than a thrall's cur.'

'If he had been the veriest dunghill cur,' Owain said, coldly
furious, 'he was not yours to say that his time had come to die.
But he was no cur, he was one of the war-hounds of Kyndylan
the Fair, until Kyndylan died by Aquae Sulis.'

'Ah yes, I had forgotten that you both contrived to come alive,
together, out of that fight.' Vadir's light eyes flicked him, like

the careless flick of a whiplash, and came to rest on the long white spear-scar that ran out of his torn sleeve. His pale brows rose a little, and the mobile mouth lifted into a half smile. 'I have never seen you stripped. How many scars the like to that one are there on your back?' he asked softly. 'Or can you perhaps fly faster than a spear?'

And he got to his feet, a little clumsy as always, and turned to speak to Beornwulf about whatever business had brought him across the Seals' Island.

Owain got up slowly, his fists clenched at his sides. But the years of thraldom had taught him that a thrall does not avenge an insult; and that lesson was more bitter than the insult itself. One of the other men, newly returned from the fields, had come to take the master's horse. And Beornwulf, interrupting his guest for the moment, was calling someone to spread earth over the blood and mess on the ground. Then to Owain he said, with a rough sympathy in his tone, 'Do what there is to do with the dog, but before that, get one of the women to salve those bites.'

Then he turned into his house-place with Vadir his guest.

12

The Sanctuary

OWAIN stood where he was, looking down at himself. He was very bloody, and some of the blood was his own. He was fang-gashed and bitten in a dozen places, but he had not known it until that moment; it was only the surface of his mind that knew it now. 'Do what there is to do with the dog,' Beornwulf had said. When any of the farm animals died, if the flesh was not fit for man, they gave it to the dogs, but when it was a dog that died, they could not do that, for it was Taboo, a Forbidden Thing, to feed an animal on the flesh of its own kind. For a dog, then, one scraped out a hole as shallow or as deep as one had time to spare for, in the woods beyond the Intake, and pushed a little earth back over, and hoped for the best.

Still moving slowly as though he had had a knock on the head and was half dazed, he went to get a spade and the narrow wooden sledge they used for carcasses at the autumn slaughtering.

Somebody helped him to lift Dog on to it—the other he left lying: let Vadir see to his own—and taking up the ropes of twisted straw, he turned to the gateway.

Half-way along the side of the forest field, which was up for barley, he found Bryni trotting beside him. 'Na,' he said, 'go home. It is time for supper.'

'I am not hungry.'

He stopped in his tracks and turned to look at the boy. Bryni's face, usually crimson when he was angry, showed white under his tan, and he drew his breath in little sobbing gasps. 'I'll kill him for this!' he said. 'I will! I'll kill him!'

Owain shook his head wearily. 'That is foolish talk. You are only ten years old.'

'I shall not always be ten years old. One day I shall be a man, and when I'm a man, I shall kill him!'

And somehow, piercing through the dull ache of his own desolation, the certainty reached Owain that it was no empty threat made in the moment of heart-break, to be forgotten to-morrow. This was a threat that would be remembered; and something must be done about it. 'Listen, Bryni. Vadir has many kin, and if you killed him they would demand your death or much wyr-gold. And because you are your father's only son, he would try to raise the gold—and with no kin to help him, for remember that when a man leaves the settlement as your fore-father did, though he may remain friends with the kin he leaves behind him, he loses all claim to their help in a man-slaying. The ruin of all your folk is too heavy a price to pay for avenging a thrall's cur.'

'Dog wasn't just a thrall's cur, he was one of the war-hounds of Kyndylan the Fair—you said so yourself.' The boy's voice broke in passionate grief, and his face was working.

'I said it myself, and if anyone were to avenge him, it should be me. Go home, now.'

'Let me come with you——'

Owain touched the boy's shoulder, kindly enough. 'Go home, I said. I shall manage better alone.'

For a moment Bryni resisted, then he turned away with a sob. 'But I *will* kill him! I *will* kill him!'

Owain stood to watch him stumbling back towards the stead-ing, hearing the desperate mutter that he was not meant to hear. Why had he spoken to the boy so? What did it matter to him if a

Saxon whelp brought ruin on a Saxon family? Slowly he turned, and went on alone, leaning forward to the pull of the laden sledge behind him.

In a little the long shadows of the oakwoods reached out to claim him, and he turned westward along the woodshore, heading for the ruined shrine. It would be less lonely for Dog's bones to lie where men had been, than quite away in the wild; and though he had been bred a Christian, a long time ago, Owain had some confused idea that Silvanus who was the God of flocks and herds and woodland things, to whom men had sacrificed in thanks for a good day's hunting, would surely receive a dog kindly and cast the cloak of his protection over him.

It was not really very far, not so far as it had seemed in the darkness and the mist, when he had come that way searching for Golden-eye on the night that Teitri was born. In a while he saw the pale glimmer of broken walls through the low-hanging branches, and turning aside into the remains of the sacred clearing, stopped before the shrine. He knew now what the shadow was that he had felt in this place before.

It did not take very long to make the hole big enough—though he dug it deep against foxes—for the earth of the oakwoods was soft and crumbling, and the ground just there was free from tree roots. And when it was done he turned to lift Dog from the sledge. But he did not like to think of Dog's beautiful brindled black and amber hide and the creamy breast fouled by the dark earth; it was fouled and draggled with blood, but that was a bright and honourable fouling; the earth would be different.

So he broke sprays of leaves from the bushes round about, and spread them in the bottom of the hole, and then on his knees lifted Dog's body and eased it over the edge. It fell soft and still lithe, and at the feel of it, pain tore at Owain like a spear turning in a wound. He settled Dog with nose on forepaws as he used to lie, and stroked his head for the last time, then began to lay the rest of the green stuff in place, with a confused prayer to the Lord of the shrine. 'O Silvanus—here is a hound, not a hunting-dog, but he was a good dog. They used to call you the Lord of all fourfooted things—Spread your cloak over him——' He was pushing the earth in again, pressing it down with his hands.

Now there was only one spray of leaves left to show; and now there was nothing left at all. He beat down the mound of earth hard and firm, and heaved a fallen column head across it to make it safer.

It was finished now, and there was nothing more that he could do; nothing left but to go back to the steading with no sound of Dog's feet padding behind him. But the entrance to the shrine was before him, full of shadows; and when he got up, he did not turn back to the steading, but went forward into the shrine, as into refuge.

He had never been inside before, being held back by a superstitious fear. But there was nothing there but quietness, after all, not even the smell of an enclosed space, for it had gone back to the wild so long ago that its smell was the same as the woods outside. Owain sat down against the furthest wall, which still stood for most of its height, and drawing his knife from his belt, began to whet it on a fallen stone beside him. Dog's blood was still on the blade, like rust, and a great patch of it, dried black now, clotted his breeks to his thigh where Dog's head had lain.

He went on and on whetting the knife, only half realizing what he did, but going on doing it, all the same, his purpose growing like a slow black cloud in his mind. It was not only that Dog was dead, and Uncle Widreth, and Teitri gone from him, but that, quite simply, he saw no point in going on any longer. If there was anything in the distance, however far off, it would have been another matter; but there was not anything; just days, and days, and days, stretching before him. It was Vadir's insult and his own failure to avenge it, almost as much as the loss of Dog, that had shown him that unchanging unbearable waste of days. . . .

The westering sun, that had been hidden all day, slipped out from under the low roof of cloud, and a shaft of light fell across the sanctuary through a breach in its wall, piercing into the darkest corner where Owain sat whetting and whetting his knife. Close beside his foot, where he had scuffed the leaf-mould aside in sitting down, something gave off a spark of blue fire.

It caught Owain's attention. Maybe it was a loose bead from a necklace that someone had left for a votive offering. Still holding his knife in his other hand, he reached out and felt about. Not a

loose bead; not anything loose at all. It was part of the floor.
Idly, he scratched up a bit more of the dark crumbling mould,
and more of the blue came to light; blue glass cubes, used with
cubes of chalk and red and yellow sandstone in the fine tesserae
that must have formed the sanctuary floor. Shape and pattern
began to emerge, a little bird worked out with rare skill, the blue
glass forming its wings and mantle; then something under it, on
which it was perching—a narrow human hand.

The act of doing something, finding something and being even
a little interested in what he found, seemed to make the dark cloud
draw off a little; and he scraped and scrabbled on, the loose black
soil formed by the drifted leaves of a hundred summers crumbling
easily away under his fingers. In a little, he had cleared a medal-
lion surrounded by a delicate border of ivy leaves and berries,
and was looking at the half-length figure of a girl with a bird in
one hand and a blossoming branch in the other. Part of the
border had been destroyed by the roots of something that had
grown through it, but the little figure was perfect, delicately
charming and full of joy. Summer, autumn, and winter would be
in the other corners of the shrine—it was a common enough
subject—and maybe Silvanus himself in the centre; but Owain
had no interest in the rest of the pavement, only in this corner,
the spring corner, which reminded him of something, someone. . . .

The shaft of sunset light had faded, and the girl's figure was
softening into the shadows. The elusive memory seemed fading
too; in another moment it would have gone from him and he
would have lost it for all time. And he didn't want to lose it, he
didn't want—something within him reached out desperately to
catch at the thing in that last instant, and then he had it, like a
bird cupped in his hands.

He had scarcely thought of Regina for years. Long ago it had
seemed to him that she must have died, and even his memory of
her had grown thin and pale so that he could see through it as
one sees through a curl of wood smoke. Now, suddenly, he was
remembering more vividly than he had ever remembered anything in his life before, Regina coming towards him, her thin
face sparkling with a kind of grave delight, holding out her

hands to him with the tit cupped between them; the jewel-blue of its cap
just visible between her palms, the blue
flash and the whirr of wings as she set it
free.

The impression was so strong that it
was like a physical touch, as though in
that moment something in Regina had
reached out to touch something in himself, to make a kind of life-line between
them, as she had done on the night that
they had found Ulpius Pudentius; but
that time it had been for her to cling to;
this time it was for him.

From that moment he knew with
absolute certainty that even if he never
saw her again, Regina was alive, and because he knew that, he could go on.

The sun was quite gone, even from
the world outside, and the shadows were
rising like water in the sanctuary, when
Owain slipped his knife back into his
belt. He scattered the black leaf-mould
again over the corner of the pavement
that he had cleared, hiding the girl and
the bird and the flowering branch; then
he got up, slowly, for his bites had
stiffened on him, and went out, stepping
round the mound of fresh earth and the
pale column head that marked Dog's
grave, and taking up the slack ropes of
the slaughter sledge, set out for the
steading.

It was almost dark when, having left
the sledge in its usual place in the big
store-shed and washed off the worst of
the dried blood, he came to the house-
place door. The evening meal was over,

but the family and the thralls were still gathered in the firelight about the long hearth. He was thankful to see that Vadir and his red hounds were not there; the Beornstead hounds lay among the strewing fern, still licking their wounds, but he felt nothing against them, nothing even against Fang now. They had merely followed the law of the pack, that when the leader's strength begins to wane, a new leader takes his place. Vadir was another matter.

He sat down beside Caedman at the lower end of the hearth, and somebody passed him the big copper stew pot that had been set aside with his share still in it, and he reached for a bannock from the basket. He even managed to eat a little though the good kale broth and the fresh-baked bread turned to dough in his mouth. Helga and Lilla had red eyes; they were both trying to spin, but Lilla kept breaking her thread. Bryni sat hunched together with his knees drawn up to his chin, and glowered into the fire, refusing to meet anyone's eyes, Owain's most of all. The men were discussing the scarcity of that spring's herring shoals, their voices falling broad and peaceable in the close warm air. No one spoke to Owain, but he felt the rough warmth of sympathy, and shrunk together inside himself much as Bryni was doing, as though he were afraid of the chafe of it against his raw places.

When he had eaten a little and pushed the rest away, it was time for sleep. The household rose, stretching and yawning, to make ready for the night, and Beornwulf himself took down the lantern and kindled its candle to make his usual round of the steading before he slept. Then, turning in the doorway, caught Owain's eye and jerked his head towards the darkness of the summer night behind him—not that he need have troubled, for of late years they had almost always shared that late round of the byres between them. Owain remembered just in time not to whistle Dog from the hearth-place and went out after him.

It was very dark, for the low cloud had shut out the stars, and in the darkness the wash of the sea seemed to draw nearer. Beornwulf walked out through the gap in the thorn hedge, as though he wanted to be clear of house-place and household before he said whatever it was that he had in his mind to say, and Owain walked a pace behind him. He rounded the corner of the steading hedge and checked beside the humped shape of the pea stack, facing seaward, and for a few moments the two men stood together in silence, the dogs about their knees. Then Beornwulf said gruffly, 'He was a good dog, and I shall miss him—as much as though he were one of my own, I dare say. But words are poor things, and it was not to tell you that, that I called you out here.'

'No,' Owain said, staring into the darkness of the marsh beyond the yellow pool of the lantern.

'I was with the King my foster brother this morning, after you rode for home. In three days' time I return to him, to set out on a long wayfaring. I think that I shall be back before summer's end, but no man when he sets out can be sure of the day of his return. I leave all things about the farm in your hands while I am away.'

There was a little silence, while the hush of the sea swelled and retreated, swelled and retreated in the dark. Then Owain said, 'Saxon master, is that wise?'

Beornwulf answered him after another silence. 'British thrall, I think so.'

'There are still Gyrth and Caedman, who have worn your thrall-ring longer than I.'

'They may grumble at your hand on the reins, but you will find that they do not question it.'

'Because you have told them that that is to be the way of it, until you come again?'

'No, because you are what you are, and they are what *they* are.'

Owain glanced round at him, and away again. 'Have I leave to ask where this wayfaring leads?'

'To the Court of King Aethelbert of Kent,' Beornwulf said. 'I was right when I guessed that Teitri was to go further than Haegel's farm; he is to go for a royal gift to the High King, and it is I that am to take him.'

It had been a very still night, but as though the name of the Kentish King had called it up, a long soft breath of air came sighing across the marshes from the sea and for the second time that day, memory was playing an odd trick on Owain; the

memory of Uncle Widreth sitting just here, on the warm side of
that year's pea stack, whittling a bird from a scrap of silvery
driftwood, and the sound of his old tired voice was in his inner
ear like the echo of the sea in a shell. 'Life is fierce and harsh to
the young, but gentler when one grows old. Only while one is
young there is always the hope that one day something will
happen—that one day a little wind will rise. . . .'

Only it never did rise. One just went on hoping until one day
one was old like Uncle Widreth.

The long sighing breath of air had died into the grass, but
another was already hushing towards them across the levels.
Beornwulf sniffed the weather like one of his own hounds, as
he turned back towards the steading. 'We shall have wind by
morning,' he said.

13

The Wreck

'AH, you may wag your heads and look unbelieving till your ears
drop off,' said the harper. 'Maybe you don't hear so much, down
here in this cursed cut-off tongue of the land. But I smelled the
Ravens gathering before Wibbendune fight, more than twenty
years ago, and I have not forgotten. I tell you, I have been snuffing
that reek again among the border kingdoms all summer past.'
And he dragged the folds of a once-gaudy cloak about him and
hitched himself yet closer to the fire.

The great pile of blazing driftwood burned close under the lee
of the boatshed; in the open it could not have lived a moment on
such a night, but leeward of the boatshed there was a pocket of
shelter from the late summer gale that came booming up across
the levels in the dark, and the very force of the wind carried the
rain slanting overhead in a roof of driving wet that only fell hissing
into the flames when the gusts dropped for a moment.

There was a constant shifting about the fringes of the firelight, dark figures looming out of the darkness and others, plunging off into the dark again, as the men who kept their ceaseless watch on the dykes and brushwood walls and the long curve of the shingle bank below the haven, came in to snatch a warm and a rest while someone else took their turn for a while. It was late, drawing on to the black hour before dawn, but there would be no sleep to-night for the men who watched the shore, not while spring tides and wild easterly gale together were piling the seas up on to the coast, bringing the old familiar danger to the lower levels.

Owain, just in from his own turn along the shingle bank (not many thralls turned out to the coast-watch, but with Beornwulf still from home, he had come to take Beornstead's share), glanced up from the fire, listened with a quickened heart-beat for what the harper would say next. But for a little while he said nothing more, only stared into the flames and cracked his long finger bones in time to unheard music. And there was nothing to hear but the roar of the gale, and under the gale—so far down that one felt it in one's bones rather than heard it—the deeper boom and crash of the sea, stronger and more menacing with every moment that passed.

'Hark to it,' someone said. 'Will you hark to it! And it's not much more than three-quarter tide yet.' And there was a deep grumbling of voices round the fire, and here and there men glanced over their shoulders as though the menace of the tide was a monstrous thing that they might see looming down upon them out of the dark. Someone threw a fresh branch of driftwood on to the fire, and the flames leapt up, casting a tawny glare over the faces of men and dogs huddled about it. The new flare of the fire-light picked out the brindled bars of Grip's hide, turning the white breast-mark to a wavering silver flame; Grip, who belonged to the boat-builder's son, was one of Dog's offspring—there were a good few, around the Seals' Island—not so very like his sire in the daylight, but now, in the light of the driftwood blaze. . . . Sharp pain struck at Owain, and he turned his gaze and his thoughts away quickly; to anything that would not carry the memory of Dog's living warmth bunched against him; to the harper at the further side of the fire.

Wandering gleemen came often enough to the High Hall of
Haegel the King, but they seldom wandered on south into the
Seals' Island, with their load of songs and sagas and their gathered
news of the outside world; and so it was, maybe, that there were
so many men, far more than need have turned out from their own
firesides, gathered about the watch-fire tonight. This one was not
a very good harper, truth to tell, but he made a cheerful noise, and
he was not grudging of himself; he could have stayed warm and
dry with the women and the bairns in Gamal the Headman's
house-place, but he had chosen to come out with the other men
and share the darkness and the storm, only leaving his harp behind where the rain could not get at it. He had even given them
one or two songs, roaring them out above the storm—he had a
great voice, even if it was not very tuneful—until somehow it
seemed as though the sheer weight of the tempest had crushed the
singing, and huddled in the shelter of the boatshed they fell to
talking in shouted fits and snatches, instead. An ugly little man
with small, dark, very bright eyes and a long inquiring nose that
seemed to quiver as one watched it, a nose, Owain thought, that
one could well imagine searching the wind for that smell of the
Ravens gathering. . . .

'The border kingdoms?' old Gamal the Headman asked, returning to the thing that they had been speaking of some while before. 'And what is it that you would be meaning by the border
kingdoms?'

'Those that border on the great Kingdom of the West Saxons,
for sure.' The gleeman looked up, and the fire set tiny flames
dancing in those small bright eyes of his. 'The little kings with a
few spears to Ceawlin's many, looking to the safety of their own
hunting runs. Too strong a neighbour to be comfortable, is
Ceawlin of Wessex, and has been these many years, and maybe
they begin to think, these little kings, that if they were to band together their spears might number as many as Ceawlin's, especially
now that there is bad blood between him and his brother's sons.
It is in my mind that someone has whispered that in their ears—
that someone is whispering it, all the while.'

'And who would that "someone" be?' Brand the Smith leaned
his huge bulk forward into the firelight, half in earnest, half

mocking in his deep rumbling voice. 'Tell us, most wise of all gleemen, since you know the secrets of so many kings.'

The gleeman shook his head, and a grin flashed across his face from ear to ear. 'Na, I am a harper who keeps his eyes and ears open as he moves from hearth to hearth, not a sooth-sayer to read hidden things in the fallen chips from an apple branch, nor an old woman with the second sight. I say that something is brewing among the little kingdoms, and I say no more.'

And suddenly out of a long past autumn evening there leapt upon Owain the memory of the King's words as he sat with his foster brother on the foreporch bench at Beornstead. 'His brother's sons will surely say "We also fought for the Kingdom, and now Wessex is great. Why then is our share so small?" and so may come trouble on Ceawlin's threshold. And that, I think, will be the chance of those who do not love Ceawlin—notably Aethelbert of Kent'. Four or five years ago that must have been, and now this little long-nosed gleeman had smelled the Ravens gathering. The queer mood of waiting that had been on him ever since Beornwulf set out for the Kentish Court quickened all at once to a sense of expectancy that was no mere echo of distant events stirring, but nearer and more urgent, rushing towards him across the dark marshes on the wings of the gale. The feeling was so strong that he half drew his legs under him as though to rise and meet it—whatever it was. Then he shook his shoulders under the folds of the heavy cloak and sank back again. The men's voices had grumbled into silence, leaving the night to the howling voices of the storm.

Suddenly the wind dropped away into a long hollow quiet be-fore the next gust, and into the quiet broke a long-drawn breath-less shout. The huddled figures about the fire were scrambling to their feet, eyes straining in the direction from which the cry had come, ears straining for another above the tumult of the gale. Owain, springing to his feet with the rest, saw a blink of yellow light beyond the thorn branches. 'This is it,' he thought, with a sudden calm in himself. 'Not Ceawlin and the King of Kent—the shingle bank is going.'

The light became the gleam of a lantern bobbing towards them.

Beside him he heard the bull voice of Gamal the Headman pitched above the storm. 'What is it? Is the bank going?'

Out of the raging darkness a voice shouted back. 'Na, na—a wreck——' and next instant a man loomed up after his voice, gasping and shaking the hair out of his eyes. 'Ulf saw her first. She nearly made it, but the waves are pounding on to the dunes at the harbour mouth. She'll beach on the Seal Rocks for sure—if she's not there by now.'

A splurge of voices greeted his words, the men of the settlement crowding close about him. 'She may still make the anchorage at Cymenshore,' somebody said, but Gamal shook his head impatiently. 'She might have done, a while since; not now—the wind's going round.'

And they glanced at each other in the swinging light, fiercely speculating. After six years on the coast Owain knew that brightening of the eyes. It was not the first time since he came south with Beornwulf that a ship, storm-caught and running for the shelter of the Windy Haven, had been driven past it to meet her death on the open coast or among the rocks of the Seal Strand. It was a gift of the gods to be half hoped for in winter, but scarcely in the summer-time. They were kindly enough men in their day-to-day lives; but a wreck was a wreck, just as war was war. . . .

'Come on, then, neighbours.' Brand hitched his rough mantle more closely about him. 'Come on, or the fish-folk beyond Cymenshore will reap it all.'

'Fair shares for them that stays to watch the bank, though,' somebody put in, and there was a general laugh.

'Aye, fair shares, but they'll be precious thin ones, if the fish-folk get there first.'

Men were already tugging their cloaks around them, plunging off into the wind and rain towards the promise of the wreck, and Owain found that he was one of them. Behind them he heard the harper laughing and urging them on, it might have been in savage mockery, as a huntsman urges on his hounds to the kill.

Then the gale swooped roaring between those who went and those who stayed, and they heard no more.

Clear of the shelter of the boatshed the wind leapt at them like a live thing, battering the breath back into their bodies. Owain leaned sideways, head down into the gusts. Low down in the east beyond the harbour bar, the first wan light was broadening. Owain saw the sea-beast shapes of the fishing boats pulled high up the keel-strand, the crouching land-beast shapes of the settlement barns and byres and house-places huddled under the thorn wind-breaks, and beyond, half lost in the trailing curtains of rain, seem-ing perilously higher than the sodden land, the white menace of the sea.

They were heading down the long curve of the coast where the sand and shingle bar of the haven came sweeping in to the land. Now they were among the dunes; they kept to the landward side when they could, but even so the boom and crash of the surf was a thing to stun and deafen all the senses, and the ground shuddered underfoot as though the great rollers were the Hammer of Thor striving to pound the land into nothingness. When they came down to the Seal Strand at last, there was light enough to show them other dark figures there before them and that they had guessed aright as to where the ship would ground.

She was hard and fast on the rocks, a small coastal vessel, black against the white-combed seas around and beyond her. Mastless and already breaking up, she was so close inshore that they could see the men on board her. That was the appalling thing, Owain thought, that they were so near that one could see the men who were going to drown; little black clinging figures that did not seem real— But they *were* real, and they in their turn must be able to see the men on shore and the gleam of the lantern fading sickly into the wild light of dawn. All so near, three or four spear-casts, maybe, not more, and there was nothing that one could do.

Steadily, remorselessly, the great waves were pitching on to the wreck—for she was no more than a wreck, now—and with each hammer-blow of the great swinging seas, something more of her would be smashed away, one less figure clinging to the tangled rigging. It was a horrible, a pitiful thing to see. Now she was just a black mass of beams and spars and tangled cordage, like the battered skeleton of some sea-monster long stranded on the rocks —yet with a few men clinging there still.

The men on shore were wading out as deeply as they dared, to catch the bales and wine-skins and tumbling spars that had begun to come ashore, before the undertow could snatch them out again. Quite suddenly, as though in answer to a summons that he neither understood nor questioned, Owain found that he had flung off his cloak and was wading out also. The low dazzle of a stormy sunrise was shining into his eyes; the savage undertow dragged at his legs and the shingle churned and shifted under his feet, and once down he would be done for; but he waded on, knee deep, thigh deep. Behind him he heard shouts of warning, but he paid no heed. He was waist deep now, he was lifted half off his feet, and next instant he was clinging to a rock slippery with green weed, the waves breaking clean over him.

A wine-skin bobbed past, dark and buoyant like a porpoise, but he let it go by and in a while saw it sucked out again. A seaman's body swept by him, dim-seen under water, and a moment later another body, uplifted on the curved shoulder of a swinging sea.

The stormy light touched the fair hair and beard, the copper-tanned skin. Beornwulf had come home in a strange way.

14

Freedom and a Sword

OWAIN caught the man as he went by. His hand slipped, but he had him now by the hair and now under the shoulder. He would have let the sea carry them shoreward together, but he remembered that wicked undertow, and kept his grip on the rocks with one hand, clamping the unconscious man against him while the great surging sea went by, and braced himself with feet clenched into the shifting shingle, to withstand the backwash that must follow. There were some men not more than a few spear-lengths away, and he yelled to them: 'Here! Brand! Hunfirth! It's *Beornwulf*! Help me get him out!'

No one heard him the first time, and he yelled again, with a kind of despairing rage. 'To me! Here to me! It's Beornwulf! Oh, for God's sake leave the wine-skins and help me!'

That time someone heard. He saw an arm upflung in answer.

When the struggle eased for a moment in the slack water between wave and wave, he shook the drenched hair out of his eyes, and saw through the flying spray that the men were forming a living chain out into the surf, working their way towards him. To leave unknown seamen to drown was one thing, but Beornwulf was a Seals' Island man, and outdweller or no, he was kin to many of them. The leader of the chain—it was Brand the Smith—was quite near now, but Owain was very nearly done; another spent wave dragging seaward would take him with it, and already the pressure of the next great breaker was roaring up behind him. It broke well out on the rocks, and the yeasty water swung boiling shoreward. Owain let go his rock and plunged forward with it in a desperate stumbling rush.

He went under, and the hissing water closed over his head. He felt a sickening blow on one shoulder, but somehow, he never knew how, he had still his hold of the unconscious man. Then there were hands on him, hands that caught and slipped and caught again. Men were shouting in his ear, they were taking some of the strain of Beornwulf from him. The backwash was screaming out over the shingle, dragging at his body as though it were an old cloak in a gale of wind, but the human chain that had hold of him held firm. And then as the intolerable drag relaxed, he grounded, and was dragged to his knees; he found his feet under him and stumbled forward up the shelving beach as the next wave crashed behind him, pouring and creaming among the black rocks.

At the foot of the dunes, out of reach of the waves, he pitched to his knees, his burden slipping from him. He crouched there, a red darkness before his eyes, and in his ears a roaring that came even between him and the roaring of the storm, like a runner utterly spent after a great race. But as sight and hearing cleared, he saw men round him, and Beornwulf lying in a hollow of the spray-wet shingle where he had laid him down.

Beornwulf lay with the stillness of the drowned, a great broken bruise on his forehead. But he was not dead, only stunned, by the look of things. Owain drew a gasp of relief as he felt under his hands, the life fighting for itself in the man's unconscious body. He got him over on to his face, and a little salt water came out of

K

his mouth, but not much. He had come shoreward on the crest of a wave and had probably not taken in much water. Owain pressed on his back to drive out any more that there might be, and felt Beornwulf's breathing waken under his hands.

He looked up at the men about him, pitching his voice above the gale. 'We must get him home. Best fetch something to carry him on; he may have ribs broken for all I know.'

After a while a couple of men came down with a sheep-fold hurdle; they had to stand on it to keep it from flying away before they could lift Beornwulf on to it. Then Owain and Brand and two other men of the settlement took up the corners to carry him home.

There was no sign of the ship now, nothing but the dark jags of drifting wreckage, and other men shouting to each other in the shallows as the bales and spars and wine-skins came rolling in. And the wind was booming round to the south, as they set out for the two-mile-distant steading. Soon it would blow itself out.

The steading was awake and busy, the thralls already going about their early morning work, heads down and shoulders hunched against the wind. Athelis came to the house-place door when she heard the dogs bark, Lilla and Helga and the bond-woman with her. The others cried out at sight of the figure on the hurdle, but not Athelis; only she felt for the doorpost behind her, and her sharp-boned face looked for the moment like a very old woman's, as she looked down at him. 'Is he dead?'

Owain shook his head. They had hurried with their burden, and the wind, though not so high as it had been, was still high enough, and he had not much breath left for talking. 'Na,' he managed, 'only stunned, I think.'

She let go the doorpost and stood aside for them to carry him in. 'Set him down by the fire,' she said; and that was all.

They did as she bade them, and stood off, panting. The three settlement men looked at each other; they had done what they could for a neighbour, and it was women's work now, and there might still be gleanings to be got from the unexpected harvest of the sea. They grinned at each other, and one by one they slipped away.

The farm thralls had come pushing in after the rest, and Bryni was there from the sheep fold, white and silent, with his eyes fixed in a kind of scared bewilderment on his father's face, and among the legs of the little throng, the dogs came nosing forward.

Athelis turned on them all, crying out in a high, strained voice. 'Off! Be off, the lot of you! Gunhilda—children—stop that sniffling and squealing! Gyrth and Caedman, have you never seen a half-drowned man before that you must stare like oxen? Bryni, if you have left the sheep all abroad and they get into the kale patch your father shall beat you for it when the strength comes back to him.'

They scattered from her like scared chickens, the dogs slinking after them, and when they were gone she turned to Owain who was still standing by. 'Now, help me to get him stripped and between blankets before he takes his death indeed.'

And so, in silence, save for the beating of the dying gale across the thatch, they set about the task of stripping Beornwulf of the few sodden rags that still clung to his body, and drying him off before they lifted him into the great box bed. 'There was a wreck, then?—And he was on board?' Athelis said at last. 'It is strange that I did not feel the danger when the wind rose.'

'We did not expect him so soon,' Owain said, 'and we did not know that he would have come by sea.'

'I suppose not, though it is quicker by sea, when it does not end in drowning. Did many come ashore?'

'Not living, I think.' Owain flung the squelching remains of one shoe into a corner. 'He came by me on the crest of a wave, and I was able to catch him before he went seaward again.'

She looked up, as though seeing him for the first time, beginning to wring the water from her husband's hair while the steam wisped up from it in the warmth of the driftwood fire. 'So? You look as near drowned as he does—Ah, and your shoulder is hurt.'

Owain glanced down at himself inquiringly. He had known, without really thinking about it, that his right arm was stiff and painful and growing difficult to use; and he saw that what remained of his kirtle was ripped completely off that side, and his shoulder was one great angry bruise. 'The sea threw me on a rock.'

'So?' she said again. 'It is maybe harder to save the life of a man than to catch wine-skins bobbing in the shallows.'

They had scarcely got Beornwulf between the soft skin rugs of the box bed, when he opened his eyes and was violently sick. He lay staring straight upward at the bed-roof overhead while they cleared up the mess, his eyes blank with the wandering blankness that one sees in the newly opened eyes of a puppy. Then slowly, bewilderment grew out of the blankness, the golden bars of his brows drew in almost to meeting point above his nose, and grunting, he began to fumble one hand up towards the broken bruise on his temple.

Athelis caught it and pressed it down again. 'No, leave it be; you will hurt it.'

'My head aches,' he grumbled, and turned it a little, cautiously, on the rustling straw pillow, to look about him. 'Where's the ship?'

'Smashed into firewood on the Seal Rocks,' Owain said.

The blue eyes came round, frowning still, but less strained, to fix upon his face. 'Yes, I remember now. Hammer of Thor! What a way to come home. . . . You were there?'

'A wreck is a wreck. Half the settlement was there,' Owain said dryly.

Athelis, bringing wrung-out cloths to bathe her lord's head, said, 'He saved your life, my man, and I think he came near enough to losing his own in doing it.'

'Ah!' Beornwulf raised himself a little, wincing, and dodged the wrung-out cloth. 'Then I have to thank him for the worst headache ever a man had without his skull flying in two—Also for the warmth of my own hearth and the light of day—' He gave a little shiver. 'It is better to be alive even with a splitting head, than drowned and wave-rolled to and fro among the black rocks of the Seal Strand.'

He let Athelis push him back on to the pillow and do what she would with his burst temple; but all the while, under the sponging cloth, his eyes were on Owain as he stood by with his own sodden rags drying on him in the heat of the fire. 'I thought at the time, that I made a good bargain with my gold piece,' he said in a while, 'but it seems that I made a better bargain even than I thought.' His voice was growing drowsy, and a little after, he drifted off to sleep between mouthful and mouthful of the milk that Athelis was trying to get into him.

Three men came alive out of that wreck, and the other two were cared for in the settlement and later sent on their way. Beornwulf slept for the best part of a day and a night, and woke on the following morning quite recovered though famine-empty, and with an air of having something on his mind. He ate an enormous meal of bannock and ewe-milk cheese, hard-boiled duck eggs and smoke-dried mackerel, and calling for Golden-eye, rode off up the old road to Haegel the King in his Great Hall.

He came riding back at dusk; they heard the horse's hooves at the gate, and the dogs barked a welcome, and Owain went out with the lantern to take Golden-eye from him. Beornwulf handed her over without a word, seemingly deep in thought, and he led the tired mare clip-clopping round to the stable, and hitched her to the accustomed ring, hanging the lantern from its hook on the low roof-beams. He slipped out the bit and gave her an arm-ful of hay and beans to keep her happy while he off-saddled and rubbed her down. Drink she had better wait for until she had cooled off a little.

He unbuckled the belly strap, then, turning with the well worn saddle in his arms, he saw Beornwulf standing in the low entrance under the thatch, with the deepening blue of the dusk behind him.

'I have been with the King, my foster brother,' Beornwulf said, 'and now that the business that took me to him is off my hands, I have time to think of my own—and yours.' He hesi-tated, for he was a man who seldom found the words he wanted easily, while Owain waited, the saddle in his arms, for what was coming next. At last he said, 'I have not forgotten my debt to you.'

'Debt?' Owain said.

'Na, not debt. When a man saves your life at risk of his own, you cannot call it a debt and pay him back as simply as though for the loan of a plough-ox or a day's threshing. It is a free gift—but you might perhaps give a free gift in return. . . . A life for a life. Would freedom seem to you the same thing as life?'

Owain felt his breath stick in his throat, and his heart began to pound under his ribs. 'Yes,' he said.

'Then go down to Brand at the smithy tomorrow, and bid him cut off that thrall-ring. He knows.'

There was a long, long silence. Then Owain said carefully, 'Let me go to Brand on the day that the King's summons comes; that for a gift. And in payment for the winter that I shall still have worn your thrall-ring, give me on the same day, a sword.'

Their eyes met, bright and coolly steady in the lantern-light. 'Who have you been listening to?' Beornwulf demanded at last.

'The harper who was at the settlement two nights since.'

'And what said the harper?'

'That there was unrest growing in the kingdoms that border Wessex. That he had smelled the Ravens gathering before Wibbendune, and knew the smell again. That Ceawlin grows too powerful for the safety of lesser kings, and that Aethelbert of Kent, who is also powerful, had little love for him. That many small kingdoms bonded together muster more spears than one great kingdom standing alone. No more than that, he said.'

'And you have put these things together, and made of them—a hosting in the spring?'

'It grows too late in the year for such a hosting this autumn.'

Beornwulf was looking at him, not quite understanding, the pale bars of his brows drawn together above his nose. 'You are not Saxon, that you should carry a sword for a Saxon king.'

'No,' Owain said, 'but against one. I am British, and my father and my brother died by Aquae Sulis. I am as good a hater as Aethelbert of Kent, and I also have little love for Ceawlin of Wessex.'

For a moment longer, Beornwulf stood in the doorway watching him. Then he nodded, and brought up his hand and smote it open-palmed on the doorpost beside him. 'Well, many a man has fought for a worse reason. So be it then, you shall have your freedom and your sword—a good sword that I had before my father died—on the day that the summer comes. Now finish with the mare.'

And turning, he strode off across the steading garth in the dusk.

Owain hung the saddle very carefully in its place, took a wisp of straw without seeing it, and started to rub Golden-eye down.

It was spring when the war-summons came: a day of wind and sun and thin shining rain, with the cloud shadows drifting across the marsh. The messenger from the King's Hall cried it to them from the steading gate without dismounting, and then rode on towards the settlement.

Owain, hearing the beat of his horse's hooves die into the distance, thought that it had been just such a day as this when Kyndylan's summons had come. Then he finished what he was doing, and went across the ten foot dyke and down to the settlement himself, to Brand the Smith.

The messenger had ridden on by the time he got there, and the place was throbbing like a nest of wild bees at swarming time. Already several men were gathered about the fiery darkness of the forge mouth above the boat strand, and the ring of hammer on anvil came from inside. Most of the men who would be answering the summons had had their weapons ready all winter past, but there were always some last things to do—a rivet to be tightened, the dint in a shield rim to be beaten out—and the forge made a good place to gather and talk the thing over in short flat sentences, now that it had happened at last. Owain waited with the rest until his turn came, then went into the fire-shot gloom of the smithy.

'I am come at last,' he said to the big brown smith.

Brand stood and looked at him, his hands on his hips, and the curling hairs on his chest turned to a russet fleece by the forge fire. 'Every day this winter, you could have come,' he said in his deep soft grumble, 'but no, you must wait and wait, and come to me at last this day of all days, when there's work enough at my door to keep Wayland himself busy for a week.'

'I had to wait until I had earned a sword,' Owain told him.

'Aye, I have heard that story. Come then, and kneel here beside the anvil.' The smith had turned away as he spoke, and was rooting among his cold-chisels for the one he wanted, and young Horn, plying the great sheepskin bellows, looked up with a grin, as he sent the fire roaring into a fiercer blaze.

Owain knelt down with his neck pressed against the side of the anvil, so that part of the iron thrall-ring rested on it. The touch of the anvil scorched his neck, and the acrid reek of hot metal made him want to sneeze. 'Hold still if you don't want to go one-eared the rest of your days,' said Brand the Smith, bending over him with the chisel in one hand and a hammer in the other.

The thing was done very quickly, though his head felt jarred loose on his shoulders, and the right ear as though it were stuffed with wool. So quickly that just for a moment he could not quite understand that he was free again, after almost eight years. He knew that it was so, but he could not feel it. He could not feel anything except a kind of quietness. He saw between the figures in the open doorway the fishing boats drawn up on the wet sand, and the hurrying cloud shadows over the marshes, and the wings of the gulls wheeling by. Then he realized that the smith was booming in his deafened ear to know if he was going to kneel there all day; and he shook his head cautiously, as though he were a little afraid that it might fall off; and got up, laughing and rubbing his neck. The men in the doorway parted to let him through, they called after him, one or two of them clapped him on the shoulder, and the sound of their voices was friendly; but he did not hear what they said, though he grinned like a fool at them.

And he headed back towards the steading to claim his sword from Beornwulf.

By evening, more detailed news, following on the heels of the bare summons, was running through the settlements like a furze fire. Ceawlin's nephews had raised the standard of revolt, proclaiming Coel, the eldest of their numbers, as King of the West Saxons.

And Owain sat late that night beside the spitting fire, nursing his sword across his knees.

15

The Truce of the Spear

'WODEN, Father of fighting men, hear now the oath of thy sons in the time that the Ravens gather. From this hour forth, until the last warrior comes again to his own or feeds his heart's blood to the death-pyre, all other loves and hates laid by, one band are we, one brotherhood in victory or defeat.'

It was the voice of Haegel the King; and the voices of the war-host roared up in response, 'In victory or defeat, All-Father, one brotherhood are we.'

Again Haegel's voice rose solitary. 'On shield's rim and sword's blade—Swear!'

A ringing rustle of metal ran through the war-host, as every warrior's hand went to his weapons, and again there came the deep slow thunder of voices: 'We swear.'

'On the dragon-prow of Aelle's war-keel—Swear!'

And yet again, the deep-voiced response: 'We swear.'

For days past they had been gathering from the furthest fringes of the South Saxon Lands in ones and twos, in whole war-bands under their chieftains; from almost every farm a father or a son or a younger brother, until now the host that thronged the vast forecourt of the King's Place, shields on shoulders and faces turned all to the threshold of the High Hall, must number close on two thousand.

From before the dark threshold where the priests gathered behind the King, a long thin tendril of smoke curled upward towards the fading fires of a royal sunset arching overhead, and the sharp tang of blood and the stink of burning horse-hair wafted in the faces of the warriors. Owain, standing well back among the younger and lesser of the war-host, caught the thick reek of it, and felt the queasiness still stirring in his belly. Only a short while since, here on the sacred ground before the King's threshold, they had given the God's Horse to Frey for his favour in the coming war; the great white stallion who was at once the sacrifice and the god who dies for the people. 'There is always a price to be paid for Godhead,' Vadir had said, on the night that the silver foal was born. He could see Vadir now, well forward among the chiefs and the royal kinsmen and the household warriors, shorter than most of the men around him but clearly recognizable by the paleness of his hair and the way he stood with one shoulder a little up, taking the weight on his sound leg; for a moment the cold hate rose in Owain, driving out all hint of queasiness. The horse had been drugged beforehand, someone had told him, otherwise they could never have brought him to the place of sacrifice at all; but even so, he had reared up at the kiss of the knife, swinging the men who held the ropes clear of the ground, and screaming, as it seemed, not in fear or pain but as a stallion screams in battle. Owain shut his eyes, giving thanks to whatever gods might hear him, that Teitri had gone to the Kentish King; at least he would not know it, when the time came for Teitri.

'On the white crest of the Sacred Horse—Swear!'

And for the last time, with a crash of weapons on shield rims, came the thunderous response: 'On the white crest of the Sacred Horse, we swear.'

Owain swore with the rest, like a Saxon warrior.

The priest was scattering something with a long horse-hair switch among the war-host, something that speckled red where it fell. Most of it fell among the warriors of the forefront, but a drop splashed on to Owain's forehead like a heavy drop of thunder rain, still faintly warm. 'That's lucky,' his neighbour told him. 'That's a sign of favour from the gods.' But it was a sign that he would rather have done without, though he would not betray himself by wiping it off.

They dragged the carcass of the White Stallion away to be given to the hounds. It was only a carcass now and somewhere in the King's horse-runs a young white stallion had become the God's Horse at the moment that the old one died. They spread sand over the blood on the King's threshold, and the thing was done.

The close-knit mass of warriors broke and drifted apart, and made for the cooking-fires where whole sheep and oxen were roasting.

Owain took his sizzling slice of beef on the point of his dagger, and drew off to the outskirts of the throng to eat it, his back propped against the low wall of the calf fold.

Above the surge of voices he could hear Haegel's herd-bull, angry about something, trampling and bellowing in his stable.

Slowly the light faded from the vast arch of the sky; dusk was creeping up over the level country, and in the King's forecourt the light of the fires began to brighten, throwing a confusion of glares and shadows over the shifting figures of the warriors and the women who moved among them with the ale jars. Owain felt queerly detached from the scene as though he alone had no roots in it. He had taken the war-oath with these men, he was bound to them and they to him, and yet he was cut off from them. He was British and they were Saxon, and between the two lay all the gulf that could lie between two worlds; but dimly he realized that there was another gulf between them also. They had something to fight for; he had only something to fight against. It was a curiously desolate feeling.

Not far from where he leaned, stood a shoulder-high column of rough stone, notched and weathered with age, on which the King's warriors had sharpened their weapons for a hundred years;

and with the main business of eating done, a knot of young warriors had gathered about it. Wiping his dagger clean with a handful of grass pulled from the base of the wall, Owain fell to watching them. The group constantly changed and shifted in the deepening dusk, as men brought up sword or spear-blade to sharpen, and stayed a while to laugh and brag and scuffle with their fellows, then wandered back to one or other of the fires, to see to the horses in the picket lines or look for a girl among the farm buildings. By and by, with a kind of defiance to his feeling of separateness and isolation, Owain pushed off from his wall and wandered over to join them.

They made way for him or did not make way for him, exactly as they would have done for any other of their fellows, as he shouldered into their midst. They were almost beyond the reach of the nearest fire, shapes of solid darkness save for the faint jink of light as they moved, in dagger-hilt or shoulder-clasp, or in the bright eyes of a laughing man.

'Listen to that brute of Haegel's bawling,' somebody said. 'He'd like to tear up the roots of the world, by the sound of him.'

'He is angry,' said another. 'Wouldn't you be angry, if we had had been feasting on your sons?'

And a third slapped his stomach and belched happily. 'And never did I taste a sweeter bit of beef.'

There was a burst of laughter, and Owain, suddenly warmed, laughed with the rest, and felt his world and theirs draw a little closer together. It was a long while since he had laughed as a free man among free men.

He had no need to be ashamed of his sword when it came to his turn at the sharpening stone. It was a plain serviceable weapon, with a grip of yellow linden-wood worn silken-dark with much handling; the balance was good, so that the thing felt alive in his hand, and the smith who made it had not forgotten beauty in the need for use, for beside the beauty of its own clean lines, the shoulders were inlaid with small four-petalled silver flowers.

Stooping, he drew the blade curving across the stone, feeling the bite of iron on granite; and the white sparks flew out on either side, bright as shooting stars on a winter's night. The throat of his

shirt had fallen open as he stooped, and a thick-set youngster beside him leaned quickly forward, and jabbed his finger into
Owain's neck, just above the collar-bone. 'You—I do not know
your name. What's that?'

Owain was aware that the thrall-ring, worn through six years,
had left an encircling stripe of white skin on the wind-burned
brown of his neck. He stiffened a little, and drew the blade again
across the great whetstone, sending up another flight of sparks so
that there should be light to see by. 'What does it look like?'

'It could be the mark of a king's gold collar, but I'd say more
likely it was the mark of a thrall-ring.'

'It is the mark of a thrall-ring,' Owain said levelly, continuing
to sharpen his sword. 'Until seven days since, I was thrall to
Beornwulf, the King's foster brother,' and he jerked his head towards the open doorway of the Hall. The young Saxons were
crowding closer round him, curious, ready for sport if sport
offered, but not unfriendly.

'So—you're British, then? I thought you were, as soon as you
gave tongue,' said the thick-set young man. 'What are you doing
in the ranks of Haegel's shield-warriors? Have you ever handled a
sword before?'

'Only in practice, not in war. I had only my dagger by Aquae
Sulis when the last of our Princes fell. There were no swords to
spare for boys.'

'They tell me that was a great fight!' A laughing giant flung a
great arm friendlywise across his shoulders, and swung him round
as though presenting him to the rest. 'They need not have sent
us Einon Hên, down from his Western Mountains; look now,
brothers, we have a Briton in our midst already, and one suckled
in war.'

Oddly, they seemed to feel nothing against him for being what
he was, and still more oddly, he did not resent the arm across his
shoulders. Maybe here, so deep into the Saxon lands, the old
enmities had grown thin; maybe it had to do with the bond of a
common enemy, the smell of the Ravens gathering. But he was
startled and bewildered by the giant's words. 'You talk in riddles,
so far as I am concerned. Who is this Einon Hên?'

'The British Envoy. Do you tell me that you did not know?'

Owain drew a sharp breath. 'No,' he said slowly, 'I did not know. And still I do not understand.'

Several voices answered him, taking up the tale one from another. 'Didn't you know that the Britons of Wales have made a treaty with us? Their swords against Ceawlin, and in return, a frontier that we Saxons will not cross? Where are your ears? It has been running through the war-host all evening! There's a British host massing beyond the Sabrina, they say, and to each of our Saxon Kings they have sent one of their great men to help on the brotherly understanding——'

He stood silent among them for a long moment, then he said in a voice so carefully schooled that it only choked a little, 'You are spinning it as you go along, like a harper's tale for a winter evening.'

'Why should we?' demanded the thick-set young man.

'I don't know. Maybe I look like a fool.'

The giant gave his shoulder a friendly shake. 'Go and look, if you don't believe us. He'll be sitting in the guest-seat.'

And Owain settled his sword back in its wolfskin sheath, and went.

There were men crowded about the foreporch doorway, passing the ale horn from hand to hand. Owain pushed through them until he came where he could look up the Hall. The vast barn-like place was flickering and flaring with fire and torchlight that was thickly cloudy as wild honey; and after the dark of the forecourt, Owain, standing on the threshold, could make out little at first but a kind of fiery cloud. Then, as his eyes grew used to the torchlight, he began to see the details of the scene and pick one out man from another on the crowded benches. Half-way up the Hall, two great raised seats faced each other across the width of it and the hearth between. In the King's seat sat Haegel with his mead horn on his knee and his small son Halfdean bolt upright and valiantly wakeful on the raised step beside his feet. But Owain looked towards the guest-seat opposite. A man sat there, with the great serpent-wreathed guest-cup of the Royal House in his hands; a small, oldish man, dwarfed by the vast carved seat until he looked like a merlin on a goshawk's perch. As he turned his head to look down the Hall, Owain saw that he had only one eye; but it was a blazing amber eye, and that too, added to his falcon aspect; for in the piercing stare of a bird of prey, one sees only one eye at a time. His mantle, flung back because of the heat in that place, was chequered blue and russet like the plumage of a kingfisher, and the grey hair that sprang thickly back from his forehead was bound by a slender gold fillet such as the British nobles still wore in the mountains, as they had done before the Romans came.

So it was true.

Owain never moved from his place by the door, until the singing and story-telling was finished and the horns drunk dry. But all that while, he was seeing not the King's Hall in the firelight, but a British war-host gathering beyond the Sabrina crossings, hearing not the voice of a Saxon gleeman but British war-horns sounding again among the Western Hills—and he was not free to answer their call.

At last men began to get to their feet, stretching and kicking the dogs aside, and to lounge out for a breath of night air to clear their heads while the pillows and rugs were spread for sleeping. Then he left his place, and slipped like a shadow after Beornwulf.

For a few moments he lost him in the darkness and the shifting throng, and when he caught sight of him again he was standing beside one of the fires with a knot of other men from the Seals' Island. He had meant to try for a chance to speak with him alone, but suddenly he could not wait, even though one of the other men was Vadir.

He strode forward quickly. 'Beornwulf——'

The other swung round. 'Owain! I was wondering should I have to seek through the whole war-host to find you——' he began.

But Owain cut in on him, a little breathlessly. 'Beornwulf—did you know?'

There was an instant's silence, and then Beornwulf said, 'About the treaty with your people?'

'Yes.'

'Not until a few hours ago.'

Briton and Saxon, their gaze met and held, steady in the light of the sinking fire; and Owain knew that the Saxon was speaking

the truth. It was no fault of Beornwulf's that the word had come
to him too late. He gave a little shake to his shoulders: since there
was no help in the thing, let it rest. 'What did you want me for,
Beornwulf?'

'Not for myself, but for the British Envoy,' Beornwulf said.
'He is an old man, and should have someone to see to his comfort
and spread his sleeping rug.'

Eagerness leapt for an instant in Owain, and then sank like a
newly kindled flame. British as he was, in Saxon war-gear and
bound by a Saxon oath, how could he face this terrible little half-
blind princeling of his own people? 'Has he no young kinsman to
serve him? No armour-bearer of his own?'

Vadir, who had been looking on with chilly amusement deepening the thin lines of his face, put in his word. 'I have seldom
heard of a hostage bringing his household with him.'

'A hostage?' Owain caught his breath. 'I had thought——' he
broke off. He had almost said 'I had thought that this was a treaty
between equals,' but he would sooner have his tongue torn out
than say that before Vadir Cedricson.

Beornwulf said loudly, before the other could speak again,
'Einon Hên comes as an envoy, freely and with honour, and being
a brave man among those who were lately his enemies, he comes
alone. . . . Go then and offer him your service; since you also are
British, there is no one more fitting among the Saxon war-host.'
He brought a hand from under his cloak, and clamped it for an
instant on Owain's braced shoulder. 'It is an honour; you understand that?'

'Surely a very great honour,' murmured Vadir, looking at the
stars.

But Owain did not look at him, though his own hands were
clenched into shaking fists at his sides. 'I understand that,' he said.

A little later, in the darkened Hall, Owain knelt before the
British Envoy as he sat on his allotted bench against the wall, un-
tying for him the thongs of his soft leather shoes. He had spread
the rugs and straw-filled pillow for the old man, and helped him
strip off his tunic, for the night was close in the Hall, and most of
the men would sleep stripped to their breeks, with a cloak thrown
over them. 'Beornwulf, the King's foster brother, told me that

you were without an armour-bearer of your own here to serve you,' he was saying, in his own tongue that he had not used for so long.

'Ah, they told me there was a countryman of mine among Haegel's young warriors.' Einon Hên leaned forward and touched Owain's neck with a bony finger, more lightly than the man at the weapon stone had done. 'And until lately you have worn a thrall-ring? Were you taken in war?'

Owain shook his head. 'Oh, no, I gave myself up without a blow struck.'

'How so?' demanded Einon Hên.

'We—a friend and I—thought to escape to Gaul, but she fell ill in the woods before we could reach the coast. She was younger than me, only about thirteen, and she—would have died, I think. She needed warmth and tending, and—she needed milk, you see.' He sat back on his heels, and raised his eyes to the old man's deep-scored face. 'There was not anything else that I could do.'

It did not seem to him at all strange, until he thought about it afterwards, that he should be talking so to this fierce little falcon of a man, freely as he had not talked to anyone since Uncle Widreth died, and as though they two were alone in the great Hall.

Einon Hên leaned still further forward on his bench, his hands on his knees, and peered down at him out of his one eye. Then the fierce half-blind stare softened, and a smile of unexpected warmth deepened the lines of his face. 'No, there was not anything else that you could do,' he said, and the long bony finger that had touched Owain's neck, touched the white scar that ran out of his sleeve. 'And yet, if you were not taken in war, I think that you have known fighting. That has the look of an old spear-thrust.'

'I was at the last battle, by Aquae Sulis,' Owain said. 'My father and my brother died there, but I was kicked on the head and the battle passed me by.' He looked up unwaveringly into the old one-eyed face, remembering Vadir's taunt. 'That is true. I did not run away.'

'No,' said Einon Hên. 'I believe that you did not run away.'

Owain drew off the soft leather shoes from the old man's feet and thrust them under the bench, and made to rise, but Einon Hên

L

stayed him. 'And now you are a free man, and our own people are massing beyond the Sabrina crossings. When the allied hosts come together, do you carry your sword over into the British camp?'

Owain was silent a moment, then he said heavily, 'I did not know until too late. I have taken the oath of brotherhood with the rest.' Another silence, and then he added, as though exploring and discovering something as he went along, 'But it is not that alone. Afterwards, if I live, I go to my own people, but not now. Beornwulf gave me a sword, and a while back I took it to the weapon stone in the forecourt, with others of the young warriors. We laughed about something—I don't remember what—and one of them flung his arm across my shoulders. I forgot to hate him, and though he knew that I was British, he did not hate me. . . .' His voice stumbled away into silence, and he remained on one knee, looking up at Einon Hên as though asking for the old man's understanding of what he did not understand himself.

The British Envoy nodded. 'Aie, aie, it is in the truce. The Truce of the Spear. I have seen it work before.'

16

Wodensbeorg

NEXT morning the South Saxon war-host marched out from the King's Place; Haegel at their head, riding with his hearth-companions about him, the lesser men who did not own a horse tramping on their own strong feet in the dust-cloud that the horsemen raised, with the pack beasts and the driven beef cattle among them; bowmen and spearmen and those whose weapon was the sword. But the horses were only for transport; the Saxon kind did not fight happily on horseback, and from the King to Owain they would all be foot soldiers when the time came to form the shield-wall.

In the open country north of Venta, three days' march by the old Roman road, they came up with the eastern part of the combined Saxon war-host. Men from the Chiltern Hills following Cuthgils, the youngest of Ceawlin's rebellious nephews: the fighting strength of all the little kingdoms east of the ancient hill track that they called the Icknield way; a score of war-bands out of Kent, but with nowhere the Kentish standard to be seen.

Haegel laughed when he saw the Kentish warriors trickling in along the road under the north chalk that had been old before the Legions came; flung back his head and laughed into the smoke of the camp-fire. 'So long as Aethelbert may sit quiet in Cantiisburg and pretend to know nothing of what goes forward, it seems that he will not watch too closely to see what the young men of his border hundreds will do!'

From time to time word reached them of how things were going elsewhere. Ceawlin was in his capital at Wilton. His sons, holding his borders from Surrey to the edge of the Aquae Sulis territory, had already taken the first shock, as Coel and Coelwulf with the men of the new western settlements came down upon them like wolves in a famine winter. They had taken the first shock and been driven back with heavy losses, and Ceawlin had gathered his host and was pressing north to their support.

Then came the word that father and sons had met, and knowing themselves to be outnumbered, had fallen back upon the ancient hill fort of Wodensbeorg, to wait for their enemies in the strongest place in all North Wessex.

That news was brought in by Coel and Coelwulf with their victorious war-bands, who came swarming round and down from the north to join the men of Kent and Sussex and the Chiltern Hills, some thirty miles short of the chosen place. Now, save for the British bands, the whole allied war-host had come together. And that night a great fire burned in the midst of the camp, and Owain, hastily summoned before his evening bannock was half eaten, stood in the full fierce glare of it, confronting the appraising scrutiny of half a score of men. Haegel he knew, and Einon Hên; the rest were strangers, but he guessed, for he had seen them ride in, that the two broad-shouldered young men with hot blue eyes and beards arrogantly cocked, were Coel and Coelwulf. He gave

them back look for look in the firelight, holding himself braced
for whatever it was that was coming. He did not know why they
had sent for him, but Einon Hên was explaining that now, in the
Saxon tongue, that the others might understand and fear no
treachery.

'Owain, to our people there has fallen a great honour, though
—maybe a costly one. Ceawlin and his whole war-host are encamped at a place that the Saxons call Wodensbeorg, turning
there to wait our coming as a boar turns at bay. It is an ancient
war-camp of our people, and like most of its kind it has more than
one possible way in, but the chief one is on the south-eastern side.
Therefore the great attack we shall unloose against them from this
side, but when it is at its height the British will take them from
the rear, striving to break in through the hinder gates, and so
carry sword and confusion into the very heart of the enemy camp.
All that has been arranged, and the thorn woods will give them
cover for surprise to the foot of Wodensbeorg; but the thing
must be timed as perfectly as a spear-throw if it is to succeed, and
the Hour of the Ravens could not be determined until the two
halves of the allied war-host had come together. Therefore the
message must go now to the British Camp—upward of two days'
march north-west of Wodensbeorg—and a man must carry it.'

Owain heard very clearly the sounds of the camp, men singing
softly about one of the fires, the squeal of a bad-tempered horse
in the picket lines. 'Do I volunteer, or is it an order?' he asked at
last.

'I think that you volunteer. You are British; the only man save
myself in all this great camp who can say that.'

The old man and the young one held each other's gaze for a
moment in shared pride.

Coel, who already called himself King of Wessex, flung the
last scrap of his supper to the hound crouching at his feet, and
leaned forward abruptly into the firelight. 'We can send a man
with you who knows the country, two men, or three, to make sure
that you reach the British Camp——'

Owain felt the blood suddenly hot under his eyes, and he cut in,
but quietly enough, 'Why not send the whole war-host with
me?'

'You are insolent, my friend.' Coel's brows snapped together.
'I do not mean to be, but I have not had my faith doubted before.'

Coel stared at him a moment longer under down-drawn
brows, then he made a small gesture as though he screwed something up and tossed it into the fire. 'All things have to have a first
time. But I was not calling your faith in question, for Einon Hên
has vouched for it. I was going to say, had you not been so quick
to put your hackles up, that we could make sure of your reaching
the British Camp, but that save for sending one man with you to
act as your guide, we should count the matter already assured. I
was also going to say that the only means we have of being sure,
completely sure, that the message has gone safely through, lies in
your return to the Saxon Camp afterwards.' His eyes narrowed a
little on Owain's face, and the Briton realized for the first time
how shrewd they were. 'Can we be certain also, that having returned to your own people, you will come back to the White
Horse Standard?'

'I will come back,' Owain said. He glanced at the British
Envoy. 'Einon Hên knows that I will come back.'

Einon Hên nodded. 'I came among you as an envoy for my
people, but more than once I have heard myself spoken of as a
hostage, by Saxon tongues.' He glanced about him at their suddenly stiffened faces, with a gleam of fierce amusement in his one
yellow eye. 'Oh yes, I may lack for an eye, but I have always had
keen hearing. Now therefore, let me offer myself for a hostage indeed, for my fellow countryman's return.'

There was another silence, and then Haegel of the South
Saxons said loudly and defiantly, 'That will not be needful!'

A murmur rose from the men about the fire; and Coel with his
hot blue gaze still on Owain's face said, 'No, that will not be needful. When you reach the British Camp, go you to Gerontius,
Prince of Powys, and tell him that the Time of the Ravens comes
at Sun-up on the fourth morning from now—the morning of
Thor's Day. That is all; he knows the rest, and if he is in position
along the woodshore he will hear the war-horns and the ring of
battle to judge his own attack by.' He was pulling a ring from his
finger as he spoke, and now he held it out to Owain; a delicate

thing of wreathed gold and silver wires, oddly womanish for the
man's strong hand, but Owain had noticed the delicacy of the
Saxon goldsmith's work often enough before now. 'This is the
agreed token. Give it to Gerontius in proof that you do in truth
come from Coel of Wessex and the allied war-host; and bring me
back his agreed token in exchange.'

An hour later, mounted on one of the spare horses—a good one,
for they would have to make fast travelling—Owain rode out of
the Saxon Camp, with the man who was to guide him riding
another; and a queer mingling of feeling within him because he
was riding to his own people, but only as a message-bearer for the
Saxon kind.

They rode through the night, and lay up through the day
among some furze bushes in a little hidden valley, while the
horses grazed, knee-haltered, then rode again through the second
night. It was open downland country for the most part, and the
Saxon knew it well. They met with no trouble, and before the
second dawn, they rode into the British Camp.

A short while later, having left his weary guide with the still
more weary horses, Owain was speaking with a tall man in the
lee of a hazel thicket. There too, a fire burned, figures standing
and moving about it, figures with Roman faces and Celtic faces;
but he was so tired that they seemed the faces and figures of a
dream. Only the tall man he was speaking to seemed quite real, a
very dark man with a cloak of British plaid hastily flung on over
an ancient legionary breastplate, his black brows bound with a
narrow golden fillet. Owain heard his own voice speaking in the
British tongue, as though it were the voice of a stranger, and even
thought vaguely how hoarse it sounded.

The man listened, his head a little bent. When the message had
been delivered, he said only, 'What token do you bring me that
you come indeed from Coel of the West Saxons?'

'The agreed token,' Owain said, and drew the ring of gold and
silver wires from his own hand.

Gerontius took it, and stood turning it between his fingers,
examining it in the fitful firelight while Owain watched him. He
was thinking that maybe if the Prince of the Cymru had joined

with the Princes of Glevum and Viroconium, that last battle might not have ended in disaster. Oh, but if it had not, it would only have stemmed the tide for a little while, not turned it. This way—he remembered the treaty—at least the Western Hills would remain free of the Saxon kind. But his world had died by Aquae Sulis, and it was hard to judge without bitterness.

A little wind was rising with the morning and something stirred and billowed at the edge of the firelight, teasing the corner of his eye so that he glanced aside to see what it was. A spear-shaft had been planted upright in the soft ground that edged the hazel thicket, and a great battle standard hung from it. It caught the morning breeze and rippled in the wind, and on the greenness of it, he saw quivering in flame and gold the Red Dragon of Britain.

Something rose in Owain's breast as he looked at it, something that hurt and shone at the same time, mingled partly of bitterness, that the ancient standard should go into battle in fellowship with the White Horse of the Saxon hordes, partly of joy, because he had not thought to see the Red Dragon of Britain, the Red Dragon of Artos, flying in the wind of any battlefield again.

Suddenly he was aware that Gerontius had turned from ex-amining the ring between his fingers and was watching him. He looked round quickly, and met the gaze of the Prince of Powys.

'Yes, you're British, aren't you, though not of the Cymru?' said the Prince of Powys.

Owain said, 'It is because I am British that I was chosen to bring you the word.'

'So it came to my mind as soon as I saw you. And you are not one of our grey-headed envoys. How do you come to carry your shield with the Saxon war-host?'

'Simply enough. I have been the thrall of a Saxon master,' Owain said. 'This spring when the war-summons came he gave me my freedom and a sword, in return for a certain service.'

'And so now you come again to your own people?'

'Only to bring the message that I have brought from the Saxon Camp. Give me a meal for myself and the man who rode with me as my guide, let us rest a few hours, then lend us fresh horses, for our own are well-nigh foundered. I must be gone again by noon.'

The other's eyes held his own, questioning a little, contemptuous a little. Then Gerontius shrugged. 'It seems the thrall-ring bites deep. If you had sooner ride into battle with the White Horse than the Red Dragon. . . .'

Owain said rather desperately, 'God knows that I would give . . .' and checked to know exactly what he would give, for he was not using a mere idle form of words. He looked again at the tattered standard as it swung and rippled in the dawn wind. 'That I would give three fingers of my sword-hand, afterwards, if I might go into battle—this battle—with my own kind. But I must go back. Later, when I am free and if I live, I will come again to my own. Not now.'

He felt as though he were being torn in two as he said it, but the words came out steadily enough, and something in them, or perhaps in his haggard face, must have carried conviction to the tall man with the gold fillet round his brows, for when he met his gaze again, it was kinder than it had been.

'There are freedoms and freedoms,' said the Prince of Powys. 'I take back what I said about the thrall-ring. And someone must go again to the Saxon Camp, to take my return token to Coel of Wessex.' With a swift gesture he pulled the great brooch from the shoulder of his cloak, and held it out to Owain. 'There, take it to the Wessex King and tell him that Gerontius and the men of the Cymru will be in their appointed place when the Ravens spread their wings. No, look at it first,' for Owain had been about to thrust it into the breast of his leather shirt.

He did as he was bid, and saw that what he held in the hollow of his hand, glowing in wrought gold and blood-red enamel, was the likeness of another dragon.

'One might almost say that you hold the fate of Britain in your hand,' said the voice of Gerontius, Prince of Powys. 'Go now. My folk will see to the food and fresh horses. May you come safe through the battle, to fight with your own people another day.'

Two mornings later the first light creeping across the high country around Wodensbeorg found two great war-hosts waiting for each other, where there should have been only brambles and bracken and the plovers calling.

It was a fitting place, Owain thought, looking about him as he shifted his grip on his buckler and felt for the twentieth time that his sword was loose in its sheath.

It had been long after dark when he and his guide had ridden in last night, and Wodensbeorg had been only a blackness upreared against the western sky. He had found Coel of Wessex beside the royal fire in the heart of the Allied Camp, and given him the dragon brooch with Gerontius's message. He did not remember much about it, he had been too weary, but he knew that Einon Hên had been there and he remembered the look on the fierce falcon face; at the time he had thought it was satisfaction, now he thought that it had been an odd kind of hope, but he did not know what for. The weariness had broken over him like a wave after that, and he supposed that he had slept until someone shook him into wakefulness before dawn. It was not a long sleep, but it must have been a deep one. His body still creaked from the long hours in the saddle, but his head and all his senses felt as though they had been washed in cold water, so that he was sharply aware of sight and sound and smell—the yelp of a raven overhead, pricking the quiet of the waiting war-host, the shape of the clouds banking low along the western sky—great flat-topped anvil clouds. Thunder before evening, he thought. . . .

Against those piled cloud-banks Wodensbeorg rose with its triple crown of turf ramparts that were old almost as the hill they circled. He could see already the darkness of massed men along the ramparts and at the gateway barricades, and the first level sunlight splintered on axe-blade and helmet-comb, though the great wings of men outspread down the hillside on either flank, and the long curved battle-line of the Allied war-host were still in shadow.

Looking along that battle-line Owain could make out the White Horse standard of Coel upreared in the centre, and away on either side the winged and taloned and serpent-tailed standards of lesser Kings spreading and lifting a little in the faint stirring of the air. Close before him, where Haegel stood among his hearth-companions, his glance caught the gleam of the new scarlet cloak

that Athelis had woven for her
lord last winter—scarlet as the Red
Dragon of Britain that was not
flying with the Saxon standards
today but waiting in the dark
woods for its hour to come. Suddenly he knew that like the men
on either side of him, he had
something to fight for, and not,
as he had once thought, only
something to fight against. He
was one with the men crouching in
the woods beyond Wodensbeorg,
waiting to go into battle for the
sake of a frontier and a free people
among the Western Hills. And in
that instant with the knowledge
of his oneness with them, he was
one with the Saxon warriors at
his shoulders. 'One band, one
brotherhood. . . .'

A few moments later, above
the waiting sounds of the host,
the quickened breathing of men,
the faint jar of weapons, he heard
the hollow booming of the war-
horns.

It was a long day and a bloody
one, and when it was over,
Ceawlin was no more King of
the West Saxons but a fox hunted
through the furze; and Owain
was still a long way from his
freedom.

He did not know that; he was
thinking of his freedom as he knelt
beside the little upland stream

washing the spear-gash in his sword-wrist. It was a shallow gash
but it had bled a lot. He was remembering the trampling roaring
struggle about the great gateway that had surged to and fro for
what seemed like an eternity; the sudden tumult in the enemy's
rear that he knew was the British attack. He was seeing again,
as the men behind Coel and Haegel broke yelling through and
stormed up against the inner defences, the Red Dragon seeming
to hover on spread wings above the battle. . . .

The British had earned their frontier. And soon now, by summer's end at latest, he would be free to seek his own people; free
to find Regina again. It crossed his mind, as he held his wrist in
the cold running water and watched the bright wisp of flowing
blood grow thinner, that the Thorn Forest could not be so very
far from here. . . . No, he would not go to look for her until he
was free—really free.

He heard a movement behind him, and looked up quickly. The
blue-black storm-clouds had crept almost across the sky, and little
uneasy puffs of wind were stirring all ways at once among the
fern and the brambles; and standing at the top of the bank, outlined against the coming storm, stood Vadir the Hault, leaning on
his spear as though it were a staff, and looking down at him. The
man had fought like a hero that day; now, though there was no
mark on him, he looked utterly spent and his face against the
gloom was drawn and white, but his pale eyes were as bright as
ever, and Owain wondered how long he had been standing there
watching him.

'Ah, here you are,' said Vadir, conversationally. 'Beornwulf is
asking for you. They have carried him into the inner berm of the
fort with the rest of the wounded.'

'He is wounded then?' Owain said stupidly, scrambling up
from his knees. 'Badly wounded?'

Vadir shrugged very slightly. 'As wounds go, it is quite a small
one. Surprising, when you come to think of it, how small a rent
in a man's hide will serve to let the life out, like Marat from a
punctured wine-skin.'

And as the first distant mutter of thunder trembled on the air,
he turned without another word, and hobbled off towards the
place where they had picketed the horses.

A short while later Owain was crouching beside Beornwulf
in the lower berm between the earthworks, trying with his own
cloak spread round him, to shelter him from the first white lances
of the rain. He had seen the wound; it was quite a small one, as
Vadir had said, round and dark just under the breast-bone, ragged
round the edges where they had tried to cut the arrow-barb out;
it did not even bleed very much, outwardly, but he knew that it
would bleed internally and there would be no stopping that.

Beornwulf knew it, too.

He lay propped against the foot of the bank because breathing
hurt him less that way, and looked at Owain with eyes as blue as
Lilla's and Helga's. 'You—have been a long time coming,' he
said.

'I came as soon as Vadir told me.'

'Ah, Vadir.' It seemed to Owain as though the man's name was
linked in some way with whatever it was that Beornwulf wanted
him for. But for a while he did not speak again, and between
them and the tumult of the camp, he heard the swish and patter
of the rain, and then far off the low growl of thunder along the
hills. 'It is growing dark,' Beornwulf said. 'I cannot see you
clearly.'

'That's the storm coming.'

'That as well,' Beornwulf said with a grim quirk of laughter on
his lips that were straight with pain. He seemed to gather himself
together for a great effort and when his voice came again it had a
hoarse urgency. 'Owain, when I set out for the Kentish Court last
year, I left all things in your keeping at Beornstead. I shall go to
Valhalla before morning—and I—should go with a quieter heart
if I might know that I left Beornstead to lie in your hands again.'

Owain was silent, not sure of his meaning, but knowing that
it was a threat to all that he had hoped for, all that he had been
thinking of beside the stream.

'It goes ill with a household that has no one but a woman at its
head—a woman and a boy; and you know what manner of boy
Bryni is—a wild young colt that will be running into trouble if he
is given his head thus early.' He made as though to raise himself in
his desperate urgency, and fell back, coughing blood. 'Stay with
him and his mother until he is fifteen and a man,' he said, as soon

as he could speak again. 'I would not ask it of you if I had a kinsman to turn to, but you know—how it is with me, that I am the only son of an only son, and—have only one son in my turn.'

Still Owain was silent, turned a little to look out over the dark distances, sloe-purple now under the storm-clouds that dropped away from the turf ramparts. Bryni was eleven now; that meant four years. Four more years, when he had thought to go free before the summer's end. It was too much to ask of anyone. There was Regina, too, but like enough she had no more need of him, and Beornwulf's eyes were clinging to his face like the eyes of a sick dog. He turned his head slowly, as though it was stiff on his shoulders, and looked down at the dying Saxon. 'Go with a quiet heart, Beornwulf; I will stay by the boy until he is fifteen.'

Beornwulf snatched a small sigh. 'So. Take my sword when they build the death-pyres tomorrow, and give it to him when the time comes. It should go with me, but it is a fine blade, and the boy will need a sword. . . . Helga is spoken for already: Lilla will be ripe for marrying in two or three more summers—it was in my mind to arrange it with Brand the Smith that young Horn should have her. Tell her mother so. Edmund Whitefang owes me something still, for his share of the boat last herring season, but— you know that. . . .' He broke off and began to cough again. Owain bent quickly and wiped the blood out of his beard, and after a while he struggled on once more. 'Have a care to anything that—has Vadir's hand in it. Nay, I've no cause, but I have— never trusted him, and—the boy hates him. You know why. There may be—trouble between them one day. . . . For the rest —do as—best you can until the boy—comes to his manhood and— can take all into his own hands.'

'I understand,' Owain said, roughly because his throat was aching. 'Be quiet now; there'll be no harm come to Beornstead or to the Beornstead folk, if I can hold it off.'

'I always—reckoned I'd made a good bargain with that gold piece,' said Beornwulf, and with that last attempt at a jest, closed his eyes.

The rain was teeming down now, and as Owain leaned forward to spread his cloak further across the dying Saxon, the first jagged lightning leapt between sky and earth, and while the white blaze of it still hung before his sight, earth and sky together shuddered to the crack and the hollow roar of the thunder.

Beornwulf opened his eyes once more. 'Hark to Thor's Hammer splitting the clouds asunder, as we split the might of Ceawlin and his sons,' he said; and the sound of his voice was the sound of triumph, though the breath rattled in his throat.

Beornwulf died before morning, and Owain took his sword as he had bidden him, and since he did not want to be charged with robbing the dead, carried it to Haegel and showed him that he had done so.

Haegel was standing to watch them build the death-pyres of thorn and furze over a heart of ash logs, and merely nodded when he saw his foster brother's sword, saying, 'Aye, it must go to the boy of course. His dagger will serve him well enough for the journey,' and turned away to bid them build this end of the pyre less steeply.

Owain went away with a rush of hot anger in his heart. But later when he saw Beornwulf laid with the other dead ready for the pyre, there was a sword at his feet, after all, waiting to be laid with his ashes when the burning was over; a great sword with a grip formed of twisted serpents that he had surely seen before, and when he looked at it more closely, he knew that it was the King's.

And when next Owain saw Haegel of the South Saxons, he was wearing a sword drawn from the common war-kist, plainer if possible than his own, for it had not even silver flowers inlaid on the shoulders.

17

The Bride-Race

CEAWLIN had escaped with his sons, and a kind of running war-fare dragged on with skirmishes here and there, until late summer came, and it was time to turn back from the war-trail, and go home to get the harvest in. But all men knew that however many summers passed before he was hunted down at last, the thing was finished. Coel and not Ceawlin wore the crown of Wessex, and Aethelbert of Kent had had his revenge.

On a day of quivering heat haze with the corn-lands ripe for the sickle, Haegel and his war-host returned to the King's farm by

Cissa's Caester. They had been shedding war-bands at every settlement, at every track that branched from the old paved road, since they crossed the border into their own South Saxon Lands; and by the time they straggled into the wide garth of the royal farm, they numbered few more than the men of Maen Wood and Seals' Island, beside the household warriors.

Women and dogs greeted them, and that night there was feasting in Haegel's Hall, and men sang triumphant songs to the bright music of the harp, though a few women wept and a few dogs pattered among the warriors, looking for masters who had not returned. Owain grew tired of the feasting before it was over, and wandered out by himself to get a mouthful of cool air and see that all was well with Wagtail in the great meadow below the King's Place where they had picketed the horses. His way back to the steading led through the apple garth; the King's trees were taller and better shaped than the Beornstead ones, for the wind did not have its way with them quite as it did out on the Seals' Island; and in the white light of the moon, the ripening apples were silver among the leaves. And just within the gate he found Einon Hên leaning against a mossy trunk and gazing up with his one fierce old eye into the branches. 'I have found in the course of a long life that there is nothing like the air that blows through apple trees for clearing a man's head from the fumes of overmuch mead,' said the old Envoy, when he saw him. 'So you also have had enough of Haegel's Mead Hall.'

'The rest seem to have struck root to the drinking-benches,' Owain said moodily, and checked beside him.

'Ah well, the long marches are done; we can all sleep off frowsy heads against the pig-sty wall in the morning.'

'Not me. I must be on my way before first light. The morning tide will serve for me to get Wagtail across the creek about sunrise, and—if I wait for the rest, the news may get to Beornstead in some garbled and roundabout way before I come.'

Einon Hên was silent for a moment, and then he said, 'Aye, and such news is heavy carrying.' He pushed off from his apple-trunk and turned back towards the steading, Owain walking miserably beside him through the rough grass. They had come nearly to the steading gate when he spoke again. 'And so the thing is finished,

M

and the war-oath has run out. In a few days I shall turn my face again to the north-westward and my own hills—And you?'

Owain stopped dead in his tracks. He had not told Einon Hên of his promise to Beornwulf, he had not been able to bear to speak of it to anyone, but the old man had turned, surprised that he did not answer. He must answer. 'I bide at Beornstead a while yet,' he said, as though it were a small thing.

'So? I thought your heart was set to go back to your own kind, when your freedom came.'

'Beornwulf was a man without near kin. He—when he had his death-wound he asked me to stay by the boy till he is fifteen.'

'You having once been his thrall,' said Einon Hên after a pause, to the night in general.

'It was not so that he asked it. If it had been, maybe I could have refused.'

'Maybe,' said the old man, musingly. 'And the boy is—how old?'

'He was eleven in the spring.'

'So. Something under four years.'

'It will pass.'

'Ah, it will pass,' agreed Einon Hên. 'I shall think of you as it passes—now and then. God be with you in the meanwhile, Owain.'

He turned about with a whisk of his chequered cloak behind him, and went in through the steading gate.

Owain turned back to the solitude under the apple trees, and walked up and down for a while. Then he too went in, and joined the young men who were spilling out now into the moon-lit forecourt, and lay down to sleep with his cloak wrapped round him, against the pig-sty wall.

He was up again well before first light, and heading down to the picket lines. He tended and saddled Wagtail with only the last of the sinking moon to help him, and in the dawn twilight he rode out through the gate of the King's Place, and turned south-ward down the old half-lost road that led to the Seals' Island.

There had been a heavy dew, and the wetness scattered like spray as he rode by. But by the time the creek was safely behind him and he came out of the woods at the edge of the familiar

Intake, the sun was up, and the open levels shone tawny beyond the paler gold of the corn-land.

The morning smoke rose blue from the house-place roof as he turned off the road towards it, and the steading was awake and going about its morning work. Gunhilda the bondwoman was coming up from the pasture with a pail of milk as he rode in through the gate—they milked in the open at this time of year—and the smell of baking barley-bannock came out to him through the house-place door. No news had reached them yet, then. Odd how it seemed as though one could be sure of that from the fact that the hearth smoke still rose upward and there was barley-bread for the morning meal. The dogs were clamouring about him as he swung down from the saddle and dropped Wagtail's bridle over the hitching-post. The horse had not been ridden hard, and it would not hurt him to wait a little before being watered and rubbed down.

And then Athelis was in the doorway, looking towards him with a smear of barley-meal across her hot forehead; the girls crowded behind her, and Bryni came running out into the early sunlight with a couple of new puppies at his heels, while Gunhilda broke into a clumsy trot towards them, slopping milk over the rim of her pail.

'Owain! You are back just in time for the harvest,' Athelis said, thrusting wisps of hair back under her kerchief with a floury finger. 'We heard that the war-host had returned to the King's Hall. Did the master send you ahead to tell us of his coming?' And then her eyes went past him and took in the horse standing riderless at the hitching-post, and returned to his face with a quick unspoken question, and he saw the colour drain out of her face.

'Come back into the house,' he said. He did not know why, but he felt that it would be better to tell her indoors—as though the roof and walls would give her some kind of shelter for her grief.

She turned without a word, and went back to the fire, the others trailing behind her; and beside the great upright beam of the king-post, swung round to him again. 'Is he dead?'

Owain nodded. 'Almost two months ago, at a place called Wodensbeorg, where we broke Ceawlin's power.'

'What do I care for Ceawlin's breaking?' she said, softly fierce.

She looked old—old as she had done that day last year when they brought the master of the house home drowned to all outward seeming, and laid him by the fire—the bones of her thin face all at once so sharp that it seemed as though they must cut through the tightened skin. But he saw that she was not going to make any outcry, as she had made none last year. If she wept, it would be later, and alone, and he was thankful. 'Little enough, I make no doubt,' he said, in answer to her question, 'but Beornwulf cared.'

'He knew, then? He was not killed outright?'

'He lived the better part of the night,' Owain told her, 'but I do not think he suffered more than his kind reckon fair payment for Valhalla.'

The bondwoman had begun to snivel and wail, and Helga and Lilla were huddling close to their mother, though she seemed for the moment not to know that they were there. But Bryni stood apart from the rest, his eyes on Owain's face and the green of them swallowed up in black. He said in a small steady voice, 'Did they burn my father's sword with him?'

It sounded wickedly callous, but Owain, who knew Bryni, knew that it was not. 'No, he bade me take it when the death-pyres were built, for you when you are of age to carry it.'

'Give it to me now, just—just for today.'

Owain hesitated an instant, then brought the well worn weapon from under his cloak, and gave it to him without a word; and the boy stood for a moment looking at it in the firelight, then with a defiant scowl at the rest of his family, in case any of them thought of following him, he turned, holding it close against him, and ran from the house-place. One sob tore itself free of him before he was quite through the doorway, and that was all.

The bannocks on the hearth were scorching, but nobody noticed them.

A white and silent Bryni brought back his father's sword at supper-time, and it was laid by at the bottom of the great kist to wait until he was a man. Owain hung up his sword and his dinted buckler above the place where he slept, and the life of the farm took him back as though the wind had never risen and he had never gone with Haegel's war-host. But his place in the life of Beornstead was a much more difficult one to hold, than it had been before. Save that he no longer carried the weight of a thrall-ring about his neck, he was just what he had always been, one of the farm men, along with Gyrth and Caedman. And yet in many ways the burden of the household and the farm, of advising Athelis and trying to keep Bryni out of serious scrapes, rested as squarely on his shoulders as though he had been the master of the house. Sometimes it made him laugh, when he stopped to think of it, though there was a bitter twist to the laughter. It was a strange trick of fate that he, Owain, son of a Roman and a British house, should find himself shouldering the care of a Saxon family and a Saxon farm, but there was not much time for thinking, except at night, and by then he was generally too tired.

They got the harvest in, and it was time to put the three lean pigs out to fatten on acorns; time for the autumn slaughtering, the smoking and the curing and the salting down. Then winter was upon them, with the dykes a constant headache, and a young colt to be broken, and whenever he could snatch a day from the ditching and dyking, Owain took the dogs and sometimes Bryni and went hunting for fresh meat. If one lived entirely on the salt stuff, which had maggots in it anyway by the spring, one got the scurvy, and if the household got the scurvy he would have be-trayed Beornwulf's trust.

Lambing came, and spring ploughing, and early summer with hay harvest and the hot smelly business of sheep-shearing. Fitful warfare had broken out again in Wessex, as soon as the winter was over, but it was only between Ceawlin and his kin, and Haegel did not call out his war-host. The barley grew white for harvest in the cornlands of the Seals' Island, and the first of the four years that Owain had given to Beornwulf was accomplished.

News always took a long time to seep down through the Wealden forests, and reach the tongue of land between the Downs and the Seals' Island, and it was autumn when a wander-ing harper—always it was a harper or a merchant who carried the tidings of the world from one settlement to another—brought word that Ceawlin was dead, and two of his four sons with him.

Ceawlin, whose shadow had fallen across South Britain like the shadow of a giant; dead in some already half-lost skirmish; the harper did not even know the name of the place, all that he was sure of was that Ceawlin was dead.

But the last coasting ship to make the Windy Haven, before the autumn gales closed the sea-ways, brought later news. The news that Ceawlin's two surviving sons had made their peace with the new King of the West Saxons, and been rewarded with a fair-sized lump of their father's old conquests, to hold under him. Aethelbert had taken the territories of Norrey and Surrey for his share of the spoils; the thing was over and paid for, tidied up and bundled away. And Owain, standing among the little crowd that had gathered to hear the ship-master holding forth, could not help feeling that the men who made the best showing in the confused and bloody story were Ceawlin and the two sons who had died with him. It was a bitter thing to have to admit, and he went back to the steading in a vile bad temper.

Another winter passed, and another, and Owain began to look about him with a queer mixture of eagerness and regret, thinking, 'Only once more I shall see the sheep-shearing here in the Seals' Island, one more harvest to get in, one more winter I shall struggle with the dykes.' And also, 'If Beornwulf were to come back, he would see that the land and the beasts are in good heart—and that young fool Bryni has not broken his own neck or anybody else's.'

That summer Helga was hand-fasted to the grandson of old Gamal Witterson, the Headman of the settlement, a good match for any girl, though she seemed not particularly interested.

Only the folk of the two households witnessed the actual hand-fasting over the hearth, but afterwards, when the feasting started, folk came from half over Seals' Island. And knowing that it would be so, Athelis had made her preparations accordingly. The trestle boards were set up before the house-place door, and loaded with great piles of barley-bread, bowls of dried fish, curds and cheese and golden-dripping honeycomb, and huge jugs of the spiced bride-ale from which the feast took its name. There was even meat, for Haegel the King had sent them a young ox.

In all the three years since he gave away his serpent-sword, Haegel had not once crossed the creek. Athelis said that he had forgotten his foster brother, but Owain thought privately, that maybe he remembered too well, and the Seals' Island no longer had the feel of home for him; and he had sent them meat before this, and corn two winters past after the harvest failed. It was a fine young ox with plenty of fat on it, and when the cold broiled joints of it were set out with the rest, Athelis, who had been afraid that Beornwulf's house would be shamed because Owain had refused to kill the pig which was not quite ready for killing, knew that there would be no need for shame, after all.

Owain came out late to join the rest, for one of their three cows was calving, and he had not liked to leave her until all was safely over. Now he stood with a cup of the bride-ale in one hand, leaning a shoulder against the foreporch wall and looking on at the merrymaking. Perhaps because he was tired, he felt cut off from the scene as he had felt cut off from that other scene in the King's forecourt before he took his sword to join the young warriors about the weapon stone. Afterwards he had come to feel himself one with those warriors—but it was different when the Ravens were gathering. 'The Truce of the Spear', Einon Hên had called it. . . .

Dusk had come like a slow-rising tide, and already the smoke of the feast-fire as it curled upward was silvered by the rising moon. The bride and groom were seated side by side on a pile of hay, and the firelight touched Helga's soft hair under the wreathed silver wires of the bridal crown that her grandmother and her great-grandmother had worn before her, and leapt on the blade of of the sword across young Wiermund's knees—always a man brought his sword to the wedding, though it was seldom needed now. Somewhere in the shadows, old Oswy was piping for the dancing that had just begun; a thin sweet piping that seemed to belong to the moonlight rather than the fire, and the young men and girls had caught hands and were spinning like a wheel about the fire, while the older men foregathered before the house-place and the women moved among them with the ale jar.

Between the piping and the sound of voices laughing, arguing, bragging one against another, Owain heard a whinny from the narrow close where the horses were tethered. Earlier, the boys and young men had been trying their paces against each other as usually happened when any feast gathered them together; and soon, quite soon now, it would be time for the bride-race, which had made a wild end to every hand-fasting in the Seals' Island settlements since the first keel was run ashore and the first hut built.

The piping ceased on a falling trail of notes, and the spinning circle of dancers burst apart. They were all over the garth now, crowding round the trestle boards. And among the rest, Owain saw Bryni and Horn, together as they generally were, with Lilla between them. Padda the boat-builder who had three cherry trees in his garth, had brought a bowl of the little fruit, rose red on one side, bone white on the other, for his contribution to the wedding, and knowing that they would go nowhere among so many, Athelis had not set out the bowl until most of the serious eating was over. The dancing had been wild, and Lilla had lost her head-rail, so that when she flung the soft heavy braids of her hair back over her shoulders, the pink lobes of her ears were bare. They seemed to have given Horn an idea, for while Bryni looked on laughing at him, he was picking over the bowl for cherries whose stalks were joined together, and with the quiet concentration with which he did all things, hanging them in the girl's ears.

It was time, Owain thought suddenly, that Athelis settled that matter with Brand the Smith. Lilla had always treated Horn exactly as she treated Bryni; but he was not at all sure now, watching them, that Horn felt towards her in the same way as Bryni did, and he had a feeling that even Lilla was ready for a change. Certainly it seemed that she was enjoying having cherries hung in her ears.

She was looking up at Horn, laughing, and swinging the skirts of her blue kirtle in time to her memory of the piping.

All at once Owain had a sudden feeling of other eyes beside his own, watching Lilla—watching her keenly. He looked round, and saw Vadir Cedricson leaning against the wall almost within arm's length of him. The moon shone full on the man's thin disdainful face, and the pale eyes, widened a little in suddenly awakened interest, were plain to see. In that moment he knew that Vadir was seeing Lilla for the first time as a man sees a woman.

Anxiety stirred in him. He had always liked Lilla better than her sister; there was more in her to like. He wanted Horn for her because he thought that the boy would make her happy; he did not want for her that look in the eyes of Vadir the Hault. . . . Then he shrugged at himself for a fool, worrying over the girl as though he were the grey-bearded father of the household; he laughed and drained the ale cup in his hand, and went to get it filled again.

As he did so, the shout went up that it was time for the bride-race. The groom had scrambled to his feet, thrusting his sword back into its sheath, and after him all the unmarried men who owned horses or had been able to borrow them for the occasion began to shake clear of the rest and jostle their way out towards the back of the steading. And when Owain looked again, Vadir was nowhere to be seen.

The girls were crowding round Helga, pulling her to her feet and thrusting her out to stand beside the fire. There were hurried farewells with Lilla and her mother, and then as a burst of shouting rose from behind the steading, they scattered, leaving her to stand there very much alone and looking suddenly frightened as though for the first time she understood what it was all about.

But almost in the same instant they heard the horsemen tussling at the gate, voices and smothered laughter and trampling of hooves, and then the dark shapes of a horse and rider swept round the far end of the house-place into the firelight, and Wiermund was stooping from the saddle to catch Helga's hand and haul her up before him. 'Up! Come up with you!' She set her foot on his in the stirrup and hopped, and the young man heaved, both of them laughing now, and then she was across his saddle-bow, and the horse which he had barely checked, broke forward out of the firelight, out through the steading gate, and in the moment's hush they heard the hoof-beats drumming away over the levels towards the settlement.

And then, hard on the heels of the bridegroom came all the rest, jostling for place at the gate and in the narrow ways between the outbuildings; and the girls ran together squealing and pretending fear. Neck and neck, the first two horsemen rounded the end of the house-place, and one sprang into the lead, a small man riding a black horse whose white forehead blaze shone silver in the firelight, and Owain saw with a swift tightening of the heart that it was Vadir.

Heedless of the poor brute's snorting terror, Vadir swung the horse in a trampling curve to the very verge of the fire, and swooping low from the saddle in full gallop, caught Lilla and swept her up before him in one swift movement, and was away into the dark.

After him dashed Horn the next rider, on Wagtail, and having missed the girl he wanted, caught up the nearest, and plunged on out of the firelight, and for a few moments the crowded garth was full of horsemen and flying shadows, shrieking and laughter, as man after man caught up a girl before him and headed for the gateway. Then the last of them was gone, and the garth seemed very empty.

So the bride would be carried off to her new home and her new life surrounded by a flying skein of horsemen, and when the loop of riders had flung themselves three times sunwise about the house for good fortune, they would come flying back over the levels, with a last draught of ale from the house-lord's own horn for whoever set his girl down first at the steading gate.

Already the rest of the wedding party were crowding out to the gateway to watch for their return, several of the men pulling blazing branches from the fire to serve as torches as they went. And Owain, on the outskirts of the throng, found Bryni suddenly beside him. 'Did you see?' Bryni sounded as though he were speaking through shut teeth, and when Owain looked round, his face even in that fitful light showed flushed.

'Yes, I saw. Horn must be quicker off the mark another time.'

Bryni's hands were clutched at his sides. 'The swine! The little swine!'

'Soft now,' Owain said, speaking quickly, under cover of the cheerful uproar in the gate. 'Any man riding in the bride-race has a perfect right to catch up any girl he chooses. You know that.'

'I don't believe he has ever ridden a bride-race before tonight; he'd scorn such sport,' Bryni said in a furious rush. 'I don't care what rights he has, if he doesn't keep his claws off Lilla, I *will* kill him.'

Owain's hand came down on his shoulder. To any of the bridal party who chanced to look that way—but they were all craning their necks out over the levels—it would have seemed a mere casual gesture, but his fingers bit into the boy's flesh until he wriggled. 'Listen to me my lad; you have had quite as much ale as you have room for. For tonight the man is a guest within your gates, and if you can't behave, I shall take you here and now and put that hot head of yours in a bucket of water to cool it.'

Bryni drew a long breath that was like a sob; but when he spoke again his voice was calmer. 'I'll behave—but he's not my guest on other nights of the year.'

Owain let his own breath go carefully. Other nights of the year must look after themselves. He released Bryni's shoulder, and pushed forward with him into the gateway.

Beyond the gold of the makeshift torches the levels lay white and quiet in the moonlight, empty to the dark barrier of oak scrub beyond the dyke; and as they strained eyes and ears to-wards it, a faint pulse of sound woke in the stillness, a rhythm soft as the beat of a moth's wings. 'Here they come!' a woman cried, as a flicker of moving darkness shook clear of the oak scrub and came sweeping down the far side of the dyke towards the plank bridge. Everyone was shouting now, shouting and waving the stumps of firebrands, and through the uproar the drum of hooves swept nearer. A second horseman was out of the scrub now, then a knot of two or three, but the first was across the dyke and head-ing straight and swift as an arrow for the tossing torches in the gate.

Bryni was thrusting his way into the forefront of the company and Owain kept close behind him. He had never doubted who the first rider would be, and now he could see the black horse thun-dering towards them, the rider bending forward over the girl held in the crook of his arm. 'It is Vadir!' someone shouted. 'Hammer of the Gods! Will you look how he rides!' and a woman cried out sharply, 'One stumble at that speed and he'll kill the girl!' But her words were drowned in the shout that the men were taking up: 'Vadir! Vadir Cedricson!'

They broke back and scattered, even as they shouted for him, and in the same instant, as it seemed, Vadir was reining the black horse on to its haunches in their midst.

Bryni sprang forward and caught Lilla as she wriggled free and dropped from the saddle-bow, and swung her away so roughly that she stumbled and would have fallen if Owain had not been there to steady her. He thought she looked ghost-white and in the moment he held her he felt her shaking, but she made no sound. Vadir laughed, softly sitting his sweating horse and looking down at the boy. 'An ill-mannered cub,' he said, as though to himself. 'Maybe thralls' manners are easily caught by those that keep thralls' company,' and wheeled his horse away into the throng as other hooves came pounding towards them.

Owain had a hand on Bryni's shoulder again as the boy would have started after him. 'Leave it!' he muttered. 'That was for both of us, and if I can abide an insult, so can you.'

Then Horn had come up, and horseman after horseman was sweeping into the torchlight, and shedding breathless, laughing, dishevelled girls. Once more the close-gathering shifted and fell back, and Owain saw in their midst, Vadir sitting his black horse and waiting, aloof and faintly disdainful, for his prize. Someone had brought Beornwulf's great drinking horn with the copper and silver mountings, and put it into Lilla's hands, and she walked forward, carrying it carefully because it was brimming with the last of the bride-ale, and Owain guessed that her hands were still shaking. The torches were spluttering out, and the firelight through the gateway turned Vadir's face to a mocking mask as he stooped to take the horn she held up to him. '*Wass heil!* I drink to you!' He threw back his head and drained it in one long draught that would have left most men gasping, and returned it, deliberately letting his hands touch hers as he did so. 'It was a race worth the riding, after all.'

And next instant he had wheeled his horse, and without word or look for anyone else was away.

Owain, hearing the rhythm of his hoof-beats change from a canter into a gallop and fade into the distance, saw that no one else felt any shadow fall across the end of the feast. No one but Bryni and Horn and Lilla. And Bryni, baulked of a quarrel with the hated lord of Widda's Ham, had turned himself to pick one with Horn, who, as he dismounted with a scowl blackening his usually pleasant face, looked more than ready for it. Lilla had disappeared, and he wondered if she was still shaking. For himself— he told himself for the second time that evening, not to be a fool.

18

Vadir

THREE days later Owain was clearing scrub along the inland edge of the shore-pasture when he thought he heard the beat of horses' hooves coming towards the steading. He went on with his work, cursing the little biting flies that bred among the oak scrub, and presently he heard the hoof-beats again, fading into the distance this time. Whoever it was, they had finished whatever they came for, and gone their way; and he worked on, thinking no more about it.

The shadows of the oak trees were lengthening seaward, and soon it would be time to be going up to the steading for the evening meal. He broke off for a moment, straightened his back and stood wiping the sweat out of his eyes. Stupid, that even now he could never see the shore-meadow in this level evening light with-

out also seeing a white stallion come trotting up the long curve of
it with the salt breeze in his mane and tail.

In the sudden quiet following the rustling and slashing of his
work, he heard the soft light pad of flying feet. For a moment he
thought that it was Bryni, but it was not the free running of a boy,
it had a faintly hampered sound and a brushing came with it that
suggested skirts, and as he turned quickly towards it, Lilla came
ducking under the low-hanging elder branches, like something
small and desperate with the hounds behind her.

Owain tossed aside his slasher, and flung out an arm to catch
her as she stumbled over a bramble root and pitched forward, and
next instant she was panting against him. He held her off and
looked at her. 'Steady then! What is it?—Look, no one is following you.'

She shook her head, seeming to gather herself together, and
stood quite still in his hands; quite still save that she still panted
with the speed she had made. Her eyes were fixed on his face, but
she did not answer.

'What is it then, Lilla?' he asked again.

She swallowed, and looked down. 'Nothing. It is nothing at
all.'

'It must be something. You're like a hunted hare.'

'No I—oh, but you can't help me. I don't know why I came.'

'Supposing you were to take a deep breath and tell me what's
amiss,' Owain said, patiently, as though she was the same age as
she had been when first he came to the Seals' Island.

She looked up slowly, her hands twisted together. 'It is Vadir
Cedricson.'

Owain felt his face stiffen. 'What has Vadir Cedricson been
doing?'

'He was up at home just now, and when he was gone again my
mother called for me and told me—he came to ask that I should be
hand-fast with him.'

'And what did your mother say to him?'

'She has not given him any answer as yet, but he is coming
again in three days; and she will say yes, I know she will—and I
am so afraid of him.'

Owain stood silent for a moment, remembering the scene at

Helga's hand-fasting, remembering Lilla laughing while Horn hung cherries in her ears, and Vadir swooping from the saddle to snatch her up for the bride-race. Why in God's sweet name had Athelis not settled matters with Brand the Smith, before it came to this? 'You should go to Bryni,' he said. 'He is your brother.'

'Bryni! You know what Bryni is, and he hates Vadir already. If I go to him, he'll do something mad. I daren't.'

'But what do you think *I* can do?' Owain demanded.

'Nothing.' Her voice was flat and hopeless. 'I said so, didn't I? I ran away to you because you were the first person I thought of; but you can't help me—nobody can help me.'

She made as though to slip out of his hold, but he said quickly, 'No, wait—let me think, Lilla; I must have a moment to think.'

And she stood still again, watching him. Owain had loosed his hold on her, and stood frowning straight before him and scratching at the old scar on his arm as he still did when he was thinking deeply. At last he moved, with a little sigh. 'I'll do what I can,' he said. 'I do not know whether I can do anything at all, but I'll try. . . . You must go home now, Lilla.'

When she had gone, he picked up his slasher again, and went steadily to work on the task that he wanted to finish before he went up to the steading for supper.

It seemed to him that evening that a feeling of strain lay over the house-place like a shadow. The mistress of the house looked white and drained, and seemed to have little taste for the good fish broth with herbs and barley-meal, while Lilla scarcely dipped in the communal bowl at all; and they took care to avoid looking at each other—not as though there was any anger between them, Owain thought, but in a kind of dreary understanding and sympathy. Even Bryni, who was not given to awareness of other people's moods, looked at them more than once without asking what was amiss, then caught Owain's eye across the hearth and shrugged one shoulder; a shrug that said as plainly as words could do: 'Women!'

These hot summer evenings no one stayed in the house-place after the evening meal, but wandered out again to their own affairs. Most evenings, Athelis, who had little enough time to spare during the day, would betake herself to tend the tiny herb patch under the apple trees behind the steading, which was her rest and her joy.

This particular evening she delayed so long that Owain, mending a piece of harness in the shade of the stable wall, and watching for a chance to speak with her alone, began to be afraid that she was not going at all. But at last she rose, and going into the house-place, came back with a newly lit lantern and her wicker creel of gardening gear, and disappeared round the end of the house.

He gave her a little while, then went and hung up the piece of harness in its accustomed place, and followed her.

She had hung the lantern on the branch of an apple tree, and was tying up tall-growing purple comfrey that had been battered by the wind. She looked up when she heard Owain's footsteps, and he thought she had a very good idea why he had come. He leaned against the branch where the lantern hung. He did not know how to break into the thing that he had come to say. Once he had begun, it would be all right. 'Mistress,' he said at last, abruptly. 'Lilla came running to me a while since. She said that Vadir Cedricson had asked for her.'

Athelis ceased all pretence at tying up the comfrey and dropped the twists of dry grass she had been using, back into her creel. 'She had no right to run to you with her troubles.'

'She was too frightened to think what rights she had,' Owain said bluntly. And then, as she did not answer, 'She told me that he will come for your answer in three days' time, and that you will say yes. Is that true?' It sounded accusing, but he did not know how to put it any other way.

She was still silent a moment, then she said, 'Yes, it is true. What else can I do?'

'You should have settled the matter with Brand the Smith years ago. You know that Beornwulf wished it so.'

She flung out her hands. 'I should have—I should have. But I did not. I suppose I wanted her with me a little longer. And now it is too late. What use to tell me I should have done this, I should have done that? What can I do now but say yes? She will do well enough when she is married to him.'

N

'Will she? I doubt it. But maybe I see Vadir Cedricson somewhat darkly, remembering that he let his dogs kill my old Dog,
and found it not unpleasant to watch.'

She said quickly, 'He was young then, not much more than a
boy; and boys are often more cruel than men.'

'He had seen five or six and twenty summers if he had seen one,'
Owain said. 'The man is twisted, body and soul, and you know it.'

She looked at him with eyes turned all to black in the lantern
light, and for an instant he wondered if she was going to strike
him across the mouth for his insolence. But she only said, 'He is
powerful, and we have no man to spread his shield over us.'

'The King would not let harm come to the household of his
foster brother, even though Vadir be distant kin to him; and
Bryni will be a man next spring.'

'The King! Haegel has spared little thought for the household
of his foster brother since Wodensbeorg,' Athelis said bitterly.
'And even if it were not so, there are harms over which the King
has no power. And as for Bryni, you know how wild and head-
strong he is. Always, whenever they meet, he is on the brink of a
quarrel with Vadir; but if Vadir takes Lilla for his wife, even
Bryni will not dare to draw knife on his own kin—and nor will
Vadir.'

'You do not think that, knowing his sister is being forced into
this hand-fasting, the boy will draw knife on Vadir *before* they
become kinsman?' He was being brutal, he knew that, remembering the thing that he had told the ten year old Bryni, the first time
he threatened to kill Vadir. But he was remembering also the
cruelty—cruelty even towards the thing he loved—that he had felt
in Vadir Cedricson on the night that Teitri was born, and he was
fighting for Lilla with whatever weapon came to hand.

Athelis was gripping and twisting her hands together. 'I do not
know,' she whispered. 'At least you will still be here. You can
handle him—a little. You are the only one who can, since
Beornwulf died. After next spring, you will be gone.'

There was a long silence. How loud the sea sounded tonight, a
hollow sounding like the echo of waves in a shell; and somewhere
within it, he seemed to catch the remembered echo of Uncle
Widreth's voice . . . 'Only while one is young there is always the

hope that one day something will happen; that one day a little wind will rise. . . .' How often that had comforted him. But it was a barren comfort, after all. He had thought, four years ago, that the wind was rising, but it had died away again into the grass; and he had waited so long, so long, for the time of his freedom to come. He was not even really young any more, and all his manhood until now had gone in waiting. It was too much for any man to expect of him; these people were the enemies of his people; Beornwulf had had full value for his gold piece. Yes, but Beornwulf had not thought of it as part of the value of his gold piece; he had asked it in the hour of his death, as a man may ask a great thing of a friend he trusts.

He looked up slowly. 'If I let my freedom wait, if I bide here until you tell me that I am free to go—would that make any difference?'

Athelis put up her thin hands to her face; then she let them drop, and looked at him again. 'Do you mean that?'

'I should not have offered, if I did not mean it,' Owain said harshly.

'No, that was stupid of me.' She had caught herself together now, and her voice was calmer. 'Owain, I can settle nothing with Brand the Smith now: that would be to bring Vadir down upon us at once; you see that, do you not?'

'I see that, yes.'

'But if you do not leave us, at least—not yet, I will tell Vadir that he must ask again in a year's time. I will say that Lilla is too young. More I dare not promise, but she shall not be hand-fast to him for a year.'

A year's respite; it was the best that could be hoped for, he knew that. Well, many things might happen in a year. Vadir might change his heart, the sea might break in over the levels one night and overwhelm them all.

'Very well,' he said. 'I will stay.'

Exactly what passed when Vadir came for his answer, Owain never knew. He was working down at the furthest end of the Intake that day. But that evening when he made his way up to the steading at supper-time, he found Lilla waiting for him among the newly made pea stacks. She was pretending to be very busy

about the evening search for eggs, which fell to her alone now that
Helga was married and away, but she gave up the pretence as he
drew near, and stood up, the egg basket in the crook of her arm.

'He came,' she said, 'and now he is gone and he will not come
again for a year.'

Owain nodded. 'That is something gained. A breathing space
at all events. I wish I could have done more, Lilla, but a year was
the best that I could do.'

Lilla was staring into the egg basket, her head drooping under
the big white kerchief that hid her hair; but after a moment she
raised grave blue eyes to his face; he had never noticed quite how
blue they were before, not bright but soft, harebell coloured. 'My
mother said that I had not any right to carry my troubles to you.'

'I'd not worry too much about that,' Owain said.

'But she was right. If I was a good girl, and—and brave and
sensible, I would go to Vadir now and tell him that I was ready to
be hand-fast with him, and not let you go on giving up your
freedom for us. But I'm not a good girl, and I'm *not* brave——'

To his dismay, Owain saw two tears spill over and trickle down
her cheeks. 'Don't cry,' he said quickly. 'Please don't cry, Lilla.
If it is for me—it will do me no harm to wait a while longer; and
if it is for you—see now, you have a whole year gained. Anything
may happen in a year.'

Lilla dashed the back of her free hand across her eyes. 'I'm not
crying, at least—not very much, and I do not know who it is
for. . . . But whatever happens, or if nothing happens at all and I
have to go to Vadir in the end, I will have had one more year—
and I will remember always and always that it was you that gave
it to me.'

The shrill cheerful sound of somebody whistling between their
teeth was coming up towards the stack garth even as she finished
speaking, and she added in a quick low tone of warning, 'It's
Bryni,' and turned away a little, to hide her face. 'See, isn't this a
big egg?'

'Double-yoked, by the look of it,' Owain said.

Better, very much better, that Bryni should know nothing of
what had happened.

19

The King's Hunting

FROM that time forward the Beornstead household saw no more
of Vadir Cedricson, and nor did any but the four who knew of it
already, come to hear of his wooing. He was too proud a man for
that.

So the months wore away and autumn brought the wild geese
south again.

That winter the farms and settlements of the Maen Wood began to be troubled by a wild boar. It happened from time to time
that wild pig would come down from the inland forests into the

tangled wild-wood among the marshes, and make a nuisance of themselves until they were killed or driven inland again. But this was a king among boar, larger, fiercer and more cunning than the common run. He made havoc in the cultivated land, rooting up fences and goring young trees; he became the terror of the forest fringes where any man might meet him as he turned home with a load of firewood in the winter dusk. And bad as the thing was now, it would become yet worse when spring drew on and the crops were sown. More than once, the men of the Maen Wood had banded together in an attempt to hunt him down, but all that they had to show for it was the death of two of their number.

And then word came down into the settlements, south to the very tip of Seals' Island where the fisher huts huddled among the ruins of the little Roman coast-resort, that the King himself was coming to try his spear against this king among boars. Let any man who wished to, hunt with him, meeting at a certain point in the forest at dawn on a certain day.

Bryni brought the news back from the settlement where he had been to pick up a new ploughshare from Brand the Smith. His eyes were bright and dark like the frost, and the colour burned under the brown along his cheekbones. 'We are going hunting with the King!' he announced.

Owain, who had met him in the steading gate, nodded gravely, when he had heard all the eager tale. 'No doubt the King will have a use for all the beaters he can get—though it is not *our* boar, south of the creek.'

'The brute might work round the head of the creek any night, and then it would be our boar, sure enough,' Bryni protested, as though he felt that the honour of the Seals' Island was at stake. 'And as for beaters——' he flung up his head defiantly—'I am son to the King's foster brother—though he seems to have forgotten it. Go you with the beaters and shout and fire the furze if you choose. *I* shall go with the spears!'

For a moment the two looked at each other in silence; and then, seeing the quirk at the corner of Owain's mouth, the boy gave a crow of excited laughter. 'Ah, but you make a jest of me—you never thought that I would go with the beaters.'

'No,' Owain agreed, 'I never thought that you would go with the beaters.'

They got out the old boar spears, and all that evening Bryni sat by the fire burnishing them with white sand, and whistling to himself between his teeth in the way that was as much a part of him as the way that Owain scratched at the old scar when he was thinking.

On the appointed day—three days later—they set off while it was still wolf-dark, for they would have an hour's walking to make the appointed meeting place. Three or four men from the settlement joined them at the old ford, and Hunna, grumbling at being roused from his sleep before the sky had begun to lighten, brought his crazy little boat across for them, and had to make two trips before they were all on the mainland bank. They left him still muttering curses, and pushed on together up the remains of the Regnum road.

Bryni strode out in front of the rest, still whistling through his teeth. It was his first boar hunt, and it was natural that he should be in wild spirits—being Bryni who was never troubled by a cold stomach—but Owain had a feeling that he was up to some devilry, and wondered whether he should have tried to make him go with the beaters after all. But the boy was a fine hunter, strong and skilled, and one of those who seem able to think with the mind of a wild animal, knowing by instinct what the quarry will do. And anyway he would have been as like to do something mad with the beaters as he was with the spears. The only thing for Owain to do was to keep an eye on him as well as he could. At all events Vadir the Hault would not have come to join the King's hunting—war was one thing, but to track the wild boar on foot through miles of wood and waste was quite another, for a man with a club foot—and that was one danger the less. Owain drew a long breath, his heart lifting to the prospect of the day's desperate sport, and settled down to the rhythm of the long loping tramp that carried them towards the King's meeting place.

It had snowed a couple of days since, half thawed, and then frozen again, and pools of whiteness lay under the trees and in the hollows and along the dykes that bordered the roadway. The feel of frost and the feel of thaw was still mingled underfoot, but the smell of the night was the cold green smell of coming thaw. The men sniffed at it, and told each other that scent should lie none so badly on such a morning.

A low dawn was kindling bars of cold yellow light across the east when they came to the appointed gathering place. The earliest comers had made a fire against the cold, and Owain, with Bryni and the others, joined the men clustered about the warmth; there were a good number of them already, and more arriving all the while; it seemed that half the farms of the Maen Wood as well as a few from the Seals' Island, had sent a man to join the King's hunting. They pressed about the fire, talking and laughing, men who had not seen each other in months, greeting each other and exchanging news, and feeling the edges of their knives and boar spears.

Slowly the light grew in the sky, and high against it, Owain looking up, could see the long lines of the wild duck in their morning flight; and soon after the first wild duck came a muffled smother of hoof-beats and a voice asking questions and a quick deep laugh told them that the King was here.

The horses were led away to the nearby farmstead, and Haegel with his hearth-companions came forward into the light of the roadside fire. He was in leather hunting dress, worn and weather-stained and dark-spattered with the marks of more than one kill; his dogs thrust about him, and he carried his own spears. He looked about him at the men round the fire, quickly and appraisingly, as though to see what manner of hunting party had gathered to his call. 'The greetings of the morning to you, friends and neighbours,' he said. 'I think we shall have good hunting today,' and he turned to speak to the leaders who had stepped up round him, inquiring as to the placing of beaters, and discussing the plans for the day, putting swift questions to the man who had brought in news of the boar's whereabouts last night. 'Over by the Black Wood, say you? So, then, if he be there yet we may bring him to bay somewhere between the neck of the forest and Bremma's Dyke.'

And so the King's hunting began, as hounds and men streamed away eastward in a slow-moving pack, heading for the Black Wood where it ran down to the sea marshes above Pagga's Ham.

The Black Wood stood like an island in the sea of marshes, black as its name even now in the light of the winter's morning; and within sight of it they checked to set on the hounds. Even as they did so a boy came running, glancing back as he ran, and shouting his story even before he reached them. 'He's still there! He would not have taken to the marshes, and the birds have been quiet all the while in the neck of the woods, so he can't have gone that way!'

There was a long wait, while the King's hunters with the great hounds still in leash went questing to and fro. And then, far over towards the neck of scrub that joined the Black Wood to the forest, a hound gave tongue. 'Sa! Garm has him,' said the King. 'I'd know that bell note of his anywhere.'

And now the other hounds had taken up the cry, and the notes of the hunting horn were blowing thin through the tangled wild-wood and scaring up the plover from the marshes. The pace of the hunt had quickened from the steady lope that it had been be-fore, and suddenly they were all running.

They were among the trees now; the low-hanging branches lashed at their faces and tangled the spears, snags of rotten wood tripped them up, and brambles clawed at them like living enemies wherever the trees fell back a little—and always the belling of the hounds and the thin song of the hunting horn sounded through the woods ahead of them. Now the beaters were drawing close; Owain could hear their shouting, a great circle of uproar, begin-ning to narrow in on itself, as he ran, head down, behind the slight racing figure of Bryni.

And then, as it seemed between one gasping breath and the next, the whole pattern had changed, and they had come to the very heart of the day's work. They were on the edge of a clearing where a great yew tree had come down in the winter gales and brought others with it in its fall; and on the far side of the open space, backed against the mass of the fallen bole, stood as though waiting for them, a gigantic black boar.

He scarcely looked a thing of flesh and blood at all, but as though he belonged to the dark earth of the wood itself, and the dark elemental spirit of the wood. He stood with lowered head swinging a little from side to side; his eyes were red like the sullen

gleeds of a burnt out fire, and the great curved tushes gleamed
against the blackness of his narrow wicked face. Yellowish froth
dripped from his jaws, and where it fell on the snow, it steamed.

The hounds, yelling in rage and hate, sprang forward as they
were slipped from the leash; from the darkness of the woods beyond, the yelling and crashing of the beaters was still closing in,
and all round the clearing the hunters crouched, each man with
the butt of his spear braced under his instep. Owain was just behind Bryni in the second line, his spear braced like the rest, in
case the boar should break through, but having made sure that his
knife was loose in his belt, for the more likely task of a man in the
second line would be to help dispatch the beast if the man in front
—in this case Bryni—ran into trouble.

The hounds were all about the boar now, yelling into his black
devil's mask as he swung his head from side to side. Across
Bryni's braced shoulder Owain saw the coarse black bristles along
his back and the redness of his wicked little eyes, and caught the
sharp stink of him on the wintry air. He trundled forward a few
steps, then Garm, the greatest of the King's boarhounds, leapt
raving at his throat, and instantly the whole scene burst into roaring chaos. The hounds were all on to their quarry now, baying
and belling as they sprang for a hold and were shaken off and
sprang again. They were no longer hunting-dogs around a boar,
but one confused mass of boar and hounds that rolled slowly forward across the clearing.

But the boar was shaking free of the hounds as he came. Garm
lost his grip, and springing in once more, missed the throat-hold,
hung for a moment tearing at the huge black shoulder, and was
flung off again; a big brindled hound lay kicking his life out in a
patch of reddening snow, and the demon of the woods, scattering
the enemies that clung to him and dragged him back, was quicken-
ing into a grotesque trundling charge that seemed to the waiting
spearmen as elemental as a landslip roaring towards them. He was
heading for the centre of the great curve of men, where the King
and his closest hearth-companions waited, crouching on their
spears. But he never reached them, for as the dogs scattered, young
Bryni straightened a little behind his braced spear, flung up his
arm with a whooping yell 'Hi-ya-ya-aiee!' and flourished it above

his head, like a boy trying to attract the attention of a friend three fields away.

Among all that uproar, the shout might have had little effect, but the sudden movement caught the great brute's eye, and his anger, which until that moment had been for the whole hunt, gathered itself and centred upon it. He swerved in his charge and came straight for Bryni.

Owain felt for one instant as though an icy hand had clenched itself on his stomach, and the next, the great brute was on to Bryni's spear-point. It drove on, carried by the weight of its own charge, until brought up by the cross-guard at the neck of the spear; but it seemed that the deep-driven blade had not found the life; not yet, at any rate. For one sharp splinter of time, Owain saw the boy's shoulder brace and twist and strain, as he fought to keep the spear-butt under his instep; then it was wrenched free, and still clinging to the shaft he was being shaken and battered to and fro as a dog shakes a rat.

'Hold on, Bryni!' Owain shouted. 'For God's sake *hold on!*' He was springing forward, expecting even in that instant to see the boy's hold broken and the black devil upon him. He dived in low among the raving hounds, his spear shortened to stab; other men were with him, other blades caught the wintry light, as he heaved aside the body of a hound and drove in his spear. Now he too was being shaken to and fro, the shaft twisting like a live thing in his hands; the breath was battered from his body, and the stink of the boar and its hot blood were thick in his throat, choking him as the world spun and rocked before his eyes. And then suddenly it was over. Whether it was his own blade or that of one of the other men that had found the life, he never knew, or whether at the last Bryni's spear had taken effect after all; the great brute shuddered, gathered itself together for one last convulsive moment of hate, and crashed down on to its side, seeming to shake the whole forest with its fall.

Owain struggled slowly to his feet, and stood panting, his spear still beside Bryni's in the boar's breast.

Two hounds lay dead; others were dripping blood from their gashed flanks. Bryni also got to his feet, ashen-white under the brown of his skin, but smiling and with shining eyes. Without a

word he set his foot on the boar's shoulder and stooped to drag
out his spear.

There were men crowding all round them; they whipped off
the hounds, and the baying died, but just for the moment nobody
spoke. Owain himself drew a deep sobbing breath that ached
under his bruised ribs, but what he had to say to young Bryni, he
would not say in front of the other men.

Then the crowd fell apart to let someone through, and there
stood Haegel the King. He looked from the white-faced boy to
the grizzly body of the huge black boar at his feet, and back again.
'You young *fool*!' His eyes were bleak, and his voice rough in his
throat with anger. 'Hammer of the Gods! If you were son of
mine I'd flog the skin off your back to make shoe-thongs, for
that piece of foolhardiness! Who taught you to think that a child
such as you are could hold the King's boar on your spear?'

Bryni turned from white to fiery scarlet under his brown, but
still he smiled. 'No one, Haegel the King. I thought it for myself.
I am sorry if the King is angry that I have killed his boar.'

Haegel looked down at the second spear still fast in the black carcass, and the stab-wounds of other men's knives, and for an instant his eye caught Owain's and there was a twitch of laughter
on his bearded lips. But the boy had been First Spear at the killing,
after all. 'As to that, the King has had other boars, and can spare
one,' he said, with the harsh note of anger gone from his voice;
and then with an abrupt change of tone, 'Who are you?'

'I am Bryni, son of Beornwulf the King's foster brother,'
Bryni said. And suddenly Owain knew that it was for this, to
bring himself to the King's notice in a way that he felt worthy,
not merely in the wildness of the moment, that he had drawn
the boar to himself.

Haegel's head jerked up a little, and for a long moment his eyes
narrowed into the wide bright eyes of the young hunter. 'So,' he
said softly. 'You are not very like your father, and I have not seen
you in four summers.'

'How should you?' Bryni said, daringly. 'The King has been
good; he sent meal in the lean time, and an ox; but his shadow has
not fallen across our door-sill since my father died at Wodensbeorg.'

One of the other men broke in angrily, but the King silenced him with a quick movement of one hand. He stood pulling at his beard, and his eyes held the hint of a smile. 'So you will tackle the King as well as the King's boar? If daring and audacity go for aught, you will make a warrior, should ever the Ravens gather again. . . . How old are you, Bryni son of Beornwulf?'

'Fourteen, my Lord King,' Bryni said, and added quickly, 'but I shall be fifteen before the blackthorn is well out.'

'That is well. I may send for you before the blackthorn fruit is set. Oh, not for war, not this time. There are other occasions than battle for which a King may need his household warriors about him.' His deep-set gaze lifted a little and caught Owain's with cool deliberation. 'And you, I remember you, the British spear among my Saxon shield-warriors. Can you still speak your mother tongue?'

'I have not forgotten the way of it,' Owain said, thinking it an odd question.

'Good.' Haegel looked at him a long moment as though storing him in his memory against some future need. Then he turned his attention back to Bryni, and putting out a foot, toed the huge black carcass. 'But we are forgetting the proper business of the day. This thing is waiting to be gralloched, and after—it is your kill, what are you going to do with it?'

'Make a gift of it to the King,' said Bryni unblushingly.

Haegel laughed. 'A truly noble gift. But keep the tushes and hide to furnish you your war-helmet.'

And he turned, stretching, and strolled across to where he had left his spears.

20

The Quiet Place

AFTER the silent and forsaken cities of Viroconium and even Regnum that the Saxons called Cissa's Caester but left deserted to its ghosts, Aethelbert's capital had taken Owain completely by surprise. Maybe it was the unwarrior-like merchant side of this King of Kent that had led him to make his chief place in the old capital city of the Cantii, instead of in some royal farm among the Wealden forests. As it was, he seemed to have brought the farm with him and superimposed it on what was there already. The general effect, Owain thought, drifting up one street and down another on his way back from the West Gate, was of a colony of jackdaws' nests built along the ledges of some once stately colonnade. The streets and many of the walls were the streets and walls of Roman Durnovaria; the reed- and bracken-thatched roofs and the middens that blocked the streets were the roofs and middens of Cantiisburg. Pigs rooted in the streets. Oxen lowed, and the smells were many and varied but mostly they were the earthy and animal smells of the farm-yard.

Standing on the corner of two streets, because he had for the moment nothing else to do, and watching the folk of Aethelbert's capital pass about their daily affairs, Owain's mind went back over the past few weeks, to the day that the King's summons had come. It was better to think about that than about what had happened this morning.

The strange thing—at least it had seemed strange at the time—was that the summons had been for himself as well as Bryni. 'For the British spear among my shield-warriors, seeing that he has not forgotten his mother tongue,' the messenger had said, quoting the King's words that he had got off by heart. Owain had puzzled over that, especially as they had been bidden to bring no weapon but their swords, and it did not seem that the gathering could be for war. Beside, the King had said that it was not for war, 'not for war this time. There are other occasions than battle for which a King may need his household warriors about him.'

The reason for his summons had been simple enough, after all, when it was told to him three days later in the King's Hall. Haegel himself had received a summons from Aethelbert of Kent —he must have known that it was coming, as far back as the boar hunt at winter's end. The High King had sent out bidding the lesser Kings, who owned him as Overlord, to a Council at Cantiisburg at midsummer. Some question of law-giving, it seemed; tribal frontiers to be settled; Owain was not at all clear about it, even now, and nor, he gathered, was anybody else. The Princes of the Allied British Kingdom would be there too, though they owned no man for their Overlord; and since Haegel of the South Saxons had a Briton among his warriors who could tell him what they said and maybe help him to understand their ways of thinking, he might as well make use of him.

So when Haegel took ship for Kent with three of his councillors and a small bodyguard of his kinsmen and household warriors including Vadir, and Bryni carrying himself already with the stiff-legged swagger of the hero of a score of battles, Owain also had been one of them. That seemed a long time ago, for they had run into squally weather and between their sailing and the time when they had landed under the ruined Roman pharos at Dubris, his memory had hung a greenish veil of seasickness. There had been horses waiting for them, and after a night's rest, during which the floor of the shed in which Owain lay had continued to heave up and down with a steep ocean swell, they had set out along the remains of the great double-track legions' road that led straight as a spear-shaft through the Great Forest to Cantiisburg. Two days they had been on that last stretch of the journey, for the roads were not what they had been when the Legions marched them; but yesterday towards sunset they had ridden into Aethelbert's capital.

Coel of Wessex and Coelwulf his brother were there already with their chiefs and champions about them, and Redwald of the East Angles had ridden in late that night, bringing his own harper in his train. All Cantiisburg was thrumming with their gathering, and the thrum would deepen and strengthen until the gathering was complete. Then, Owain thought, strolling on again, the Council would begin, and if Haegel really needed him, there would be something for him to do. He was not used to finding his hands empty of work, and felt lost because of their emptiness.

It was because he had nothing to do that he had wandered out to look at the King's horse farm just beyond the West Gate. At least he had told himself that that was his only reason, because if he admitted to himself that he was going hoping for a glimpse of Teitri, he would have known that it was a stupid thing to do. Teitri was gone: let him go.

Well, he had had his glimpse, of a white stallion running among his mares, so far off that it might have been any white stallion—if he had not known by his heart rather than his eyes that it was Teitri. He wondered, if he sent the old shore-bird whistle down the horse-pasture, whether Teitri would remember anything at all; and knew that he must not put it to the test.

'I've had the care of three God's Horses in my time,' said the horsemaster leaning on the fence-timbers beside him; a red-faced man whose voice grated on the ear, 'but never one the like to that. If he doesn't kill his man before he goes back to Frey, I don't know the look in a horse's eye. He came to us out of the South Saxon Lands.'

'I know,' Owain said, almost under his breath. 'I've seen him before.'

He felt, rather than saw, a shadow beside him, and there was Vadir the Hault, his gaze also going down the long horse-pasture, following the flying shape like a white wind-blown point of flame. So he too, had not forgotten. . . .

Then Vadir looked round. His cold bright eyes met Owain's for an instant, then passed him by, and he said to the horsemaster in that silken voice of his, 'Our friend has not told you it all. It was he who brought the God's Horse into the world and he who gave him the training that is permitted. Before he came to his greatness and his terror, the God's Horse would come to his whistle—like a little dog. Doubtless he has been wondering whether the old whistle would call him yet—if it were not sacrilege to whistle to a God.'

Owain had felt as though something precious and infinitely private to himself had been torn free of its covering and held up naked to a jeering mob. Vadir had meant that he should feel like that. Curse him! He had turned from both men without a word, not trusting himself to speak, and come away.

Still raging and miserable he rounded a street corner, dodged aside to avoid a half-grown pig that ran squealing across his path, and all but blundered into a man going the opposite way. For the moment, as he dodged him again, he saw no more than that he was a small old man and that his hair was grey. 'Your pardon, Old Father,' he said, and would have gone on. But in the next instant a hand gripped his shoulder with unexpected strength and swung him round, and he found himself looking down into one brilliant amber eye that blazed up at him past a great beaked nose. 'It seems that my memory is better than yours,' said the old man, 'for I have not forgotten my British armour-bearer in the Saxon Camp!'

Owain stood looking down at him with an incredulous delight and an odd sense of being rescued, as the face of the stranger changed before his eyes into the face of Einon Hên. He brought up his hand to cover the old man's on his shoulder. 'Einon Hên, by all the winds of heaven! I did not expect to find you in Cantiisburg, and I was thinking of something else.'

'It must have been a thought to hold you very deeply,' said Einon Hên, 'for I've a face not so easy to forget as most men's.'

'I was thinking of a foal I saw born a long time ago,' Owain said. 'Are the Princes of the Cymru already here, then?'

o

'Not yet. Nor is the time yet come for me to seek my own hills again. Since the treaty it is well that our people should have an ambassador among the Saxon kind. Almost three years I have served the Cymru here in this place—and it is good to hear a British voice again.'

'For me also,' Owain said. 'For me also, Einon Hên.' The passers-by were jostling against them, two dogs had started a fight, and a child on a door-sill, bowled over by the pig as it wandered indoors, was howling dismally. He raised his voice above the tumult: 'Is there some quiet place where we might talk? May I come with you?'

The old Envoy looked at him a moment, silent in the uproar of the narrow street. 'There is a quiet place—one quiet place in all Cantiisburg.' His face quickened into a smile. 'I was on my way there now, and I should be most glad that you come with me.'

They went up one street and down another, Einon Hên leading the way and Owain following behind. Close beside the old Governor's Palace, where Aethelbert had made his Hall, they came through a crumbling gateway from the street into a little courtyard full of the dappled shade of a mulberry tree. A door stood open in the far wall, between the broken columns of a small portico, and quiet seemed to lie on the place, as tangible as the shadows of the mulberry leaves.

'What place is this?' Owain asked, glancing about him.

'The Church of Saint Martin. Come.' The old man spoke as though it was so natural, that for the moment the younger one, following him across to the doorway, accepted it as natural too, that there should be a Christian church here in the midst of Jutish Cantiisburg—a Christian church that was not a ruin but still in use; for as they entered, the whisper of incense came to meet them, mingled with the smell of age and of shadows, and at the far end, beneath the glimmer of candles, the figures of three women were kneeling before a priest.

Einon Hên hesitated, as though he had not expected to see them there. 'My Lady prays late, or the day is still younger than I thought,' he murmured. 'Let us wait here.' And going quietly down the two steep steps he turned aside into the shadows just within the door, drawing Owain after him.

Standing aside, with the old man, Owain looked about him.
The church was a very small one, and bare as a little white barn,
save that on one wall someone long ago had painted Saint Martin
giving half his cloak to the Christ-beggar. The colours had faded
into the cracked plaster, but the soft buff pink of the Saint's cloak
that had once been the true warrior scarlet still seemed to glow
with an inner fire. The murmur of prayers in the Latin tongue
reached him in the quiet. It was the first time that he had known a
Christian place of worship since the summer when his world had
fallen to ruins. He remembered all at once the grey stone preaching cross in the hills, and behind all the silence of the service the
deep contented drone of bees in the bell heather; he remembered,
as he had not remembered them for years, Priscus and Priscilla,
who would have shared their cloak with him. . . . Slowly the
sore hot places of his heart grew quiet within him.

A faint movement from the old man beside him recalled him
to the present moment. The priest had gone, and he saw that the
women had risen and were coming towards the door, two of them
dropping back a little into place behind the third. And looking at
the third woman, Owain knew who she was, for he had seen her
last night from his place far down the High King's Hall. Her place
had been as high as his was low, and there had been many women
gathered about her and the gleam of a Queen's gold circlet about
her head. She wore a plain gown now, and her head-rail was held
by a circlet of blue silk. A woman with a face like a horse, but a
very gentle horse.

She was at the foot of the steps when she saw them in the
shadow of the doorway, and checking, she turned to them with a
gesture of her outspread hands. 'Ah, Einon Hên! God's Greeting
to you!' and her voice made Owain forget that she looked like a
horse. It was a beautiful voice, low-pitched and vibrant.

'God's Greeting to *you*, Madam,' said the old man, bending his
head.

'And this? You have brought a friend to us?'

'I have brought a friend. A Briton like myself, and his name is
Owain.'

'Owain,' said the woman, in her low voice. 'If this were my
house, I would make you most joyfully welcome to it, as I would

have made Einon Hên long ago. But it is God's, and so the welcome is surely His.' Her whole face was soft with joy, and suddenly she held out her hands to them, and to the women beside her, as though gathering them all in. 'See, we are a growing company! There are six of us now, with good Bishop Lindhard my chaplain—and soon, so soon now, surely we shall be a multitude!'

And smiling at them like a mother, and gathering up the trailing skirts of her kirtle, she went on up the steps, her women behind her; and they heard the steps of the three across the courtyard, and a door which Owain had not noticed behind the mulberry tree opened and shut.

Alone now in the empty church with the altar candles out, Owain said, 'I did not know that the Queen was a Christian.'

'And has always been free to follow her own faith, here in Aethelbert's Court. That was in the bond, when Aethelbert went asking for a Princess of the Frankish Kingdom, to be his Queen.'

'And what did she mean when she said that soon we should be a multitude? I have seen no sign that the Jutes and Saxons are weary of their own gods.'

But Einon Hên did not answer directly; at least not then. He was still looking after the Queen, very kindly, as a man might look after a child he was fond of. 'Poor simple woman,' he said, and turned and led the way up the little church towards the sanctuary.

After they had made the morning prayer they went out again into the courtyard, and sat on the raised stone curb about the foot of the mulberry tree in companionable silence as though they had been friends all their lives. Presently Owain found that the old man was looking at him questioningly. 'If you did not think to see me here in Cantiisburg,' said Einon Hên, 'assuredly I did not think to see you. Have I miscounted? It has been in my mind all the while that this spring was the time of your freedom.'

'No, you have not miscounted,' Owain said. 'The boy turned fifteen before the blackthorn flowered.'

'So you are free now?' The question within a question was so quietly spoken that Owain could pretend not to have heard it, if he wanted to.

'Not yet,' he said. He sat quite still, looking down at his hard

brown hands lying across his knees; and then he found that he was
telling Einon Hên the whole story, about Lilla and Vadir Cedricson and his promise to Athelis her mother in return for a year's respite. 'I don't know that it was any good. The year is almost up
now—he might have asked again by now, but that he also sailed
with the King. God knows what will happen when he *does* ask,
and—God knows when I shall see my freedom. I have waited for
it so long that sometimes my heart grows sick with waiting; and
when it comes—if it comes—I sometimes wonder if I shall know
what to do with it.' Suddenly he turned to the old man beside
him, and stretched out his hands in an oddly pleading gesture, as
though he were afraid that the other might blame him for turning
so long from his own people. 'But what else could I do?'

Einon Hên was silent for a long while, considering him out of
that one fierce falcon's eye, and his silence seemed to fill the little
courtyard. 'You could have broken your faith with Beornwulf
and taken the freedom that was yours by right,' he said at last.
And then quickly, before Owain could answer, he went on, leaning forward, his arms across his knees: 'Owain, has it ever seemed
to you that a strange thing is happening between the British and
the Saxon kind? It is three generations since Artos died, and the
years between have been lost and dark and very bloody, so that if
one looks backward it is as though one peered through night and
storm, to catch the last brave glimmer of a lantern very far behind. You who were at the last fight by Aquae Sulis saw the last
light go out. Yet I remember how we spoke once, you and I, of
the Truce of the Spear; I believe that there are other kinds of truce,
more binding, and some that may change and grow and
strengthen. . . .' He had been watching the play of the sun spots
through the mulberry leaves, in the dust at his feet; but he turned
his head abruptly, and fixed Owain with a glare. 'Now this
Beornwulf turns to you, a Briton, in his last and sorest need of a
friend, and for four years of your life, and maybe more to come,
you have shouldered the weight of a Saxon household, and you
sit there and ask me, as you asked me once before, "What else
could I do?"—And that, do you know, is a thing that I find more
filled with promise than any treaty between Aethelbert and the
Princes of the Cymru. Almost it is as though, looking forward

this time, one might perhaps make out another gleam of light— very far ahead.'

Owain looked at him, frowning a little and scratching at the old scar, questing after his exact meaning and waiting for what he would say next. But the silence lengthened and the old man had returned to watching the sun spots in the dust; and there was nothing more after all, that could be put into words. Owain went back to the still unanswered question that he had asked earlier. 'What *did* she mean—the Queen—when she said that now there were six of us and soon we should be a multitude?' For she had meant something; it had been no mere pious hope.

Einon Hên advanced one foot and with great care and exactitude trod on a sun spot as though he expected it to remain underfoot like a yellow leaf. 'I have no idea,' he said.

And with that, Owain knew that for the present at all events, he must be content.

The days went by and the gathering was complete, and the Council met in Aethelbert's great Mead Hall, while the young men, left to their own devices, wrestled together and borrowed horses to race against each other, and got bored. One day the Council met, two, three, the talking and arguing dragging on around the table at whose head sat the tall stooping man with eyes that one could not see into, who was Aethelbert of Kent. But little seemed to be accomplished, and Owain, standing behind Haegel's seat, his gaze moving from Coel of Wessex to Redwald of the East Angles, to the Princes of Gwent and Powys, to Einon Hên in his place beside the High King, had a strong feeling that all these vague questions of laws and frontiers were no more than an excuse to gather the Rulers together for some other purpose. He wondered what it could be. Not war: a handful of Kings each with his bodyguard behind him did not make a war-host.

At evening, when the business of the day was over, Aethelbert's Mead Hall returned to its proper use, and the Kings and the Elders feasted on the long benches, while the young warriors gathered about the great fire in the forecourt, making merry on their own account, drinking deep, and tussling with each other like puppies, or thronging the foreporch doorway to listen to the songs and sagas of the harper sitting at Aethelbert's feet.

On the third evening—Owain never forgot it—it turned wet at twilight, and they had crowded up into the lower end of the Hall, packing the beggars' bench and squatting with the hounds about the lowest of three long fires. The smell of the wet earth breathed in at the doorway to mingle with the tang of wood smoke and the smells of men and hounds and mead. Ingwy, Aethelbert's harper, had taken up his harp when they called for it, and plunged into the great Saga of Beowa the Sun-Hero, and how he slew the Winter-Fiend; and the Hall that had been loud with voices and laughter had grown hushed to listen, for it was the best beloved of all the sagas that Hengest's folk had brought with them across the North Seas. Only from time to time as the excitement and the splendour mounted, the warriors joined in, thumping fists and ale horns on their knees in time to the leaping rhythm that Ingwy beat out upon his harp as a swordsmith beats a bright blade on his anvil.

Even Owain, whose ear was not tuned to the Saxon way of music and story-telling, felt his heart quicken and the hair lift on the back of his neck as the crisis of the saga drew near and the Winter-Fiend came padding closer through the dark.

Ingwy swept a discordant crash of notes from his harp, to herald the Monster's arrival—and in the same instant, as though the ancient story had called it up, there loomed into the open doorway of Aethelbert's Mead Hall, a huge shapeless Thing.

The hounds sprang up baying, and a long gasp ran up the Hall, men's hands leaping to their weapons. The harper fell silent between word and word, and for a long moment a hush that prickled in one's marrow held the Great Hall.

Then the Thing in the doorway strode forward into the light of the fires and torches, and a gale of laughter roared up to the rafters as the men on the crowded benches saw in their midst no fiend from the Twilight World, but only a big man in a wolfskin cloak with a hood that he had pulled well forward against the wet.

Other men loomed behind him in the dark of the foreporch. He strode on up the Hall, drops from his wet cloak spitting in the fires as he came, the hounds sniffing about his heels. He kneeled at the High King's feet, stiffly, as a man who has been long in the saddle. And Aethelbert leaned forward in his great raised seat, his hands on the snarling dragon-heads of the front posts, and looked down at him with those curiously veiled eyes. 'Edwulf the Coast Warden—you bring me news of some sort by your seeming. What is it, then?'

The Coast Warden was a bull-necked man with a bull voice, and his answer boomed clear to the far ends of the Hall. 'Aethelbert the King, I bring news that a party of holy men, Christians out of the Frank-lands, have come to shore at Ebbesfleet. They were but two score of them, unarmed and seemingly no harm in them, so we let them come to land. Their leader sends you greeting in the name of their God and of their Holy Father in Romeburg, and begs your leave that they may come before you.'

'So.' Aethelbert bent his head, but Owain, watching, had a feeling that he had known what the man would say. 'And this leader, what like is he? And by what name is he called?'

'A tall proud man with cold eyes,' said the Coast Warden. 'I should judge him strong in his own esteem. His name is Augustine.'

21

Dawn Wind

EARLIER that morning there had been mist across the marshes, but it had blown away now, and the levels lay clear and pale under a high drifting sky. And the crumbling rampart walls of the old coastal fortress stood up, staunch and menacing even now, against the winding waterways that cut Tanatus Island from the mainland.

Owain stood with Bryni among the half-moon of warriors about the great chair of carved black oak in which the High King sat, enthroned amid the emptiness of the marshes as though he were in the High Seat in his own Hall. They had had to get the chair there on mule-back, and it had given the men in charge of it more trouble than almost all the rest of the Camp together. But since Aethelbert had chosen to hold his first meeting with the holy men here, close to where they had landed, before allowing them any further into his kingdom, and had determined that the meeting must be out of doors where it would be harder for them to work any enchantment on him, there had been no help for it.

Only one thing had given more trouble on the road from Cantiisburg, and that was Frey's Horse, which Aethelbert had also
determined to bring to the meeting place, that he might have the
strength of his Gods with him in case of need. Owain could hear
him now, neighing and trampling in a burst of fury at his picket
ropes; he had not been near the white stallion again since the
morning at the horse farm, but he knew Teitri's voice among all
the other horses of the Camp.

He looked away past the waiting figure of the High King
to the harsh grey mass of the fortress. Rutupiae, his own people
had called it; it had no name now, it was just the Romans'
Burg. How much it had seen, the old fortress: the first invading
waves of the Sea Wolves, the last Roman troops in Britain; and
now . . .?

The faint sound of chanting reached his ears, carried on the
light sea wind; and there was an answering stir among the waiting
Saxons. Beyond the old land-gate, something was moving and he
saw the blink of polished metal. And slowly, winding into view
through the gates of the ruined fortress where they had lodged
while they waited for the King, came a long line of figures, pied
black and white like plover. At their head walked a man carrying
a tall silver cross, and behind him another, bearing aloft a picture or
a standard of some kind, on which even at that distance the colours
shone like jewels and behind again, leading all the rest, walked a
very tall man who carried himself like an Emperor. 'A tall proud
man with cold eyes and strong in his own esteem,' the Coast
Warden had said; and even if he had taken last place in the line of
monks, Owain would have known that he was Augustine, the
leader.

The chanting swelled louder as the company wound out over
the bridge and causeway, and drew slowly nearer along the paved
road. Words began to take shape out of the rise and fall of the
chanting; the stately words of the Litany: 'Kyrie eleison,' Owain
heard, 'Kyrie eleison. . . .'

He saw Aethelbert beckon to Bishop Lindhard, the Queen's
chaplain, who stood beside him in golden alb and white and green
dalmatica, and ask a question. He saw the Bishop shake his head,
making some low-voiced answer, and knew as clearly as though

he had heard the exchange, that the King had asked, 'This singing —is it a spell?'

Standing there among the Saxon warriors, Owain had all at once a strange sensation, a kind of weeping in his breast. His faith had meant a lot to him when he was a boy; it had been bound up with the Britain that had stood sword in hand against the inflowing Barbarian hordes; but later, it had worn thin, even as his memory of Regina had worn thin. The only time he had prayed with power since he came to manhood, had been to Silvanus, on the day he buried Dog. But now it seemed to him that a glorious and a shining thing was happening; he had a feeling of great wonder, and the shadows of the clouds over the marsh were the shadows of vast wings.

The foremost of the band of monks, he who carried the cross, had reached the place where Aethelbert of Kent sat with his Kings and councillors about him, astride the road into Britain. The chanting had fallen silent. The cross-bearer moved to the left, he with the great many-coloured banner of Christ in Glory moved to the right, and the tall man came between them with hand upraised in blessing, and walked to the footstool of Aethelbert's chair, without waiting for Bishop Lindhard who had stepped forward to bring him to the King.

For a long moment nothing moved save that the silken standard with its gold-wrought figure rippled in the light sea wind. The two men looked at each other, eye into eye; and Augustine did not kneel. Then Aethelbert rose to give the other man the courtesy of a host to the guest within his gates.

But somehow, as he watched the scene that followed, Owain's winged moment slipped away from him, and the shadows drifting across the levels were only cloud shadows again.

Augustine had begun to speak in clear measured Latin, Bishop Lindhard translating for him as he went along. His voice was hard and strong as a sword-blade, but not so flexible. The monks had gathered in a great curve behind him, just as the warriors stood behind the Kentish King, and the King's white boarhounds sniffed distrustfully at the hem of Augustine's habit as he spoke.

'The Greeting of God be to you, and the Peace of God be upon you, Aethelbert the King. We are come to you from our Holy

Father in Rome, from the blessed Gregory himself, to bring you his word and his greeting under God. . . .' It was a friendly speech and a long one. Owain had enough Latin left to understand most of it, without Bishop Lindhard's stumbling translation. Now he was telling them how, years before, when the Holy Father was only a simple monk, he had seen in the slave market in Rome, some Anglian boys who had been carried off by pirates, and hearing that they came from a people who did not know the Lord God nor His Son, had held it in his heart ever since to bring them into the Fold of the Faith.

It was a touching story, but somehow it failed to touch Owain.

'We are Jutes, along this coast,' said Aethelbert, fingering his beard, and Bishop Lindhard translated for him as he had translated for the stranger monk.

Augustine made a small inclination of the head. 'Yet Jutes and Angles and Saxons, you have all the same need of the joy we have to bring. We come to you and not to the Angles, on the threshold of this great venture, for the sake of the Lady Bertha, your Queen, knowing that she is of our faith and has been free to follow her own ways of worship, here at your Court. Because of that, it has seemed to us, and to the Holy Father who sent us forth, that this is the place ordained for our coming at the outset.'

Aethelbert listened, still fingering his beard, and Owain knew how his eyes would be narrowed on the stranger's face. 'There is truth in what you say,' he agreed, when Bishop Lindhard had translated again. 'And for another reason, it may be that you have chosen wisely. Five Kings stand here with me today, five Kings and the Princes of the Welsh in the far west.' (He used the Saxon term, and Bishop Lindhard stumbled over it, for there was no Latin equivalent, until Einon Hên moved out from the group about the High King's chair and gave the British 'The Princes of the Cymru, the Land of Brothers'.) 'Five Kings, and the Princes of the Welsh in the far west,' said Aethelbert of Kent, 'and there is no Lord of the Angles nor yet of the Saxon kind who could make such a boast.'

Augustine bent his head again, and it seemed to Owain that there was a hint of irony in the way he did so. 'Great and powerful is the royal line of the Oiscings. That also, we knew in Rome, Aethelbert the High King.'

'And it seemed to this Holy Father of yours that a strong King with a Queen already of your faith might spread the shield of his protection over you; might stretch out his arm to help this work that you have at heart?' Aethelbert's voice suddenly became sharp as the bark of a fox on a frosty night. 'Well, Holy Man, what would you have of me?'

'No more than your goodwill at first,' Augustine said. 'Grant us leave to enter your kingdom, and give us a small plot of ground where we may raise a church and welcome those who come to join us in the Faith of Christ.'

Somewhere close behind Owain, a man growled behind his shield rim to his neighbour: 'Are we to leave our own Gods, then, who were good enough for our fathers, and who led us to victory, and go running cap in hand to this God that the British worshipped, who stood by and let them go down into defeat? And all because a shaven-headed priest says so?'

And his friend replied with a smothered laugh, 'There's no accounting for the strange ideas that folk will get. My grandsire thought for fifteen years that he was an ash tree and could not sit down.'

Augustine heard the laugh, and his proud gaze, frowning a little, flicked towards the place from which it had come. For the first time he included the men behind the King in what he had to say, and Owain felt as he had not done until that moment the strange monk's power and his magnetism. 'There will be many who laugh at first, but we are come, my brethren and I, to relight the candle of the love of Christ in this land of Britain where it has so utterly perished into the dark; and though we seek to make but a small beginning, remember that a spark falling on tinder is a small beginning, yet it serves to kindle a fire that may light and warm a king's Hall!'

'The candle of the love of Christ, in the land of Britain where it has so utterly perished into the dark.' Among those who stood about the High King, the Princes of Gwent and Powys glanced at each other. Owain remembered again the grey finger of the preaching cross and the little priest whose soul had seemed to be on fire, and Priscilla in her valiant Sunday necklace of blue beads; and he thought, 'This is a great man, and he loves God, but he is without understanding and without humility.' And in proportion to the joy of the shining moment he had known so short a time before, he was suddenly wretched.

Augustine was still speaking of the Faith and the Master he served, while the Jutes and Saxons muttered among themselves. But Owain was no longer listening with a whole heart; something had smudged the radiance, and there was growing on him the certainty that there was more to all this than showed on the surface.

But the stranger monk had done now, and Aethelbert was speaking. 'I have listened to you, and heard what you have to tell, and what you have to ask. As to what you have to tell, I understand little of it. I do not understand your three Gods in one, nor do I see how this God of yours is better than our Woden and Thor of the Hammer, and Frey who brings our beasts to birth and our corn to harvest. But as to what you ask: for the sake of the Lady Bertha my Queen, who will grieve and doubtless make my life a burden if I send you away, you may come to Cantiisburg and build your church there, and welcome whatever men are fools enough to come to you, into the faith of this White Christ of yours. And I will hold back my priests from killing you, if that may be.'

Augustine seemed to grow taller yet, as the King's words were translated; he flung back his head, and his hands went upward in a gesture that seemed at once triumph and supplication; and for a moment there was a light on his face that was not the cool daylight of the marshes. He cried out in a great voice, 'Thanks be to the Lord our God!' And behind him, the monks raised the paean that the soldier-bishop Germanus had raised for a war-cry against the Sea-Wolves of this very coast two hundred years before: 'Alleluia! Alleluia!'

Later, the cooking pits were opened and the carcasses of baked sheep and oxen dragged out, and Aethelbert of Kent feasted with his guests while the shadows of the ridge-tents and branch-woven cabins stretched out long and cool across the grass.

But Owain, who was in no mood for feasting, grew weary before the mead had gone round more than once. He threw the mutton-bone he had been chewing to the nearest dog, and getting up from his place beside one of the fires, turned away towards the dunes and the grey ramparts of the old fortress. Bryni, digging hot marrow out of an ox-bone with the point of his dagger, grinned up at him as he passed, and watched him go, but nobody called after him; he was always something of a lone wolf.

Behind him he heard the voices and the music of the harp falling further across the levels until it was no more than a dim wash of sound in his ears. He crossed the causeway, skirted the whale-backed hump of Rutupiae Island, and dropped down through the soft sand towards what had once been the harbour. There was nothing there now but an odd snout of rotten timber thrust here and there above the drifted sand to tell where busy wharves and slipways had been, and a long curb of worked stone below the watergate that must have formed the edge of the main jetty; and the water that had once been deep enough to take the war-galleys and the great troop-transports of the Empire had sunk away, shallow even now at high tide, as the harbour mouth silted up before the encroaching sand.

And there, below the crest of a long curved dune, he found Einon Hên sitting solitary, his great beaked nose towards the sea. He hesitated, ready to turn away without a word, but the old man looked round with a hint of a smile in his one golden eye, and the young one sat down beside him, knowing himself welcome.

'I have been all day and for so many days past striving to make myself a bridge between two worlds. But the Saxons will never understand the ways of our people, and nor now will Rome, and I am very weary,' said Einon Hên, after a companionable silence.

'I thought it was in your mind that Saxon and Briton drew closer to each other,' Owain said dully, looking out over the wet sand.

'Closer yes, but always there will be a gulf and it is still a wide one.'

Another, longer silence followed. At last Owain said, 'This that has happened today—it was what the Queen meant, when she said that soon we should be a multitude?'

The old man looked round at him quickly. 'It is the beginning of what she meant.'

'And Aethelbert knew?—Perhaps he sent for these men himself?'

'You think that?'

'Don't you?'

'I—think so, yes,' said Einon Hên, very quietly.

'Einion Hên, what lies behind this that we have seen today?'

The Envoy had begun to draw careful patterns in the slope of the dune with a bony forefinger, but the loose sand ran into the traced lines and filled them up. 'I do not know,' he said at last, 'but this is how I read the signs: I think that the thing has grown two-fold like the sides of an arch, and that what we saw today was the keystone where the two sides come together. . . . Long ago, before even Artos's time, Rome came crumbling down, and when it rose again from the ashes, all was changed. The power of the Legions was gone for ever, and in its place was another kind of power, the power of our Christian faith. All the provinces of the Western Empire were lost, but they might be won back still—into another kind of Empire; only now the work must be done by the Church, and not the Legions. So much for the first side. For the other—think back four years, to Wodensbeorg. Aethelbert of Kent has cleared his enemy from his path, he is Overlord of all the southern half of Britain, save for that which lies beyond Sabrina, and he is already linked through his Queen with the Frankish Kingdom, the great Christian Kingdom of Clovis. He is a wise man, and he comes to see that for such a ruler as he is, there is much to be gained by becoming one of this new Empire of the Christian faith. So—perhaps—he sends word to Rome, saying, "Come, and I will be converted to your faith, and bring my people with me." And Rome sends back word, "Gladly we will come." ' He drew two sweeping lines in the sand, and stabbed the bony finger with meticulous care into the exact place where they met. 'The arch is complete, and what men may build upon it, God knows.'

Owain was watching a yellow horned poppy close to his foot as it swayed in the light sea wind. 'And so, knowing the appointed time of this coming, Aethelbert gathers his lesser Kings under

pretence of a frontier council, that he may make a worthy showing of his power before these emissaries of Rome. I never quite
believed in that Council.'

'No?'

'No. But if it is as you say——' Owain spoke slowly, thinking
the thing out as he went. 'If it is as you say, why did he greet them
so grudgingly? Why not fall into an ecstasy and be converted on
the spot?'

'Because he is not a fool. He cannot be sure how his kings and
chieftains will receive the faith of Christ, and he cannot afford to
receive it while they hold without weakening to Frey and
Woden. He must give the thing time to work, he must feel his
way. He is a patient man; he waited more than twenty years to be
revenged for Wibbendune. When he can be reasonably sure that
it is safe, maybe in a year's time, maybe more, he will listen to the
Queen's pleading and suffer a change of heart, and come to this
Augustine, seeking baptism.'

The silence that fell between them was the longest yet. So long
that the evening light across the marshes was beginning to fade
when Einon Hên cocked his one bright eye at his companion, and
said, 'My friend, you look as though the taste of sloes was in your
mouth.'

Owain laughed ruefully. 'The taste of one's own foolishness is
just as sour. I thought this morning, just for a wing-beat of time,
that—that something wonderful was happening. And all the
while it was no more than a piece of statecraft being played out.'

Einon Hên said very quietly, 'But even a piece of statecraft
might hold your "something wonderful" at its heart.'

And Owain looked at him quickly, remembering that this was
a man who knew the feel and balance of statecraft as doubtless he
had known the feel and balance of a sword when he was young.

'We spoke together a few days since—you remember?—of
looking back through the storm and darkness of these years, to see
the last gleam of a lantern far behind; and I said something to you
then, I think, of the hope of other light as far ahead. For the space of
two men's lives at least, we have stood alone, we in Britain, cut
off from all that Rome once stood for, from all that we thought
worth dying for. And today we have joined hands with those

P

days of the Long Wandering, before the Saxon-kind became the things again—a light clasp as yet, and easily broken, but surely it will strengthen, both by the ways of statecraft, and with every man and woman who comes—as they will come, though the time for the Queen's multitude is not for a long while yet—to Augustine and the Christian Church.' He abandoned the patterns he had been drawing in the sand, and sat for a few moments completely still, his head up and the breeze off the sea lifting the grey hair at his temples. 'Not the dawn as yet, Owain, but I think the dawn wind stirring.'

22

Frey's Horse

I T was dusk when Owain came again over the lip of the dunes, and
a faint mist had begun to smoke up from the ground. He saw the
red flare of the camp-fires across the marsh, and the sound of
voices and harp music came to meet him; but still, as he checked
among the furze bushes, he could hear the soft long-drawn hushing of the tide beyond the dunes.

'Not the dawn yet, but I think the dawn wind stirring.' The
old Envoy's voice was lingering in his ears, as Uncle Widreth's
had lingered there. He thought suddenly that they would have
liked each other, those two old men, if their ways had crossed.
'Not the dawn yet, but the dawn wind stirring,' and again, 'Even
a piece of statecraft might hold your "something wonderful" at
its heart' . . . The wry unhappy mood of the past few hours had
fallen from him, and he felt quiet, as one feels after relief from

pain; something else too: deep within him, almost below the level of his being aware of it, was a sense of change, like the change in the wind at winter's end. Ever since the last stand, by Aquae Sulis, he had felt himself at the end of something. Now, standing among the dune furze bushes in the dusk, he knew all at once, that he was at a beginning.

Scarcely aware of moving forward again, he walked on towards the camp-fires.

The royal fire burned before Aethelbert's great ridge-tent in the midst of the camp, and there the High King sat in his chair, his white boarhounds at his feet and his kings and councillors and the black-robed holy men about him; while Ingwy his harper knelt beside the flames, chanting to his harp the high and far-off deeds of Scyld the Father of his People when the world was young.

At the lower fires where the young warriors gathered, they were making their own more uproarious amusement. They also had a harp, belonging to one of their number, and were passing it from hand to hand as they passed the mead jars, beating out the rhythm of their thoughts as they asked each other the long elaborate riddles beloved of the Saxon folk.

A tow-headed young man with a strong merry voice had the harp when Owain came up, and was ranting out his riddle to a circle of laughing listeners.

> *White of throat am I, fallow grey my head;*
> *Fallow are my flanks, and my feet are swift;*
> *Battle weapons bear I! Bristles on my back*
> *Like a boar's stand up. With my pointed toes*
> *Through the green grass step I——*

'A badger!' somebody shouted. 'It's a badger!'

'A badger's head isn't fallow, it's striped,' someone else objected, 'striped black and white like the holy men at the King's fire yonder.'

'I say it's a badger for all that—isn't it, Osric?'

'You're too sharp, you are,' said Osric, grinning. 'I wonder you don't cut yourself!'

And Bryni, who had been sitting beside him, staring idly

across the fire at a couple of dark-haired Britons of Gerontius's
bodyguard, sprang up, putting out his hand for the harp in his
turn. 'I've made a cunning one—listen!' His eyes were very bright,
and his voice was thick and a good deal louder than usual.

> *Swifter than swallows, darting through blue air,*
> *Winged I am, mightily, but no bird am I.*
> *Battle-sark I wear, many-scaled, shining,*
> *But no fish spawned me, in green depths under foam.*
> *Flame is my breathing——*

Vadir Cedricson yawned and did not trouble to hide it. 'If you
sing in honour of our western strangers, remember to make your
dragon red.'

Bryni broke off between one word and the next, and glowered
towards him. 'You said, Vadir Cedricson?'

The other smiled. 'I said if you sing in honour of the western
strangers, remember to make your dragon red.'

'Are you sure that I was not going to?'

Vadir raised pale brows. 'My grandsire never did, so far as I remember. He used to ask that riddle after supper, at least twenty
times a year.'

'That's a lie, for I made it up myself, since supper!'

'Maybe if you had made it up before supper, you would have
remembered where it came from.'

'I'm drunk, am I?' Bryni said furiously, and flung the harp
aside so that it fell with a jangle of jarred strings. 'So then—I'll be
drunk as a hero by moonrise, if I choose, but *you* shan't tell me
of it!'

'No?' said Vadir, in a voice as smooth as silk.

'*No!*' shouted Bryni.

The thing had flared up before Owain was well aware of it.
Now he cut in. 'Don't be a fool, Bryni, you *are* drunk, and so is
he. Let it go.' But the boy did not seem even to hear him; the
blood was burning scarlet along his cheekbones, and his eyes
were stormy. 'No one tells Bryni Beornwulfson when he's
drunk, not even his nearest kin; and thanks be to all the Gods in
high Valhalla, you are no kinsman of mine, Vadir.'

Vadir got slowly to his feet; he could move quickly enough

when he chose, despite his lame foot, but at the moment he did not choose. Slowness could be more maddening. He was as drunk as Bryni, but he showed it less, and he could always goad the boy to madness.

Yet now, maybe for the first time in his life, he said a thing which Owain, watching him, was fairly sure that he had not meant to say. 'Not yet,' said Vadir Cedricson.

While the words still hung on the air in the hush that had fallen about the fire, his pale eyes flickered, as though he would have called them back if he could. But the pride which had made him hide from his world the fact that he could want any girl badly enough to wait a year for her, forbade him to deny the thing now that it was said.

In the silence, Bryni took a long menacing step towards him. 'And what is it that you mean by that?'

Smoothly, deliberately, Vadir told him.

'That's another lie!' Bryni said, when he had finished.

'No, just something that maybe the women did not trust you to know.'

'It will be a long time before Lilla comes to your hearth, Vadir.'

'Ah, I hope not. Your mother thought her too young last year, but by the time for the autumn slaughtering——'

Until then it had been no more than a wordy quarrel. Now, quite suddenly it became deadly. Bryni turned from hot to cold. He said, through shut teeth, 'Slaughter month is a good choice, Vadir. But men can die as well as cattle. Do you think I'd let you have Lilla, you crooked little man?'

The hush about the fire became a tingling stillness, and in the stillness Owain saw a devil looking out of Vadir's eyes. He made no sound, but he moved with the swiftness of a striking adder, and something flashed in the firelight, in his hand that had been empty the instant before. Bryni's knife was out in the same instant, and they sprang together. Blade rang on blade and the sparks flew up. Then Owain had leapt in from behind and caught the boy's knife-wrist and dragged it down, while other men fell on Vadir, and between them they dragged the two apart.

'Drop it!' he panted. 'Drop it, Bryni! Remember where you are!'

For to draw weapon at such a gathering was one of the things for which there was no forgiveness.

It was all over. Bryni stood panting, with the blood dripping from a shallow gash in his upper arm. Vadir stood still and unresisting in the grip of a man on either side of him; he breathed through nostrils that flared and trembled like those of a stallion, and his eyes glittered between half-shut lids; but he had control of himself again. He said quite quietly, the words falling small and deadly chill, 'I will have your heart's blood for that.'

'But not here, and not now,' put in a huge man of Aethelbert's following, whose very size seemed to give his word some weight among the rest. 'The High King's feast-fire is no place for the settling of blood debts.'

Owain flashed him a quick look of gratitude. But voices were rising from the men about the fire, the hush was passing from them and the mead in their veins leaping up again. They were in a mood for anything that offered excitement, and they came crowding in on the two who stood hackles up in their midst. Then one of the Britons struck in, stumbling a little over the Saxon tongue. 'In my tribe, when a quarrel rises at a time or a place such as this, where it is forbidden to draw blade, we have a way of settling the matter, all the same.'

Instantly a dozen voices together were demanding more. 'And what way is that? Tell us, then——' while both Vadir and Bryni, breaking their narrowed gaze from each other's faces, turned towards him.

'The two whose quarrel it is, draw lots,' said the Briton, 'and he who draws the shorter corn-stalk is accounted clear, but he who draws the longer corn-stalk must put his own life to some chosen hazard before the next sunrise, or be called coward henceforth by the men who were his brothers.' He looked about him at the faces in the leaping firelight. 'It is an old custom, and it is a good one. When the thing is ended, it is ended. There is no place left for a blood feud.'

Owain felt suddenly a little sick, but the others were crowding round, eager as young hounds on a scent, and Bryni, his eyes suddenly at their most blazing green, cried out, 'Well, what is there to wait for? We've no corn-stalks to hand, but grass-stems will serve just as well.'

'Here, then.' Osric, who had asked the badger riddle, stooped without more ado and plucked up half a dozen stems from the trampled grass beside the fire. He handed the grass-stems over to the dark Briton, who arranged them with care in his closed fist, the heads sticking out between his thumb and forefinger, and held them forward into the firelight.

'Now, draw.'

Bryni drew first, scarce looking what he did, and held up a grass-stem that ended about three finger-breadths below the feathery brown head. Then Vadir took a limping pace forward and chose his stem with deliberate care; and held it up also. Owain saw with sharp relief that it was almost twice as long as Bryni's. 'It's Vadir!' the shout went up. 'Vadir has it!' Bryni gave a cry of disgust, and tossed his grass-stem to the breeze which carried it to the fire's heart; and Vadir stood looking about him with an odd smile on his thin lips, holding his grass-stem as though it were a flower.

At that moment, above the quick rise and fall of voices, they heard again the angry neigh of the God's Horse.

Vadir flung up his head and laughed, wildly and recklessly. 'So. To me falls the hazard, and most welcomely; but I'll choose my own. Brothers, I'll ride you Frey's Horse, that has never known mortal man on his back before.'

For the second time that evening, and more deeply than before, a hush fell on the warriors about the fire. Even Bryni was silent. And looking at Vadir standing there, a little sideways as he always stood, his eyes bright and the lees of the wild laughter making thin lines about his mouth, Owain, who hated him, paid tribute within himself to the man's insane courage. For this was a terrible thing that he was taking to himself; it was not alone to pit his magnificent horsemanship against a virtually wild stallion, but to pit himself against his Gods, if he believed in any Gods at all. If he had not been drunk, surely not even Vadir would have claimed that particular hazard.

'So be it,' said Aethelbert's man, while the dark Briton opened his hand and let the grass-stems drift into the flames.

'And your blood be not on the hands of any here, but on your own head.'

And the hush was lost in a roar of voices. Men were pulling brands from the fire to serve as torches; with Vadir borne in their midst and the firebrands whirled aloft they began to stream off towards the hind part of the camp.

Frey's Horse was tethered by a strong flaxen halter to an ancient thorn tree such as grew here and there on the higher ground of the marsh. He was standing alert, his head turned towards their coming as though he waited for them. He stamped and snorted at the torches, tossing his head so that his mane flew up like the crest of a breaking wave; but he was not afraid. He had never, save once, been afraid of anything in all his proud life, and Owain, remembering the tottering grey foal that he had brought into the world, was pierced by his beauty as by a sword.

His ears were pricked forward in curiosity, his eyes bright in the torch-flare that was staining his whiteness with gold as the young warriors crowded closer; and again, pawing the ground with one round hoof, he flung up his head and neighed defiance at them.

Vadir said, 'Get back, you fools, unless you want your brains dashed out. Somebody get me a lick of salt.'

One of the men ran back towards the cooking-fires, and returned with a palmful of greyish salt. Vadir held out his hand for it, and then without a glance at the men around him, he limped forward alone.

'A whip,' somebody said quietly, out of the dark between the torches—it was odd how quiet they had all become. 'You'll need a whip.'

'The pommel of my dagger will serve as well, if I have a hand to spare,' Vadir said, still without looking round. He halted at arm's length from the stallion who watched him as though with scornful interest, and held out the salt on his palm. Frey's Horse advanced his head, snuffed at the man's hand, and dropped his muzzle into the salt. Men had brought him licks of salt before, and he knew the sound of their voices in his ears, and even perhaps remembered dimly a time when he had not been so terrible, and men had dared to draw their hands down his nose as this man was doing now.

'Don't do it, Vadir,' somebody cried out sharply. 'You haven't a chance!'

But if Vadir heard him, he paid no heed.

He was moving slowly, quietly, round to the horse's side, and there was a strangeness on him, a kind of exultation, the look of a man face to face with something that he has been waiting for all his life. 'Two of you come here and hold him,' he ordered coolly, 'and be ready to cut the halter when I say.'

After a moment's hesitation first a Saxon and then a Briton ran out to him and caught the white stallion by mane and halter rope, and even as he began to snort and rear, Vadir made a perfect steed-leap. He seemed to barely touch the quivering white shoulders with his hands, and next instant he was astride his mount. 'Now!' It was like a shout of triumph.

A blade flashed in the torchlight, once, twice, and the halter leapt apart. The two men sprang back and ran for their lives as Frey's Horse reared free.

This had never happened to him before, this Thing, this Terror on his back. Fear was on him as it had never been before even in the winter of his breaking, but more than fear was fury. Screaming with rage he reared up and up until it seemed to the men watching that the stars in the green summer sky were no more than the sparks struck from his lashing hooves; then he plunged earthward, whirling and bucking, mane and tail flying in a white spume as he sought to fling off and break and pound into nothingness the thing that clung to his back as though it were a part of himself.

Vadir clung as though indeed he were part of Frey's Horse; with clenched knees, and hands twisted into the roots of the flying mane. The watching men would have been roaring him on to victory, but a kind of awe held them, and the wild excitement swept through them silently like a soundless wind. Frey's Horse was rearing and plunging, the ground shivered under his hooves and his screams of fury seemed to tear the night in two. And all the while the whirling moon-storm of battling horse and man remained in one place. More than once the God's Horse would have broken out of the torchlit circle and gone thundering into the night, but the ruthless hands on his mane and head-gear wrenched his head further and further round and up, until he could only swing in a circle, far back on his haunches.

Afterwards, Owain wondered why Vadir did not let him go, trusting to his own horsemanship to be able to hang on until the horse had run himself to a standstill and exhaustion gave him the mastery. Maybe it was because he was determined that he and not his mount should choose the moment. If so, he delayed too long. Suddenly, so suddenly that for the first time it seemed that Vadir was not prepared for him, the stallion whirled about and plunged towards the thorn tree.

The low-hanging branches seemed to swoop to meet him. Owain heard the brute's terrible scream of triumph, and a sharp human cry cut off hideously short; and Frey's Horse plunged on riderless, then, trampling and shrieking, swung back to come at something that lay still on the ground.

Conscious of a vague surprise at himself, Owain found that he was running, flinging himself forward to come between Vadir and the trampling hooves. He heard a roar of voices all about him, men were closing in with flaring torches, and in their midst, he had sprung for the short end of the severed halter, and hung on. If he lost his hold and went down under the murderous hooves, he would be not only trampled on but savaged into wet red rags. He knew that, and he knew that swung and shaken like this, he could not hang on long. His one hope was that, even now, through the killer rage in the great savage heart, he might be able to reach Frey's Horse and make him remember, and with the last breath almost gone from him, putting out the whole strength both of his body and the love that he had felt for the long-legged colt, he cried his foal-name over and over again. 'Teitri! Teitri!'

He saw the wild white head upreared above him, fiendish against the darkness, and then Bryni was beside him with, of all mad weapons, a bundled-up cloak in his arms, and as the great head came down with flaming eyes and bared teeth towards Owain's straining shoulder, he thrust the bundle into the horse's open jaws.

The folds clogging his teeth and half choking him seemed to give him a moment's pause, and break, as it were, the bright circle of his rage.

Screaming again, he went up in a rearing half turn, swinging dizzily on his hind legs; he shook his head, savaging at the thick folds and flinging them aside. But the fire of his panic fury seemed sinking, and all at once it was as though the familiar voice crying his foal-name pierced through to him. Slowly the great lashing forefeet came down, and Frey's Horse gave one last convulsive plunge, and stood still.

He was trembling from crest to tail, his milky hide black with sweat, the whites of his eyes wild in the fierce light of the fire-brands, and his breath snorting through nostrils that seemed as though they brimmed with blood. But the ears that had been laid viciously back were swivelling forward to catch the tones of a dim-remembered voice.

'Teitri! Back then! Sa sa, get back, my bold heart!' Owain was sobbing for breath, talking to the trembling stallion pantingly, in the British tongue, as he had talked to him when he was a foal. 'Softly, softly now, get back—back I say!' And all the while, with his hand on the arched nose, he was urging him away from the man who lay so still under the low-hanging thorn branches.

Suddenly, like a child that is very tired, the God's Horse ducked his head and muzzled against Owain's heaving breast.

After that the thing was quickly over. Someone had brought one of the God's Horse's mares to lead him away, and Owain watched him go, then turned back to join the knot of men round Vadir Cedricson. He was quite dead; from the look of him his neck had been broken by the branches, and he must have been dead before he hit the ground. Bryni was there also, no longer drunk as a hero, but stone cold sober, as he knelt beside Vadir's body. 'I always said I'd kill him, didn't I, and I suppose in a way I have,' he said, looking up at Owain with a face nearly as white as the dead man's.

'It was Frey that killed him,' another man said, and there was a mutter of agreement.

But Owain did not hear him. 'You and I, as surely as Teitri; but himself most of all.'

He was aware suddenly of a voice that asked questions in a tone like a fox's bark, and other voices that answered the questions. But it all seemed far off and meaningless, outside some barrier, and for the moment, even Bryni shut out, he was alone with the broken body of his enemy. He saw with a piercing vividness the white dead face, he heard the sea wind in the thorn branches and smelled the saltness in it, and the sweetness of bruised marsh grasses.

He had hated Vadir Cedricson, and now the man was dead, and because he was dead, Owain himself was free. But in those first moments he remembered the bond of the shared task that had been between them on the night that the silver foal was born.

A hand came down on his shoulder, and someone was bending over him. 'Come—up with you. It is the High King.' He stumbled to his feet and turned about. There within arm's length stood Aethelbert of Kent, a knot of his hearth-companions behind him, and at his side, tall and austere, the stranger monk, Augustine.

Aethelbert spoke no word, and nothing moved about him but his beard stirring in the wind. And looking into the veiled eyes Owain felt the anger in him, for though it might be in his mind to abandon the faith of his forefathers for a faith that could be more use to him, he had not quite abandoned it yet, or he would not have felt the need to bring Frey's Horse with him to this meeting. But at the same time he saw that the King would not deal with the affront to the God, as doubtless he would have liked to do, because of his wish to stand well with the Emissaries of Rome, whose God was one day to drive out Woden and Thor and Frey of the White Horse.

Clearly he had asked all that he needed to ask, and had already said all that he could allow himself to say on that matter, for when he spoke at last, it was only to demand, with a glance towards the body under the elder tree, 'Was he a friend of yours?'

'No,' Owain said.

'The more fool were you, then, to risk an ugly death for him. But it seems that you have some power over the horse-kind. I never yet saw any man handle the God's Horse in his rage, and win him to quietness, let alone live to tell of it after.'

'I knew him in his colt days, and he remembered me again. There is no more to it than that.'

Aethelbert nodded, and turning to the man who stood beside him looking on, began to say something; then with an exclamation of impatience, looked about for someone to translate for him. But at the moment, Bishop Lindhard was nowhere to be seen. Owain said quickly, 'I have yet something of the Latin tongue. Tell me what you would say to the Holy Man.'

'I would have spoken only some foolishness concerning the wisdom of making friendship with the mighty. If you can indeed speak his tongue, tell him the meaning of what he has seen, for he is a curious man who asks many questions.'

Owain turned to the man at the High King's side, and found the cold masterful gaze already on his face. He began in careful Latin, 'Holy Father——'

But before he could get farther the other leapt in. 'Ah, you speak the Tongue! I thought from the first moment that you were no Saxon.'

'I am British, of the Roman stock. My Latin has rusted for we used it seldom in daily speech, even when I was a boy; but our priests still use it for the services.'

'Of the Faith too, then, as well as the Tongue.'

Owain met the imperious gaze a little challengingly. 'The faith of our fathers has not so utterly perished from Britain as maybe Rome believes,' and felt, when he had said it, like a small boy who has loosed a bird-bolt at a man in armour.

Augustine merely bent his head in answer, and said, 'Now tell me the meaning of all this that I have just seen.'

'So the High King bade me do,' Owain said. He gathered his thoughts together, and in as few words as might be, he told Augustine what he asked, while Aethelbert looked on, fingering his beard.

When he spoke of Vadir drawing the longer grass, the monk broke in again, with a gesture of one hand towards the crumpled body. 'And this was the hazard chosen for him?'

'No, it was the hazard he chose for himself. He knew the stallion as I did from the day he was foaled. There was a link between them always—I believe——' He fumbled for the words he wanted; his head felt thick. 'I think he was fated.'

Augustine was silent for a moment, and his eyes had the look of a man gazing into a far distance. 'Fated, yes,' he said at last. 'The High King was telling me a while since, how in the elder

Saxon-kind, whenever the people sought new pastures, they would send a white horse ahead to lead them. And now the White Horse leads them again, out of old things, into the new.' His gaze flashed back to Owain's face. 'Say to Aethelbert of Kent for me that I have seen Frey's Horse who was as far beyond all other men's handling as though he were the North Wind, bend his neck in acceptance under a Christian hand; and I take it joyfully as a sign from my God.'

But when they had taken Vadir up, his head hanging, and carried him away, and the young warriors went back to the fires, they threw mead into the blaze for Frey, before they returned to their drinking again.

For as Einon Hên had said, the time for the Queen's multitude was not yet.

23

Three Women

WHERE the old paved road plunged into the woods, Owain checked and looked back over open country. The Intake was shining with the pale gold of stubble under a high tumbled sky. He had stayed to help them get the harvest in; but now harvest was over and it was time to go.

Bryni would have come with him the first few miles, but he had not wanted that. No long-drawn farewells at all that he could help. He had not even gone for the last time to look at Dog's grave or the girl with the bird and the flowering branch. He had simply picked up his cloak and the old well worn sword and his small bundle of belongings and taken his leave of the household— all save Lilla, who at the last moment was not there—as briefly as though he would be back by nightfall.

This was his true leave-taking, this pause between the Intake and the Wild, and the last look back towards the familiar steading beside its wind-shaped apple trees; and when he turned his face northward again and went on into the woods towards the ferry, a part of his life would be finished and laid away behind him, and he would be walking forward into the future.

A little rustle among the bushes of the woodshore made him turn quickly, and Lilla stepped out on to the old paved road, with burrs clinging in her yellow hair. Owain's heart sank a little. 'Why, Lilla! What brings you out here, then?'

'You,' she said breathlessly. 'I hoped that you would not be gone beyond my catching up with you. I came to bid you the Sun and Moon as your path.' And then in a little rush: 'No I didn't; I came to say—don't go, Owain.'

Owain's heart sank further. 'I must go, Lilla.'

'Why? We are your people—the nearest people you have. I can scarcely remember the time when you were not here, and nor can Helga and Bryni; the hearth will be desolate without you.'

'You'll be going to a hearth of your own, soon. I don't belong here, anyway.'

She was silent a moment, then she came nearer and put her hand urgently on his that held the bundle. 'Then let me come too. I don't mind where. I'll belong wherever you do, if you'll let me come too.'

Owain was silent also, looking into her small round pleading face. Then he shook his head. 'I've a girl of my own, you see.'

She dropped her hand as though it had been stung. 'Where did you find her? At the Kentish Court?'

'She was my girl before ever I wore your father's thrall-ring round my neck.'

'That's a long time,' Lilla said, her eyes huge and grave on his face. 'Do you think that she will have waited for you?'

Q

He looked down at her very kindly. 'I don't know. But I am going to see.'

'And if she has *not* waited——'

Again he shook his head. 'No, I shan't come back, even if she hasn't waited. It is as I said: I don't belong here. And you—you want a good steady lad of your own age, like Horn.' How pompous and grey-bearded that sounded. Well, if it made Lilla laugh at him, as he knew Regina would have laughed at him, that would be something.

But Lilla did not laugh. She only said in a small flat voice, 'I suppose you are right. I suppose I never really thought that you would let me come with you.'

'I know I'm right, but thank you for wanting to come, all the same.' He gave a little hitch to his bundle. 'You must go home now and I must be on my way.'

'Yes—it is no good starting on a wayfaring with the day half spent. The Sun and the Moon on your path, then, Owain.'

'And on yours, Lilla. Life be kind to you.' He knew that she wanted him to kiss her, so that she might have it to remember, afterwards. But the less she had to remember the better for her and Horn. So he only took her by the shoulder and turned her round. 'Go now, and don't look back, and I won't look back either.'

He stood for a long moment to watch her walk away, feeling completely wretched, because he knew that she was crying. Then he hitched up his bundle again, and turned northward into the trees.

Weeks later, brown and ragged and travel-hard, lean as a winter wolf, Owain stood among the hazel and wayfaring scrub of another woodshore, looking out over cleared land, and knew that his memory had not played him false. He had remembered every detail of that long road south with Beornwulf; he had turned it round and followed it northward in his mind so often in the early days, and again in these last few months; and now here he stood, just where he had stood turning for one last look back before he stumbled on after his new master, eleven years ago.

But he had had slow travelling, sometimes hunting as he went, sometimes stopping to put in a day's work on a farm in exchange for a meal and a night in the corner of a hay loft; and once his memory had been unsure and he had taken a track that carried him too far westward and cost him two days to get back on to his proper trail again. And already summer was falling behind; the first yellow leaves were falling from the birch trees, and in the open land before him the autumn ploughing had begun.

For a little, standing there on the woodshore, he did not want to go forward, thinking suddenly that Lilla had been right: eleven years was a long time.

Then he shook his shoulders and took a new hold of his bundle, and strode on into the driftway that led up through the cultivated land past the steading gate. He looked about him eagerly as he walked, in case Regina was working in the kale garth or the orchard plot; half expecting her to know that he was near, and come running to meet him, ready to take up again the journey that they had had to lay down here so long ago. But they would not make for Gaul this time, even if they had had the gold. Gaul had been a plan for despair and defeat, for the black darkness. It was different now. 'Not the dawn yet, but I think the dawn wind stirring.' It came to him suddenly, but as though it were a thing he had known for a long time, that he would take her to Priscus and Priscilla.

But she was not in the kale garth nor the orchard plot, and she did not come running. He was at the steading gate now, and the dogs were baying at the ends of their chains. A woman with children clinging about her blue skirts appeared in the house-place doorway and cried out sharply to quieten the dogs, and then seeing Owain, stood waiting for him with her hands on her broad hips, as he came up past the midden. She was a plump pretty creature with a full pink mouth and eyes as blue as her kirtle and as hard as pebbles. 'If you want my man or his father,' she said without a greeting, 'they're down at Ella's stead, helping with the thrashing.'

'Good fortune on the house and the woman of the house,' Owain said. 'I was not wanting your man or his father. I come seeking a girl—a girl called Regina. Is she here?'

The woman stared at him for a moment, and then laughed in

his face. 'A girl called Regina? Why, she was years older than I
am.'

'Was.' Owain had a sudden feeling of coldness in the very
midst of him, that made it difficult to breathe. 'Is she—not here any
more, Mistress?'

'Not now. She was here until not much more than a moon
since. Then she ran away.'

The cold clutch on Owain relaxed, leaving him a little sick.
'Why?' he demanded.

She looked at him sharply and consideringly. 'Who are you,
then? What business is Regina of yours? I have never seen you
round here before.'

'No, you would not,' Owain said wearily. 'I have not been able
to come back until now. It was I who left her here.'

Her eyes widened, and she gave a snort that was between
laughter and scorn. 'So! I've heard that story! She always thought
you would come one day.'

'Why—did she run away, Mistress?' Owain asked again.

She looked at him in silence a moment, while the children
stared bright-eyed and curious round her skirts. Then she seemed
to make up her vixenish mind. 'I'll tell you. My man's mother
made a waiting-woman and a friend of her, and that was a fine
thing for her so long as the old woman lived, but she died at hay
harvest, and then my man would have taken Regina for his other
woman. The Great Mother alone knows why, for she was thin
and thorny as a bramble spray and none so young as she used
to be, either.'

Owain was remembering the boy like a handsome bull calf,
who had thrust forward to stare at Regina as she lay unconscious
beside the fire. 'And so she ran away,' he said.

'Yes, and I helped her. If she had wanted him, I'd have poisoned
her.' He saw how hard the blue eyes were, and believed it. 'As it
was, I gave her a cloak and some food and a knife, and told my
man that she lay sick in the woman's quarters, for three days after
she was away. He beat me for that, but I didn't care.'

Owain was not listening to that part of the story. 'But where
to?' he burst out. 'Where would she go? What would she do? She
had no one to turn to——'

The woman shrugged. 'She said she would go, and she went northward. I know no more than that.'

'But did she not tell you what was in her mind to do? If she thought that I would come, did she not leave any word for me?'

'Maybe she did not know herself what she would do, or maybe she feared that if I knew, *he* might drag it out of me. She need not have feared, if *that* was the way of it.'

Owain stood looking at her, trying to be sure if she was telling the truth; but the hard eyes met his without any shadow of guile in them, and he could think of no reason why she should be lying. Slowly he straightened his shoulders, and hitched up his bundle. 'Then I'll be on my way, Mistress.'

She shrugged again. 'As you please. Do you want a drink of milk before you go?'

'Not in this house, New Mistress, since the Old Mistress is no more here to give it to me,' Owain said, and turned and trudged away.

Outside the steading gate he checked a moment, then set off north-westward following the stream without any very clear idea of his direction, save that he wanted to get away from the farm. Once he was clear of the farm he would be able to think. He felt so dazed that it was not until he was actually among the scrub of the woodshore that he remembered the other thing he had left here: his father's ring.

He found the great thorn tree just as he remembered it, standing out from the forest, with its crown of branches spread triumphantly against the sky. It was so old that the years since he left the ring in its keeping had made no difference to it at all, only the leaves that had been green with early summer were tinged with russet here and there, and the berries turning darkly red. He found the place, where one of the twisted roots thrust out from the bole, and squatting down beside it, pulled his knife from his belt and began to poke through the moss and leaf-mould. In a little the knife point found something, but it did not feel as a ring wrapped in rotten cloth would feel, more like a stone, and the point grated on it. Just a stone in the ground, yet he did not remember to have come up against a stone when he buried the ring there, and however he probed about, he could find no trace of the ring itself.

He dropped the knife on the moss beside him, and thrust his hand into the hole he had made, feeling about and working the damp crumbling earth with his fingers. Something soft and cold and many-legged twisted under his thumb and ran, but still he could not feel the ring—only the thing like a stone that was just about where the ring should have been. It was rounded and regular. Suddenly he knew with a little jump of the heart that it was too regular for a stone; whatever it was, it was man-made.

He worked it free with his fingers, and pulled it out. It was a tiny earthen pot such as the women used for salves and unguents, and the narrow mouth had been sealed with a lump of streamside clay. With his heart racing, Owain picked up his knife and dashed the hilt down on to the little pot. It fell in shards like the petals of a brown flower in his palm, and in their midst, he saw a lock of hair black as a rook's wing, twisted close and tied with a strand of scarlet thread.

So Regina had left word for him after all, in the best way she could, seeing that she could not write. And as he poked the broken shards back into the hole under the tree-root and flattened the earth back over them, Owain was trying desperately to think out what it was she had tried to tell him. In the first place, she had taken his father's ring, and left the strand of her hair in its place to tell him, if ever he came that way, that it was she who had taken it. (So she must have seen and understood, in that brief moment when her eyes were open, what it was that he was doing among the roots of the thorn tree.) And that could surely only mean that she was hoping for him to find her again. And *that* could only mean that she had made for some place where he would think of looking for her. She could not have gone seeking him, for she would not have known in all South Britain, where to seek. For a moment he wondered whether she might have gone to Priscus and Priscilla, but he did not think he had ever told her about them—they had not talked much about things that were past, they had been too busy living from day to day. And then with the suddenness of the blue flash of a jay's wing through the undergrowth, he knew that she would have gone home to Viroconium.

He flattened the torn moss back over the loose earth, and thrust his knife again into his belt. He untied the scarlet thread, and knotted the long strand of black hair again and again round his wrist, as the best way that he could think of, to keep it safe. Then he got to his feet, picked up his ragged bundle, and set off for Viroconium after Regina.

He did not attempt to retrace the way that they had come so long ago, but simply headed north-westward as well as he could and as fast as he could, until he struck the great double-track frontier road that he had followed twice before. After that it was simple enough, so far as finding the way was concerned. But it was a gruelling journey, none the less, for he was hunted on by sharp anxiety for Regina, who had always been afraid of the world outside her city walls: Regina alone in the ruins of Viroconium, if indeed she had got so far, after eleven sheltered years that must surely have made her unfit to fend for herself in the wilds. Every time he stopped to hunt for food the delay was maddening to him, and often he went hungry on a handful of blackberries, rather than stop to hunt at all. It was wild country here in the west, too, still border country for all the treaties that man might make, not like the long-settled lands further east; and once he saw the smoke of a burning farm in the distance, and never knew whether it was a Saxon or a British blaze.

But the day came at last, a still autumn day, turning towards evening, when Owain came loping wearily up the straight stretch to the South Gate of Viroconium. The yellow poplar leaves were drifting down. The gravestones of the old burial ground had sunk into a tangle of elder and wild rose, and the brambles had arched out to engulf the road.

It looked as though no one had passed that way in a hundred years, and Owain's heart sank a little. But that was foolishness, he told himself; one girl would scarcely have left a cleared track behind her—nor her footsteps marked with the little three-fold clover, like the Princess of his childhood's legends. He passed the turf banks of the Amphitheatre, and came to the crumbling gate-arch, and went through into the city.

The wilderness had been kind to Viroconium. It had come flowing in like a slow green tide—like the compassion of God, Owain thought, looking about him—to cover the sorrow and the scars.

In the year that Kyndylan died, his city had been raw with the newness of its ruin; but now the silent streets had become green ways, and everywhere, wherever he looked, was the soft grey smoke of seeding willow-herb. The horror, too, was gone, and Owain thought that under this in-flowing of the Wild, the old man with his bag of gold must surely sleep as quietly as the standard bearer of the 14th Legion whose headstone had long ago collapsed into the brambles.

He walked on slowly, listening and looking about him as he went, towards the heart of the city and the Palace of Kyndylan the Fair. He was thirsty, and he turned aside from the street, heading for the gap in the wall and the old short cut that would take him by the grotto; maybe there was still water to be had there. The garden of Kyndylan's Palace had been a flowering wilderness when last he came that way; now it was a tangle of hawthorn and elder and run-wild roses, so dense that in places he had to cast about to find a way round and through and between the thickets.

A thrush gorging on the elderberries flew off with an alarm call, as he ducked under a bush, but somewhere ahead of him a robin sang on quite undisturbed, and ahead of him also, he heard the trickle of falling water. He came round a tangle of bushes and found himself on the edge of the well-hollow. Below him the three steps, mossier than he remembered them, led down to the grotto under its overarching hazel, and the water still fell through the bronze jaws of the lion mask, into the basin and away under the stones and ferns. And standing with her head turned expectantly towards the sound of his coming, the crock that she had been filling still in her hand, was a woman.

A tall very thin woman in the rags of a russet kirtle, her face brown-skinned and narrow under the heavy masses of black hair knotted about her head, who stood looking up at him out of black-fringed eyes that were as pale as rain. There had been birds all round her feet, but they had taken fright at his coming, and burst upward into the hazel tree, so that the branches over her head were full of the rustling of their wings.

'Regina,' Owain said.

She did not smile, or make any movement to set the crock

down. 'Owain,' she said. 'I knew that you would come one day.'
And that was all.

Owain went down the three steps into the grotto, and took the
crock from her and set it down. Her hands were cold as though she
had been holding them in the running water. 'I came as soon as I
could,' he said, 'and I followed on as soon as I found your message.'

'I hoped you would understand. I could not have left the ring
there, anyway, lest they cleared the land properly one day and
found it; but I hoped that if I left my hair to tell you that it was I
who had taken it, you might guess where I had gone, and follow
after.' Her hands had gone to her neck as she spoke, where something hung on a scarlet thread under her kirtle. She pulled it up
and bit the thread through, and gave it to him. 'There—take your
father's ring again.'

He took it from her without a word, knowing the familiar feel
of it without looking, and slipped it on to his signet finger. It
fitted now, as though it had been made for him. And all the while
he never stopped looking at Regina, trying to join this woman
who was 'thin and thorny as a bramble spray and none so young
as she used to be' on to the girl he remembered and had somehow
expected to find again.

Regina's gaze went downward as though she were looking for
something just behind him, and suddenly she asked, 'Where is
Dog?'

'Regina—it is eleven years.'

There was a silence, filled with the fluttering and calling of the
birds overhead and then Regina said, 'I had forgotten. . . . Do I
seem as changed to you as you do to me?'

He nodded. 'We shall have to learn each other all over again.'

'I think it should not be too hard,' Regina said, softly as though
she were consoling a child. 'I think I should have known you
again, under the change, even if I had not been waiting for you;
and I am still here for you to find me.'

In the little grotto the light was fading. 'It is late,' Regina said.
'We must go home and cook supper. . . . Thank you for your
strike-a-light, Owain. It has lit me so many fires to warm me.'
She gave a little quick sigh as though she was not aware of it.

'We should have a blue olivewood fire tonight—but I dare say an ordinary one will cook the supper just as well.'

'I have a hare in my bundle that I caught yesterday,' Owain said.

'And I have two eggs. I saved yesterday's—as though I knew that you would come today.'

'Eggs? How did you come by two eggs? Regina, how have you fared for food all this while?'

'Well enough. You taught me how to set a snare, remember, and autumn is a good time for food. And as for the eggs——' Her face that had been so still, was suddenly shimmering with delight. 'There's a little outland settlement over in the woods beyond the Virocon. They must lose quite a lot of hens to the foxes. They'll never miss one little brown hen more.'

Owain stared at her for a moment, then flung up his head with a joyous crow of laughter. 'Yes, you were right! You were right! You are still there, Regina!'

He stooped for the crock, which now held three hazel leaves floating on the surface of the water: but Regina was before him. 'No, you have your bundle—besides, the crock needs knowing. See, it is cracked here, and if you tip that way it dribbles, but it was the best I could find.'

She held out her free hand for his, and they climbed the three steps together and turned as they had turned so often before, towards the furthest corner of Kyndylan's Palace.

'The roof has fallen in,' Regina said. 'I have made a kind of shelter in the old corner, with branches and grass. It is not very good, but you could make it keep the rain out.'

'I'll make it keep the rain out.' Owain hesitated, then looked round at her as they walked. 'But not for long. We must be on our way in a few days, Regina, while there is still time left before winter closes down.'

'Are we still going to Gaul?' Regina asked carefully, after a few moments.

'No. That was for the dark; now, there's a dawn wind stirring.' Owain tipped his face a little, as though feeling the wind on it as he walked, and his hand tightened on Regina's. 'We are going southwest into the hills. There was an old man and an old woman there; I do not think I ever told you about them, but they were kind to me once, and they'll welcome you for my sake, until they have time to welcome you for your own, if they are still there.'

'And if they are not still there?'

'Then we'll build a turf hut and light a fire in it, and in-take a patch of hillside, and I'll find a sheep to go with your little brown hen,' Owain said.